Indian
HIPPIE

Indian HIPPIE

Gautam Shankar Banerjee

PARTRIDGE
A Penguin Random House Company

To order additional copies of this book, contact
Partridge India
000 800 10062 62
orders.india@partridgepublishing.com

www.partridgepublishing.com/india

DEDICATION

My mother and father Asha Banerjee and Santosh Chandra Banerjee, who have put me on the right path; Devdan Sen and Anne Bomze; all those who had given me their time and mind; all the policemen, Naxalites and others, who were killed in the bitter struggle; all the lovers of peace and harmony, brotherhood and humanity.

CHAPTER - I

Akshyay felt relieved as he stepped out of the train on to the platform of Rishikesh railway station. He stretched and kicked his legs in the air and untied the knot of sticky long hair. The long journey through the arid plains of North India had been monotonous and tiring. His seat had been beside the window of a three-tier coach. He had, off and on, dozed off to a fitful sleep, the full-throated cries of hawkers waking him up with starts at wayside stops. The hawkers were selling tea, peanuts, puris, cold drinks and other eatables, which one finds almost in every railway station of North and Eastern India. The barred windows had framed the moving countryside beyond, which was like a backdrop to his train of thoughts.

Images of the past had flitted in and out of his mind. He had thought of his father and about his life. His father had died barely two months ago in Calcutta in his ancestral house, and he had set out for Rishikesh to fulfill his father's last wish. He recalled the day when he had called him to his bedside.

"My son, I will not live long. There is something I have to tell you."

"What is it? Why do you say you will not live long? I am sure nothing will happen to you. If you take the medicines properly, you will soon recover. You have been refusing to take them, haven't you? I have heard that you have been drinking on the s . . . That's what Abdul said." Akshyay bit his lips as he realised that he should not have spoken.

"Oh! Has he? I had told him to keep it a secret. The fellow has betrayed me? I'll have him ticked off . . ." Mr. Choudhuri gasped for breath, as he tried to raise his head. He had difficulty in breathing. His right hand clutching his chest, he lay back and sighed, "No! No! I'll not say anything to him. He has been with us for a long time. Perhaps, he has done the right thing."

"He was only trying to hold you in check. He could not see you wasting away."

"I guess so. Now let me tell you what I have to. You have been wasting your life too. I had put you in a good boarding school so that you could come out a successful young man, fit for a good job in a multinational company. Instead, you have turned the other way: taking drugs, going for pop music and behaving like a hippie. This must change.

You must give up drugs and lead a normal life. You will have to pass out of college and try for a good job."

Akshyay had kept silent. He had not wanted to protest or argue with his father, now that he was so frail and sick. His face was pale and his cheeks were shrunken. He was no more the strong tall person with a butterfly moustache, waiting to take him back home for the annual vacations. He had also remembered him as the tyrant who had kept his mother away from him. His sweet dear Mum . . . she had suddenly gone away from his life, when he had been a young boy of nine or ten years. He had heard that she was mad, but neither his father nor his aunt, the two persons living in the house in Calcutta, ever told him, where she was. He had also never dared to find out from his perpetually angry old man.

The feeling of silent anger had for that moment changed to a sad one, as he noticed the entreaty in his eyes as he looked at him, trying to form the words and speak coherently. He repeated, "You have dropped out of college. You are into pop music, wasting your time and energy in everything but study . . . It's the effect of drugs. Your aunt told me so. You have been taking drugs and you have also gone in for pop music, with a drug-like passion." Mr.Choudhuri's face had been intensely emotional. "You must go to an ashram. It's the only way to get cured of drugs. I know a Swamiji there. Our family has been regularly contributing to the ashram. Swami Ananda will take care of you for a few months; and I am sure you will come back a sane person, motivated to succeed in life. I must have your word that you will go to him. You must give me your word. You must."

Mr. Ramen Choudhuri had taken Akshyay's hand in his and kept on looking at his face, with eyes that had seemed to be on the brink of tears. After he had controlled himself, he had said, "I have kept a letter for Swami Ananda and some money in the drawer there; you can pick it up later."

Akshyay felt visibly moved that day. There was no way he could refuse him. He had to give his word that he would visit Rishikesh and meet Swami Ananda.

A few days later his father had died and then his life had begun to fall apart. He had suddenly felt lost. He had always had a dislike for his father, as if he were a yoke on his shoulders, which he could not off-load. Even when completely immersed in his music sessions, his image would suddenly assail his consciousness like that of a surfing whale in the ocean. Sometimes he would return home late from his rock joint or from a date with one of his girlfriends. He would then invariably find his father sitting around with a glass of whisky in the drawing room, as if he were a part of his fledging conscience.

A feeling of guilt would often creep over his mind, especially if the delay would have been due to a fling with one of those crazy girls. His good looks and that he belonged to a well-known family, with much property around town, made him stand like a Star. His family had acquired landed property during the British Raj, in the wake of the Zamindari system in Bengal, and had wielded considerable power and prestige in the past. One of his ancestors, his great-grandfather had also been a famous social reformer. He revolted against Sati: the system of burning of brides on the funeral pyre of their husbands. He stood up against the social stigma attached to widow remarriage. He fought relentlessly against the unfavourable attitude towards sending women for higher education, and the caste system. Naturally, Akshyay had the aura of his family background around him and although he wanted to, he could not get rid of it.

His father's death had suddenly cut off the final link with the family and the past. He had suddenly become free: the cause of his revolting nature having vanished overnight. He had been against the strict and severe family traditions, ever since he had begun to hold his father responsible for his mother's predicament. His father became the symbol of the aristocratic family that must have sat heavily on his mother's slender form. He could still visualise the thin arms and the long fingers that had held his chubby hand so often. His mind was full of negative images of his father and with his death; there was a sudden void. In his final moments, his father had however, appeared to have changed: no more domineering and angry but submissive and sad. Now that there was nothing to revolt against, he had found his rock band and LSD becoming farcical and meaningless. The Beatles group had also begun to break up; what was wrong if their group broke up too?

The musical apple cart overturned; he had to find other ways of giving vent to his talent. A friend had guided him to a classical music guru, in line with George Harrison's stint with Ravi Shankar and the song 'Jai Guru Deva'. Getting to learn the sarode or sitar had already become the in-thing. He had therefore begun to take lessons in sarode and had soon picked up some of the basics. His knowledge of guitar came to his aid, speeding up the learning process rather than slowing it down, as normally is the case when one tries to learn similar subjects.

However, playing sarode, alone, could not excite his sensibilities and therefore, he had to be bit by the travel bug and the destination had to be Rishikesh; again, following the Beatles. His father's last wish was there, to bolster his desire. It also served as a handy excuse for convincing his no-nonsense Aunt Monica. She did not at all savour his idea of his going to Rishikesh: a place, according to her opinion, full of fraud sadhus and certainly not the place for a success-seeking individual.

However, against her aunt's wish, he was at Rishikesh, to seek his future. He was not sure how he should gain from the visit, but as it was, it was the destination of the Beatles and Mahesh Yogi. There were many freaks and junkies all heading for Rishikesh. He had to be there too. He had always wanted to be like a Westerner. In his looks and demeanour, he was almost one.

There were other reasons for getting away from the city and his house. For one, he had wanted to avoid the company of his nagging aunt. She had a strong dislike of his ways, which she hid under a garb of benefaction. Furthermore, the city of Calcutta with its myriad problems had become unbearable. It had always been a pleasant thought: that of leaving the city. A third reason was that his Aunt Monica, would keep on trying to rake up the subject of the will and property, over dinner. That would only serve to remind him of his father's death and, of course, the formidable wealth of the family. It was only in the presence of the family lawyer that one could discuss the subject. Therefore, he had avoided talking about the will. When finally, his aunt announced his cousin, Abinash's, expected arrival from London for a settlement, he decided that his reaction should be to get away.

However, now that he had finally arrived at Rishikesh, he felt the past floating behind like a distant dream. It was already far away. He could hardly control a smile as he looked back at the train. It reminded him of the harrowing journey. It was over at last. There were very few passengers on the platform. Most of them had disembarked at Haridwar, the more illustrious pilgrim spot. Akshyay wondered how long he had been standing around, daydreaming. He should get going. He recollected that he had read about the river. With his sling bag on his shoulders, he eagerly headed for the ghats, for a cool dip in the Ganges.

The road from the station was straight and flanked by shops. They were selling everything, from vegetables to pictures of Gods and Goddesses. After all, these were for the pilgrims who come during the summer months, to visit the different shrines in the Tehri Garhwal and

Garhwal districts of the Himalayas. The road was strangely bare: most of the buses carrying pilgrims to the Himalayan shrines, having left early in the morning. Therefore, the tongas[1] idled by the roadside and the tangawallas sat around chatting and smoking.

No sooner than he reached the ghat[2], Akshyay stopped involuntarily at the first sight of the river. The sound of the river leapt up over the stones and silvery waves to greet him. Akshyay quickened his pace and then broke into a run. He stopped where the water lay still between the stones, untouched by the torrential flow. He kept his bag on a dry round stone and took off his red kurta and yellow pyjamas, and with his gamcha[3] round his waist waded knee-deep into the river. The flowing waters, trying to carry him off, swirled round his feet. The current was strong and the water was cold. He looked at the river coming out from between the foothills and for a moment he saw the mountains rushing towards him over the curling and roaring waves. He shook off the illusion and felt the cold entering through his flesh and transporting him to the ice-capped Gangotri glacier. The sound of the river, gurgling, gushing, roaring, tingling, was like the jhankar[4] of a million sitars and the lahara[5] of thousand tablas. Akshyay waded a few feet farther and dipped his head into the running water, which seemed to wash away the sense of fatigue in his mind and body. He climbed out of the riverbed, full of round stones of a variety of shades and sizes, water dripping crystals from the strands of shoulder-length, light-brown hair. He felt a certain lightness, and as clean as a cloud, as he put on a fresh set of white kurta-pyjama.

It was almost ten o'clock when he again slung the bag across his shoulder and set out for the ashram.

"Hi!" A voice addressed him.

Akshyay turned to find a tall, blond, youth in kurta-pyjamas, with a garland round his neck, smiling and coming towards him.

"Like some hash, man?" He asked as he came near.

"No thanks, I've just had a dip in the river as you can see, and all I want now is some grub."

"Oh yeah! Now I'll have to get stoned, all alone."

"Well some other time I'll give you company. I've just come from Calcutta and . . . Are you, by any chance, staying at the Swiss Cottage? I've a letter for Swamiji, who's staying there."

"You're just right. I have been staying at the Swiss cottage for about three months, now. It's a far-out place, and, Swamiji too, a hell of a nice guy. I vouch for it."

"Could you direct me to him? I plan to stay in Swiss cottage."

"Where do you come from?" The young man suddenly asked.

"Well didn't I tell you? I come from Calcutta."

"Yeah? I thought you're from London or you know, from somewhere in Britain."

"Well very often people think I'm French or British . . . you know: one of the European countries, but I am very much Indian. The colour of my eyes and probably my long hair . . . I have just looking for peace here. Calcutta's become one hell of a place now. I couldn't take it any further."

"I don't know whether Swamiji would allow you to stay there since the place is only for Westerners. He may consider your case differently."

"Oh, don't worry about that. Swami Ananda can never refuse me after he considers that it was my old man's last wish. He asked me to stay in the ashram."

"Let's go then. I'll walk down with you and get you fixed up. I think you'll like it there. The cottage is near the river bank."

They started walking through the maze of cobbled lanes between the dharmashalas[6], shops and houses and on to the main road. Some distance away from the hub of the market area, a stone and mud track dropped down towards the rumbling river. The Swiss Cottage was on its right-hand side. A gate in the brick wall served as entrance. It was open. The sound of the river muffled their tread.

Instructing Akshyay to wait in the garden, the young man whose name was Allen, went into the square house that had numerous doors and windows provided for single rooms for the hippies. The whitewash on the walls was incongruous to the greenery all around. The green grass of the lawn encroached on the narrow path that led to the house. Marigolds in full bloom stood nodding in assent on either side. On the left, a mango tree stood laden with fruit. On the right, on the cemented seat around a Banyan tree, a young woman sat in padmasan[7].

The rays of sunlight that filtered through the leaves and fell about her, set aflame her flowing hair and lent an aura to her white face. The image of a thousand spotlights bringing to sudden relief the parading female forms in a fashion show, came to his mind. A closer look revealed her closed eyes and her slightly raised eyebrows. Her slender, shinning, extended, arms, rested on her knees, palms facing out, in the typical lotus posture. Akshyay advanced a few feet forward and when he was just about ten feet away, she woke up from her trance. He found himself looking into her large, brown, eyes and rapidly sinking into their softness into some unknown abyss. There was no sense of fear or doubt or scorn, or anger or lust, from which he should shy away. He lay like a child rocking in a cradle of peace and joy and basking in the gaze of love. Their eyes blinked and Akshyay said, "Hello! Hi!"

"My name is Sarah," she said. Her lilting tone of voice seemed to say; 'Didn't you know?'

"Did I disturb you?" Akshyay asked, not quite apologetically, but with a smile playing on his lips.

"Not really. I never knew when I had opened my eyes. I thought that you are an Avatar, standing before my mind's eye."

"I'm Akshyay. I have just come from Calcutta. Allen told me to wait here. He's gone to see if Swami Ananda's around."

"Oh! There he comes!" She said with a hint of elation in her tone. She looked in the direction of the house, unlocking herself from the yogic posture.

Akshyay turned and saw a middle-aged person in saffron kurta and lungi, approaching with Allen at his side. Though of average height, he walked in long strides. His cheerful face broke into a wide smile as he reached near.

"Welcome to Swiss Cottage. I heard you would like to spend some days here?"

"Well Swamiji," Akshyay began, "I have a letter from my late father. I suppose you knew him." He took out the envelope from his side bag and handed it over to Swamiji.

Swami Ananda opened the envelope and began to read the letter. Halfway through, he looked up and said, "We'll discuss the issue. Come follow me." He turned and began to walk towards the ashram building.

Akshyay took one look at Allen and then at the girl. He wanted to talk to her, but he did not know what to say. He could only let his eyes follow Swami Ananda, who had already started walking in long strides. Akshyay had to make an effort to drag himself after him. Though he succeeded to some extent, his mind lagged behind. It sought to delve deeper into the brown eyes that had held him captive a few moments back.

CHAPTER - II

The Swiss Cottage got its name from its owner, a Swiss lady. It was a haven for foreign tourists. They came in large numbers, mainly from Europe, in the wake of George Harrison's trip with Mahesh Yogi, which brought Rishikesh into the tourist map of the world.

The house, into which Akshyay entered, was a single-storied white building. There were rows of back-to-back single rooms enclosing a square, cemented, courtyard, which had a samiana to serve as a ceiling. There was a garlanded clay image of Radha—Krishna, on a pedestal, and opposite to it, Swami Ananda's room, across the courtyard. Swamiji beckoned to Akshyay to sit on the modest bed, while he pulled the chair from under the table and sat down to read the letter again.

"I must inform you that my father passed away about two months back," Akshyay said, after the Swami had finally read it.

"I am sorry to know about that. He had always patronised the Mahananda Ashram. Until last year, when I left it, we received cheques from him every month. May his soul rest in peace!" He looked up at Akshyay and with a quizzical look on his face, asked, "How is it that you are bringing this letter after two months?" Before Akshyay could answer, he continued, "Of course, you must have planned to come here earlier but then Mr. Choudhuri passed away and . . ." Swami Ananda hesitated.

"You are right," Akshyay prompted. "His sudden death delayed my departure; and then, there were property matters to tackle. My father had the major share. My aunt and a cousin, who lives in London, are the two other owners."

"I hope it is all settled," Swamiji said.

"Not really. According to the will, as far as I know, none of the owners have any right to sell the property, not even his share, other than by consensus. It means that the will locks up all the money. The rent we get is pretty low, based on the price-line of the British days. It is only some cash that my father left in the bank that has kept me going. All the money I earned, playing for the rock band, got blown up."

"So you had been with a rock band?" Swamiji asked.

"I was the lead guitarist, and instead of going to my classes, I spent the time at my disposal with the other members of the group, practising the tunes. They used to come over to my house and on many an occasion, we strummed through out the day, much to the annoyance of my aunt and the neighbours. The trouble began when money started pouring in and all those crazy girls. I popped LSD one day and saw myself creating a forest on a barren earth. I carried full-grown trees on my shoulders, planting them one by one. I couldn't sleep. I raved in the house and everyone thought I had conked out like my mother. My father wanted to send me to the Ashram to you . . . But then I learnt, from the reply I received to my letter to the Ashram, that you had left. That's how I came here, directly."

"God's will," Swamiji said, looking up and closing his eyes. The authorities of the Ashram did not like me patronising the so-called 'hippies'. I had many a fight, until the Swiss lady, who built this place, called me over one day. I felt I could serve people better, running Swiss Cottage, and looking after the young people, who come from distant lands in search of peace and tranquillity in a tormented world. The dharamsalas and ashrams don't allow foreigners to stay there. It is another thing that those very Westerners would not, in any case, be able to adjust to the living conditions prevailing there. At least, there are beds here and most important: attached baths. Come, let's go and see your room."

As they came out of the room, Swami Ananda pointed to one corner of the courtyard, on the left-hand side of the Radha-Krishna image. "That is where the kitchen is. We've got two cooks here. They are Gaur Brahmins. The food is strict vegetarian."

"Whatever it is; I am dog hungry. I've not had anything since morning. Further, the dip in the Ganges has made me even more hungry."

"Wait a minute then. I'll tell them right now. Panchu! Hari! Where are you?"

An old person with white hair came out of the kitchen room.

"Swamiji, have you called me?"

"Could you quickly make some parathas for our guest here", Swamiji said, and then, turning to Akshyay lowering his voice, "that is Panchu." He is the Ashram cook, and very good too. Now, let's go to your room, on the other side," Swamiji said, taking Akshyay's arm. "Let's go."

The room was small. A single bed covered with a white bed-sheet, and a chair and a table were the only furniture in the otherwise bare interior. Akshyay had wondered why most of the rooms had locks hanging from the doors like bats from a tree branch. Swami Ananda had told him that Allen and Sarah were the only foreigners staying now. Just a week back the place was full. The Government had recently permitted foreigners to go up to Rudra Prayag. Therefore, most of those who had been staying at Swiss Cottage had left for that Garhwal town, lodged between the turbulent Alakananda and the gently flowing Mandakini.

When Swamiji had left and after Akshyay had devoured the parathas, he came out of the room to have a look at the garden. He suddenly noticed Sarah coming in his direction. The sunlight was still behind her flowing hair and graceful body, and her eyes were on him.

"Oh! Your room is right next to mine. That's very warm. It's almost a week now; we've been very lonely here."

"Yes, it will be good for me too," Akshyay said as he watched her taking the key ring from the folds of her sari to open the door of her room.

"Why don't you come in and sit? We could have some tea. Have you had your breakfast?"

"Yes I have just had some parathas," he said and hesitantly followed her into the room.

"Sit down, will you? I'll go and get the tea," she said, and went out of the room.

Akshyay sat wondering how fast things were moving. The images of the girl in the padmasan posture and the river between the hills flashed across his mind. Other images from his past sprang to life, one after another, like bulbs in an assembly line. As the images of the past surfaced, he re-lived the pain and suffering of his early childhood and youth. The agonising fear and loneliness came back to his mind. He recalled that he had taken up music to relieve the pain, in the strumming of the guitar and drum. Now the recollection was like a drug that heightened the pain. It overshadowed the images of the flowing river, the girl under the tree and the eyes into which he had sunk. He scrambled out of the rocks and began to cut his passage through the dense undergrowth, when Sarah returned, tray in hand.

"Here's the tea," said Sarah and handed over a cup to Akshyay.

"You are from America, aren't you? Swamiji told me that you are."

"I'm from New York and you?"

"I'm from Calcutta. I'm Indian."

"Really! You don't look at all like one. Oh yes! I think you do. You must be from the Aryan stock, which had come to India ages ago; settled down here and produced the Vedas, Upanishads and Bhagabat Gita."

"Well, I'm not too sure about that. However, you could be correct. From where did you learn these theories?"

"Swami Ananda told me and then I read some books on India. There is one book by Persival Spear and there is a German writer called Zimmer. I wonder why the Universities don't teach the Upanishads and Gita, instead of funky subjects?"

"You were in the University, weren't you?"

"I was, but I dropped out. I concluded that the university would not help me in any way. There were many people dropping out each day in search of freedom and peace, away from that concrete wall. One day I told my father that I was leaving. He kept quiet and looked on helplessly, as I moved into Jack's flat. He used to play the flute and after seven days I got bored. I told Jackie that I've heard Krishna's flute and that I could not resist the call. My old man was good enough to give me the dollars to buy a ticket to Europe. I've been through Greece, France, Liverpool and even Morocco. I have learnt to walk over broken glass. I landed in India three months ago."

"How did you land up here?" Akshyay asked.

"New Delhi, with the unnerving immigration office and the ogling crowd was a nightmare. The places in the tourist circuits generally don't interest me. You know, the Taj Mahal and Pink City and all such legacies of an inhuman civilisation, which have sought to stifle the wisdom and beauty of ancient India. I heard that Rishikesh was one of the few places where the Ganges still flowed free; a place where people seeking peace, were heading to. They asked me a hundred questions on why I wanted to go to Rishikesh. They just wouldn't let me, until a friend got me a certificate from an ashram here. That very night I took the train to this place. It's been very peaceful here. The people are good. The river is lovely and powerful, driving away all the evil thoughts. I feel spaced-out here."

"I feel the same way too," Akshyay said, carried away by the narrative. "What are you doing this afternoon? I want to go to the opposite bank of the river. The Geeta Bhavan is located there."

"Why don't we go right now? For me there isn't any lunch: I'm fasting today."

"That'll be groovy."

"I'll just change my dress. I'm still not quite used to the sari," she said and started unwinding it, and as it dropped on the floor, she stooped to collect it. She kept the sari on the bed and picked up a gown. She was in her petticoat and her back above the slender waist completely bare. Akshyay didn't know what to make of this. He could see her straight but shapely back, and arms. The skin was whiter below the neckline and as she lifted her arms to slide into the gown they exposed for a brief moment the sides of her swinging breasts. Akshyay experienced a drawing in of his stomach walls and a pounding in his chest but before they could overpower him, Sarah turned with a beaming smile and said, "Are we ready to go?"

CHAPTER - III

The winding road entered the looming foothills ahead. The sun was already high up in the clear sky and the journey through the six kilometres of road seemed long. Akshyay wanted to call a tangawalla but Sarah preferred to walk. Occasionally, a few trucks carrying supplies to the Garhwal towns zoomed by and he drew Sarah to the side of the road, close to him.

They came across a disturbing crowd of people, beggars, pandas and even freelance photographers, on the lane that dropped down from the main road and led to the Lakshman Jhula. Akshyay put a protective arm round Sarah's shoulder and led her through the crowd. He noticed the river below strangely calm, as if held in check, by the high mountain walls on either side, which also supported the hanging foot over-bridge.

When they reached the opposite bank, they took the less crowded road flanked by trees to the Geeta Bhavan. Sarah felt exhausted and wanted to rest. The long walk in the hot sun had been tiring. Walking through the rows of sickly beggars, most of them lepers, she felt like staggering wearily through the pathway leading to Hell.

They sat on a bench, on the side of the road under a mango tree. Sarah took a deep breath of fresh air and tried to visualise the river flowing through her mind. Akshyay sat watching her as she closed her eyes and relaxed her body. When she regained her energy she asked with a frown on her face, "Why are there so many beggars here?"

Akshyay looked away wondering what to say and then came out with, "Pilgrims come to this place from all over India and many of them consider giving alms, a way of atoning for their sins."

The reply did not satisfy her and she shot back, "What is the Government doing about these people? I have seen them everywhere: at railway stations, bus stops, and temple premises. How can the Government allow this?"

"The society accepts this. What can the Government do? We are a democratic country and the Government expresses the will of the people," Akshyay said, becoming conscious of his nationality and realising at the same time that what he said did not hold water. He realised that the argument was going out of hand and becoming complex. He would have to take it to a different level. Before Sarah could open her mouth, he began, "Just a minute, I really don't claim much knowledge on the subject. In any case, the answer lies in Hindu Philosophy and Thought, which runs through the very blood of the Indian people. These people are beggars or lepers or whatever because of their Karma."

"Do you accept this theory in principle?" Sarah asked, sitting up and turning to him somewhat agitated and with a quizzical look in her eyes.

"Don't be upset," Akshyay said, trying to calm her. "Neither do I subscribe to that view nor the people of this country. It's all at the subconscious level. How else can you explain the indifference to the persistence of poverty, ignorance, and unemployment through the ages?"

"Social and historical factors are responsible," Sarah said emphatically. "The constant subjugation, the caste system, the oppression, the invasions, all put together."

"I don't deny that social and historical factors were responsible. However, the real reason for the callous indifference, and the obtrusive presence of poverty, is the all-encompassing Hindu view of life. That is what I was trying to say," Akshyay said, conclusively.

Sarah kept quiet, not knowing how to react. "What was the Hindu view of life?" She thought. She had been reading some of the books on the Bhagabat Gita and Yoga philosophy, which Swami Ananda had given her. In spite of that, she could not relate what Akshyay just said to what she had read or heard. They sat on the bench in the shade of the mango tree allowing their bodies to be cooled and their minds to drift. Sadhus with trisul and Kamandulis passed by without as much as noticing them. They saw some groups of pilgrims trudging along. There were even some tourists and newlywed couples holding hands, on the way to Gita Bhavan. They could not see the river tumbling along but they could hear its sound, mingling with the rustle of the leaves of trees and the chirping of birds. Then, at a sudden change of the breeze, it would, like a crying child demanding attention, drown all other sounds and roar in their ears.

Akshyay felt the sound breaking into his consciousness: stirring, throwing up images of isolation and fear. Scenes of his childhood flashed across his mind. He saw his father sitting on the bench in the school playground. His head bent, his chin was on his chest and his arms dangled loose. The vacations had begun, but he could not partake in the joys of holidays and freedom. While the other children eagerly waited for their parents to arrive, he would be waiting in the empty dormitory and gazing at the Kunchenjunga. He would want to stay on in school. How he dreaded the vacations and his aunt's long face in the lonely house in Calcutta! He saw himself waking his father up when all the other boys had left. On the journey from Darjeeling to Siliguri they would not talk to each other. When he would pick up some courage to broach the subject, his father would just, with a wave of hand, say, "Don't talk to me about your mother."

He saw his mother tugging at his arm on one side and the Principal, on the other. He could hardly remember how old he was then or which class he was in—the whole episode lay, buried deep down in his mind: layer upon layer of plaster and shock absorbers. Even then, the images floated right in front of his eyes with as much clarity as if they were memories of yesterday.

"I want to take my son. You leave him alone," his mother was shouting. Her eyes were red and her hair flowed loose. She was wearing a black gown that covered her up to her bare feet.

"No! You cannot take him. We've received a telegram from his father to keep him here because his mother . . . You have gone mad," the Principal said, as she tugged his arm, again.

"To hell with you. He is my son and I'm taking him. Come Akshyay let's go. Let him go . . . You let him go," she shouted. Then she suddenly broke down, "Let him go please." There were tears in her eyes and she let go of his hand. He saw his mother standing in the corridor outside the Principal's office weeping and the police arriving. The image blurred and came back again.

He was in the Principal's house staring out of the windowpanes at the Kunchenjunga. There was Urmila, the principal's daughter to comfort him. He spent time with her learning to play the guitar. She was eighteen and beautiful. He was only ten but he would feign innocence and brush up against the softness of her shapely bosom. He would feel the coolness of the flesh of her bare arms on his hot pulsating temple. He would sit and watch for hours in the evenings by the fireplace, her long nimble fingers drawing out lilting tunes from the guitar and wouldn't know when he would drop off to sleep.

"Hey, Akshyay!" Sarah exclaimed and touched his shoulder, realising that he had been daydreaming. Akshyay woke up from his reverie with a start and turned towards Sarah.

"How long have we been sitting here?" He asked, awakened.

"About half an hour, I think" Sarah said with a shrug. "About what have you been dreaming?"

Akshyay did not answer but kept his eyes fixed on the ground. The gamut of feelings, relating to his boyhood experiences came rushing back like a huge wave.

I was just thinking about my mother. She had flipped out when I was very young and I don't know where she is now.

"Why, what happened to her?"

"I don't know, but I guess she could not get on with my father. My old man loved drinking and every evening he would go for his drinking bouts and come home dead drunk. The servants would help him up the stairs. My mother must have suffered from loneliness. You see; I had to go away to a boarding school. One day she came to take me home after the vacations and that was the last I saw of her. I could make out that she was mad. I was the subject of a tug of war between my mother and the Principal. My mother was screaming and crying at the same time over me until the police came and took her away. That was not really the last I saw of her . . . . She keeps entering my mind."

Sarah kept quiet for some time thinking about what Akshyay had just said and then said, "Why couldn't you find out where she was? Mental diseases, such as those arising out of depression and loneliness, are curable."

"I learnt that my father had sent her away to some mental hospital but I don't know what happened to her. My father did not talk about her and I never had the heart to ask my aunt, who would not spare an opportunity to rail against her and call her names. I could never endure that and preferred ignorance . . . . Let's go now. We can walk up to Geeta Bhavan and then take the motor boat to the other side."

They got up from the bench and started walking and after half an hour reached the sprawling white marble building: Geeta Bhavan. The Birlas built the structure for the benefit of pilgrims. The walls had the entire Bhagabat Gita inscribed on them. Akshyay looked about reading the Sanskrit slokas trying to decipher their meanings. It was a pity he thought that his school or college did not care to teach these slokas. Whatever he had learnt was due to his efforts. It was also an offshoot of the impact of George Harrison's interest in Oriental thought. His reading of the Bhagabat Gita had been only through an English translation. He noticed Sarah looking at the inscriptions blankly and felt all the more frustrated at not being able to come to her aid. His face lit up however, when he recognised one of the slokas and promptly began to recite the words.

"Yada yada he dharmashya glanirbhabati Bharata Abhyuthanam adharmashya tadatmanan srijamyaham.

Paritranaya sadhunan binasaya cha duskritam Dharmasansthapanathaya sambhyabami yuge yuge".

What does it mean? Is it something to do with dharma?" Sarah asked.

"Yes," Akshyay began, "Krishna is explaining to Arjuna at the battle field about the incarnation of Supreme Power, whenever unrighteousness predominates in the world, to protect the virtuous and destroy evil."

"I think the world badly needs such an incarnation: there is very little of goodness left."

"Yeah, there appears to be no direction. The world is in turmoil. Poverty and unemployment are on the increase. The symptoms of deception are everywhere."

"The need for change has become an obsession. Scores of young people, all over the world, are dropping off and going in search of green pastures, for freedom. That's why I have come to Rishikesh. The mechanised life in the US is unbearable. In any case, there is something funny about this Geeta Bhavan. I'd have liked it to be one of those ancient places."

"This place is the handiwork of one of the biggest industrialist in the country who builds temples, which could like factories churn out religion for the masses. I don't dig this industrialisation of religion at all."

"Let us go from here," Sarah said. "I had never imagined Rishikesh could be so tiring. Even the river seems to have lost her power here. No wonder the motor boat can sputter over her."

They walked out of the Geeta Bhavan and a crowded motorboat ferried them across the river. A pair of them was in service ferrying pilgrims. The river flowed with a lesser current here. When they reached the other side, they sank into one of the waiting tongas.

It was with some effort that they could extract themselves, from their seats, when the tonga stopped. Their minds were still racing over the running road with the rhyme of the horse's hooves, the squeaking wheels and the curses of the Tangawalla.

CHAPTER - IV

It was evening. Swami Ananda, Sarah and Akshyay sat in the garden, on chairs, pulled out from some of the rooms. Panchu had brought in the cups of tea, which they sipped in a common relaxed mood.

"So how was the trip to Geeta Bhavan?" Swami Ananda asked Sarah.

"It was quite an experience," Sarah said, with a shrug of her shoulders. The image of rows of beggars and lepers on the way to Lakshman Jhula leapt back into focus and like blinkers narrowed her vision.

Swami Ananda could make out from her facial expression that she did not savour recounting the trip and so he did not pursue the subject. He turned to Akshyay instead. "Why don't you take a bus to Rudraprayag? Sarah can accompany you."

"I would not like to go anywhere for some time now," Sarah interrupted, "I just remembered that my visa would expire in a week's time and I don't know what to do." The marks of anxiety appeared on her face.

"Why?" Swami Ananda said, "We are here to help you out. I could write to a very senior government officer in the foreign ministry. Getting an extension won't be a problem."

"But Swamiji", Sarah complained, "I just don't want to go to Delhi. That place puts me off completely. You can't imagine, what kind of hell I passed through there!"

"But there is no way; you could avoid it. You have to go to Delhi."

"I know," Sarah said thoughtfully, wringing her fingers and lowering her eyes.

They fell silent and became conscious of the river rolling along and the chirping of birds returning home. The western sky gently pulled a blanket of darkness over itself. Sarah's mind raced after the failing light as if making a last ditch attempt to find a tension-freeing idea before the dark night could envelope the firmament. She wanted to stay on at Rishikesh. She practised meditation every morning and did yoga under Swami Ananda's tutelage. Devouring Panchu's parathas for breakfast, she would walk the cobbled lanes of the town and witnessed the sight of sadhus in the temple courtyard. She was aware of the constant sound of the river and sat on the bank watching the rolling waves. All this had tied her to the place. She could not even think of leaving Rishikesh even for a few days to go to Delhi to get her visa extended.

Swami Ananda could understand her predicament. He looked thoughtfully from Sarah's face to Akshyay's, trying to find a solution. Akshyay, who had been attentively listening to the conversation, and in silence, also got caught up in the search.

Swami Ananda's face suddenly lit up in the waning light as an idea struck him.

"Why Akshyay", he began, "there is an easy way out in which you can help."

"Me . . . . In what way? I don't have any connections with the visa office Swamiji and I don't like the bureaucratic ways."

"You didn't get me. I wanted to tell you that you can marry Sarah and then her visa gets extended automatically.

She does not even have to go anywhere. We can send a letter from here and I know the Deputy Commissioner of this district. I am sure he will forward it. There is no reason why he wouldn't."

"But . . ."

"No ifs and buts. You can surely marry her. Sarah is a wonderful girl and just the right type for you. You will be a terrific pair; and by the Grace of God, all your problems, will be over. What do you say, Sarah?"

Sarah, who had been somewhat in a daze and lost in her thoughts, suddenly woke up, saying, almost spontaneously, "You are right Swamiji, you are right!"

"You mean you agree to the proposal?" Akshyay asked, surprise, looking at Sarah in the eyes and trying to read her mind. "Do you really want to marry me?"

"Why not? You are a wonderful person. Our wavelengths are similar." Sarah said.

"But I am not sure about being able to support a wife. I'm not quite ready for marriage, you know, and I am still unemployed. I dropped out of college and I am . . . You could call me a freak."

"Don't worry about that; I have been a freak too. I won't be a load on your shoulders. Ours could be a contract marriage if you like. You help me to stay in India, as long as I want to; and you gain entry to the US. What do you say to that?"

Akshyay became silent. This unexpected proposal had thrown him off-balance. He did not know what to make of it. He had come to Rishikesh for some peace of mind. He wanted to be away from the pressing problems of everyday living in a city like Calcutta. There were myriad problems there of poverty, slums, unemployment, Naxalite violence, police atrocities, the milling crowds. There was also the long face of his aunt in the frighteningly lonely house, where the ghost of his father, in his dreams, kept going menacingly at his poor, insane, mother... His future was undecided and he had allowed it to remain that way. The life that he had left behind, even though temporarily, did not interest him. He asked himself whether he wanted to go back to it. Did he want to renounce the world? He recollected that whenever the question had come up, he had promptly snubbed the idea with an emphatic 'no'. He had scant respect for people who renounced the world instead of facing life's problems and overcoming them. Not that he did that himself, but he was very much in love with the earth's beauty. He liked to hear the chirping of birds in the morning. He liked to see and feel the changing seasons, the snows of the Kunchenjunga, the purifying sensation of a dip in the Ganga, the music and poetry of life. He was aware of the sheer ecstasy of living—all too intensely pleasing to be discarded. There was a host of problems that needed solving and much work at hand, which he had kept pending to return to, when he would gain some strength and confidence. Right now, he was weak and in need of rest. The marriage proposal, if agreed to, would transport him back to the life he had left behind.

Yet as he looked at Sarah, the image of her beautiful face, which had been so full of love, floated before his eyes. He knew that she possessed an intellectual mind, which was also loaded with sympathy for the poor and weak. He pictured her graceful gait and recalled the feel of her long fingers when he had held her hand on the motorboat and again he saw her undressing in the room. The intense physical sensation that he had experienced then welled up within his body and like a wave engulfed him.

Akshyay got up from the chair and walked a little distance away. He wanted to hide the agitation in his mind, in the darkness, which had already descended all around and silenced the birdcalls. As he stood with his back to Sarah and Swamiji, he became aware of the sound of the river thundering down the valley. It reminded him that life goes on and within a few seconds the waves of agitation and turmoil in his mind and body seemed to ebb. He became conscious of someone beside him. It was Swami Ananda.

"I know you are in trouble, Akshyay," Swami Ananda said, with a knowing smile on his face. "But I am sure: you will not regret marriage to Sarah. She has a unique personality, wherein both rationality and emotions coexist in equal proportions. I am sure she will provide you with the support: you desperately need."

"It is true she is a wonderful girl, but I was here on a different trip altogether. I was looking for direction: a way of life, which would differ from the mundane existence."

"I have offered . . . Sarah has offered you, a new direction. Marriage to her would change the complexion of your life. Your existence will become purposeful. Come on now. Don't hesitate any further. You can't keep Sarah waiting . . . Come." Swami Ananda assumed an authoritative posture as he said these words and led Akshyay by the hand to where Sarah was expectantly sitting. She had never proposed marriage to anyone before. She did not quite understand why she had agreed to the marriage proposal in the first place. Probably it was something prompting her from within or perhaps it was because she had started falling in love. She could not be sure what it was, but now that she had extended her hand, she desperately wanted Akshyay to hold it. She looked at Akshyay anxiously as he approached. Akshyay looked at her soft, large, eyes and her pale face. He broke away from Swami Ananda and came close to her and grasped her hand.

"I want to marry you Sarah . . . I love you Sarah . . . I want to marry you Sarah," he said in a voice charged with emotion.

Sarah got up from her chair and slowly disengaged her entwined fingers, from Akshyay's grip. She stood in front of him, her eyes, unwaveringly fixed on his. Then, in a quick movement that caught Akshyay by surprise, she encircled his neck with her arms and kissed him full and long on his lips.

CHAPTER - V

Allen woke up Panchu early in the morning and between them they plucked all the marigolds in the garden. The yellow flowers lay in a heap on the floor of Swami Ananda's room and Allen volunteered to make garlands with them. The idea, of participating in a Hindu marriage, quite thrilled him.

The news of the marriage had spread all around the town. Nevertheless, only a few, who knew Swami Ananda and Sarah, talked about it. Among those who knew Sarah was a young Sikh: Avtar Singh. He came forward with the proposition of arranging a Benarasi sari at half the cost. He also lent a helping hand to the marketing; delivering invitation letters to the different ashrams, shopkeepers, grocers, and others, with whom either Swiss Cottage had dealings or Swami Ananda.

The bhoja would be simple: a curry of potatoes and peas with puris and a laddu for dessert. They expected around two hundred guests. It was not possible to invite more people or to arrange for a sumptuous meal due to financial constraints. In any case, there wouldn't be any criticism for this.

Akshyay had only about rupees two thousand with him, with which he had planned to stay for about three months at Rishikesh. He would now have to curtail

41

his stay and go to New Delhi to his cousin's place or to Calcutta. Meanwhile, Swami Ananda took a thousand rupees from him. Sarah contributed two thousand rupees. With this small budget, he began arranging the wedding.

Swami Ananda had called both Akshyay and Sarah to his room in the morning. Sarah was the first to arrive and Akshyay later, ushered in by Panchu, who went to call him. Both of them were strangely reticent and Swami Ananda had to virtually dictate the terms. All along, Akshyay and Sarah were unusually shy and sensitive to each other's presence. Swami Ananda had no difficulty in getting their assent when he summed up the proceedings from the note pad. "So Akshyay gives rupees one thousand, Sarah rupees two thousand and I will arrange rupees one thousand from the Swiss Cottage fund. That makes rupees four thousand. A Benarasi sari with blouse and veil for Sarah will cost rupees nine hundred and fifty. The cost of a gold necklace and earring: two thousand rupees. Rupees three hundred will fetch a dhuti and kurta for Akshyay. Another two hundred will take care of the marriage ritual in the Shiva temple and dakshina[8] to the pujari[9]. That makes a total of three thousand four hundred and fifty. The remaining amount: rupees five hundred and fifty, to feed the guests; and who knows, some savings as well." He had looked up by turns at Akshyay and Sarah, who were staring at Swamiji and listening to the accounting as if it were some testament read out by a judge. "Well", Swami Ananda said at last, "what do you think of that?"

"It's okay", Akshyay said, and for the first time speaking directly to Sarah, continued, "what do you think? Isn't it a fine budget? I had never thought that a Hindu marriage could cost so little."

"It is indeed," Sarah agreed. "I wonder why marriages in India aren't less expensive?"

"People will someday realise the folly of spending thousands of rupees in marriages, specially when they can't afford it. We have to rid the society of the evil dowry system, which has vitiated our lives." Swami Ananda said this as he got up to leave. "Get yourself ready for the marriage, day after tomorrow. According to the Hindu calendar that is the only date this month. And I think: the quicker the better."

Afterwards, Swami Ananda took Akshyay aside and told him that he had allotted him a room next to his own, because for the next forty-eight hours, the bride and bridegroom should not meet each other. This was a great relief to Akshyay. He had a feeling that he would not be able to confront Sarah. He would not know what to speak. Sarah also had been experiencing a strange transformation of her personality after that fateful evening. Alone in her room the night before the wedding she had tried to look into the life that she had chosen for herself.

Things have begun to move fast. Swamiji had proposed the marriage and she had jumped into it, without as much a second thought. She had at first felt amused at imagining herself in the role of a Hindu wife. She would have to look up to her husband as God and give herself up completely to his whims and wishes, forgetful of her self and desires. There was no visa problem to solve, no sense of insecurity, and no mad desire to break away from the mechanical life of civilised Western society. She saw herself as an Indian woman, waiting for her husband to return home before she could take her meals. The image of Akshyay's face floated in front of her eyes. It was an innocent face: the light-blue eyes set on a wide forehead, the shoulder-length hair. It was the same image of peace and innocence, that she had seen during her meditation trip and had thought to be that of an Avatar's. There appeared to be some affinity between the meditation trip and the role of a Hindu wife. She wondered whether following the code of a Hindu wife, would be like undergoing a course in self-discipline. 'Should she back out from such a rigorous course?' She thought. The change of dress, the vermilion on her forehead and in the parting of her hair, and the conch-shell bangles—the lifestyle would be very different from what she had seen in the West. Even then, she thought: Akshyay was quite Westernised and in appearance too . . . Anyone would mistake him for a Westerner, for his long hair, fair skin, blue eyes and hippie clothes. The life she was heading for was a mystery to her. She had developed a strange reliance on Akshyay, who was like a strong ship on which she would set sail on a wide, wide, ocean.

The lagna was between 7:00 and 10:30 in the evening. The tongas decorated with marigold, with the bride and bridegroom, set out of Swiss Cottage. The small procession had Allen, Avtar Singh, and Swami Ananda walking ahead of the tongas and a group of sadhus following behind. Sarah, in the typical bridal dress of Benarasi sari, gold necklace and conch-shell bangles, sat with the anchal covering her head. No one could tell whether the radiance of the Banarasi sari or the dying rays of the evening sun flushed her face. Her eyes, however, were downcast and the light veil revealed them, to those among the bystanders, who craned their necks for a better view.

Akshyay sat in a white kurta and dhoti on another Tonga. Though they were close enough, they hardly looked at each other. Their eyes had not met, even once, after they came out of their rooms for the journey to the Shiva temple. They had both been fasting since morning, and Akshyay's dip in the Ganges had further sharpened his senses. He was acutely aware of Sarah in the bridal dress, sitting in the Tonga ahead of him, the evening sunlight glowing on her sari and necklace. He was sensitive to the eyes of the curious people who stopped by to watch the quaint procession. It seemed to affect his mind, which began to vacillate between his perception and those of others. His mind assumed some degree of steadfastness, when he noticed the calm and steady gaze of the sadhus walking behind the Tonga. For some time he sat with his mind like a sieve, impassive to visual external stimuli. However, the scent of marigold mixed with attar and the rhythmic sound of clattering horses' hooves, attracted his attention. Through the rest of the journey, he sat with his mind in a state of trance.

When the procession reached the Shiva temple, the evening sunlight was on the fluttering triangular flag on the spire. The river gleamed in the reflected light about two hundred meters away and applauded with its rumblings the sudden ringing of the temple bells, which gleefully greeted their arrival.

Swami Ananda led Akshyay and Sarah inside the temple. The stone floor was damp, as well as the walls. The Shiva Lingam beneath the apse, glistened in the dull light of the oil lamps, placed on parapets along the wall. The smoke of incense sticks rose in thin strands and mingled with the air that flowed into the temple. The Pujari, who was sitting on his haunches, arranging the paraphernalia of items for the marriage ritual, rose up to receive them. He was an old man with a white beard and long white hair.

"They are just like Radha-Krishna", he said with a smile and then, turning to Akshyay and Sarah added, "here, come here and sit." He pointed to the asans placed side by side in front of the Shiva Lingam. "Who will give away the girl? Will you, Swamiji?" He asked.

"Yes," Swami Ananda said, and sat on the asan placed beside Sarah's, facing the Pujari, who was on Akshyay's side. The sadhus sat in the covered area, supported by pillars, outside the apse, and a crowd of curious women in their wet and dripping saris assembled at the doorway to watch the proceedings.

The Pujari pronounced the Sanskrit mantras and Swami Ananda repeated them. The mantras echoed and hummed on the stone walls. Akshyay tried to comprehend the meaning of the slokas and repeated them when his turn came to do so. Sarah sat spellbound in the dank and dark, eerie atmosphere, which was yet full of strength and vigour because of the mantras. In the intonation and incantation of the slokas, she could hear the hymns sung in churches and in synagogues.

"I hereby give away Sati to Akshyay," Swami Ananda said at last and the Pujari asked Akshyay to repeat his acceptance.

It was then time for exchange of garlands. The sadhus stood up and rung the bells; the women at the doorway gave jokar[10] and some of them even blew conch shells. Akshyay and Sarah, renamed Sati, both stood up, and facing each other, exchanged the marigold garlands, helped on by Swami Ananda and Avtar Singh. Their eyes were moist. Akshyay and Sarah's eyes were moist too and downcast with self-consciousness, but on Swami Ananda's insistence, they looked at each other. Their eyes met and for a brief moment the sound of the ringing bells and the echo of jokars seemed to melt away from Akshyay's mind. Instead, she experienced a strange feeling of his consciousness merging into hers. He was no more alone; Sarah's personality was bonded to his. The scent and feel of the marigold garlands and the whirlpool of sounds, of bells ringing and echoing mingling with the shrill sound of jokar mesmerised Sarah. She saw in Akshyay's eyes an image of deep-rooted strength and serenity, to which she clung, even as she lowered her eyelids into the din all around.

The marriage over, the procession started back and reached Swiss Cottage around 9 p.m. Swami Ananda led Akshyay and Sarah to the courtyard and made them sit on the asans placed facing the Radha Krishna idol. The guests, many of whom were already waiting for the bridal party to arrive, then came to see and bless them. The sadhus came in one by one and touched their heads to bless them. Many of the other guests also blessed them for a prosperous and happy married life. Some of the guests just sat in front of the couple and looked on with unflinching admiration. Avtar Singh stood at one corner and joined in echoing the utterances of some of the people he knew. These were mostly words of admiration: 'How lovely the couple looks!' . . . . 'Oh! 'Don't they look like 'Radha-Krishna'?' . . . . 'How fair they are!' . . . 'The bride looks like a goddess!'

Allen and Panchu served the food in talpatta plates. Everyone relished the puris and potato curry. Panchu's puris were hot: crisp and soft in the right proportions. The sadhus and the other guests had as many puris as they could and left Swiss Cottage, one by one and in-groups, it to its quietness once again.

A room next to Swami Ananda's was now for the married couple. Panchu had placed the two single beds together. Rajanigandhas covered the pink bed-sheet and wound round the leg posts and bedstead. A vase of flowers and incense sticks on a stand, were on the table, which was covered with a plain light-blue tablecloth.

After the guests had left, Swamiji, the bridal couple, Allen, Avtar Singh and Panchu, sat to eat together. Swami Ananda thanked Allen and Avtar Singh for their great help. After dinner he led Sarah and Akshyay to the room with the nuptial bed for the Suhaag Raat[11].

At the doorway, he made them stand side by side and blessed them. Akshyay bent down and touched Swami Ananda's feet in obeisance. Sarah also bent down, following Akshyay, but Swamiji stopped her for a brief moment, before allowing her to touch his feet. He suddenly remembered that she had become a Hindu wife. He then ushered them into the room and asked Akshyay to close the door.

Akshyay paused as he turned the latch. The room was small. He felt he was about to shut himself out from the rest of the world and from his own fitful and agonising past. Sarah was already sitting on the edge of the bed waiting for him. He turned with excitement and curiosity to what lay in store for him.

Sarah looked up as he turned, wanting to say something, but she did not utter a word. Akshyay came and sat beside her and after a while picked up her hand. Holding it tightly, he said, "What . . . How do you feel Sarah? Are you feeling tired?"

"No. Not really. It was quite an experience, for me," she said. "But I liked it all . . . So much love and benevolence, so many sadhus to bless us . . ."

"Yeah, I am also having the same thought. I've never had people doing so much for me. They were all there, Panchu, Avtar Singh, Allen, Swami Ananda, and then, above all, you . . . Sarah. I am fortunate to have you as my wife." He lifted her hand to his lips and then with his right hand on her shoulder, pulled her near, so that her face was close to his, and said, "I will never leave you."

Sarah said nothing, but smiled in reciprocation and kissed him passionately on his lips.

Akshyay suddenly felt his heart pounding and his blood warming up to the touch of her arms and shoulders, which seemed to enter his mind. He felt he was fast receding, sinking into a pit of soft white flesh. He felt a strange sensation all over his body as he went down on the bed rolling Sarah over him. Sarah made no attempt to resist, allowing him to get herself over him. Akshyay felt Sarah's weight over his body, but its softness was overwhelming: the softness of her firm breasts on his chest; her round thighs and knees pressed on his groins. Akshyay lost control of his limbs, as the sinking sensation again overtook him and he grappled with her body like a drowning man. Sarah allowed herself to sink with him.

Gasping for air, he broke away from her wet mouth and still found her body all over him. The sheer weight of her body brought him to his senses and he managed to off-load her. They lay side by side and Akshyay saw that Sarah had closed her eyes. He raised her head and kissed her closed eyelids and then her cheeks, nose and ears and again her lips. His pounding chest was now on her breasts and his hand held her head as he showered kisses on her face. In between, he muttered, "I love you, Sarah. I shall never leave you, Sarah. I love you Sarah."

His trembling fingers began to reach out and fumbled at the buttons of her blouse and under the folds of her sari. Sarah guided his fingers, and soon the lights went out. The two bodies merged into one another, enveloped in a wave of surging passion.

CHAPTER - VI

A week passed by in which Akshyay and Sarah lay ensconced in a couch of pleasure. It was a new sensation for both of them as there was no sense of guilt or remorse in their union. Their minds were in perfect harmony with the impulses of their bodies, like the bellow to the fire.

It was a different kind of trip for Sarah. She also experienced her personality merging into his and losing itself. There was however no need to come back: to be restored to the Jewish-American psyche unlike Akshyay, who did not quite change with marriage. For Akshyay, marriage so far, was a comforting experience. He clung to Sarah more for succour than for pleasure.

Life for both Sarah and Akshyay was carefree and yet within the framework of the ashram's discipline. They went for early morning walks along the bank of the glittering river and bathed in the cold clear percolating water. Afterwards, Sarah would sit in padmasan and meditate under the Banyan tree, while Akshyay would sit in the room and read books on yoga and Hindu philosophy that Swami Ananda had given him. In the evenings they listened to Swami Ananda's talks. He spoke on the teachings of the Bhagabat Gita: the purpose of life, categories of human beings, action, duties, and dharma. At night, after dinner, which Panchu served in their room, in accordance to Swamiji's orders, they cuddled into each other's arms and went to sleep.

That morning, a knock at the door woke up Akshyay. "Who's there?" He asked, rubbing his eyes, looking at Sarah's sleep-balmed face above the pink bed-sheet, to check whether she was awake. She was not.

"Baba, there is a telegram for you," He heard Panchu's voice. Akshyay crept out of the bed; opened the door, and peeped.

"Give it to me and go get some tea, if you can." He looked at the telegram and read, "Return immediately matter urgent, Monica." Akshyay closed the door and frowned at the thought of going back to the city and to see the long face of his aunt.

"What's it?" Sarah asked, her eyes still closed, and turning on her side. "Why don't you lie down with me for some more time? Come on." She opened her eyes, caught hold of Akshyay's hand and pulled him down on the bed. Akshyay could not react to her entreaty; his face wore a mask of thought and anxiety.

"It's my aunt's telegram. She wants me to go back to Calcutta immediately. She has not given the reason, but it must be something to do with my mother or the property. I have to leave today. I wonder whether you would agree to go with me."

"Of course. I am your wife and I have to go wherever you take me," she said, much to Akshyay's astonishment.

"But didn't you say before our marriage that you hated going to Delhi? Was it not your inability to even think of going to Delhi that prompted you to accept me as your husband? Calcutta is even worse, you know. It's congested and dirty: unlike New Delhi, where there are vast open spaces and parks, and less of factory chimneys and slums."

"I know, but I don't mind going to Calcutta. Allen was telling me about the Kali Temple and the burning ghat, where Allen Ginsberg had spent a year and composed 'Vietnam'. I should also like to see Belur Math and the Ram Krishna Mission. I have heard about them back home and of Swami Vivekananda."

Akshyay was at a loss whether to take for her words. He had known her outwardly as a good-natured, frank, modern American girl, interested in India because of the current trend. He never thought for a moment, that she could really want to participate in the Indian way of life that involved thinking in the idiom of Hindu philosophy, which so permeated traditional society. Her words were not compatible with his image of her. He considered her to be like any other person from the West: insensitive to the traditional values of religion and customs, which was an integral part of the vast majority of Indians, and a large cross-section of the orthodox Christian, Muslim, and even the Buddhist world. In short, he thought that her character and personality to be like his own and that was why they had clicked. He failed to understand how the marriage could so transform her personality. How could she change herself to be like a traditional Hindu wife, ready to follow her husband's footsteps, and sinking all her desires and wishes for the sake of her husband's pleasure? He could not help asking again, "Do you really think that you want to go to Calcutta and rather not stay back for a week or two till I come back?"

I've already told you that I'd go with you. Now, don't you worry your head about me? Come get in."

Akshyay was about to get under the sheet, when there was a familiar knock at the door again and Panchu's familiar voice called, "Tea, Baba, tea."

The scheduled departure of the train was in the afternoon. A pall of gloom spread over the ashram premises as the Tonga arrived to take Sarah and Akshyay away. The bright afternoon sun seemed to have dried up all the cheer. Even the Banyan tree, under which Sarah used to sit for her meditation trips, stood still, refusing to sing to the tune of the soft breeze. The impending departure of Sarah, who was the only woman in the ashram, was the cause of all the woe. Panchu shed tears as he handed over packed puris and vegetable curry, to her, for their dinner on the train. Avtar Singh and Allen helped Akshyay pack their baggage, with averted eyes.

Sarah's possessions were few. She had a sleeping bag, two sets of kurta and gown, and a lungi. Apart from this, the Banarasi sari and blouse, a few cotton saris, tooth powder, soap-case, a towel, some books and pamphlets on Yoga and India—all these were to be packed into a rucksack. She preferred to wear a red-bordered white cotton sari bought from Avtar Singh's shop, for the journey. Akshyay had only his sling bag in which he carried his things. These included one set of kurta-pyjama, a gamcha, toothbrush and paste, two sets of undergarments, a bed-sheet and the marriage dhoti-kurta. The packing over, Akshyay and Sarah went to meet Swami Ananda, who was waiting for them in his room. Akshyay touched his feet and Sarah followed suit.

"Swamiji, it is time for us to leave," Akshyay said.

"I wish you happiness and prosperity in your married life." He looked at Akshyay and then at Sarah and smiled.

Sarah said: "Swamiji, I have some money in the bank and some more is expected by this weekend. Please arrange to withdraw the amount and sent to me by money order or bank draft." She handed over a cheque of rupees five thousand to the Swami.

"Sure I will. Do you have enough money for the road?" He asked her and turned his eyes on Akshyay.

"We have enough. I've got five hundred rupees and Sarah has about two thousand", Akshyay said and quickly, as if by impulse, added, "there'll be no problem. I'll look after her and try to keep her happy." He glanced at Swami Ananda to see whether he acknowledged his statement or agreed to the prospect, but he could not make out anything from the Swami's bright eyes and beaming smile. Akshyay waited for some words from Swamiji, but the latter said nothing. He only smiled benignly at them. The sudden silence surprised Akshyay. He decided to break it, blurting out, "Swamiji, the tonga is waiting . . . good-bye."

"Good-bye," the Swami said. "Allen will see you off at the station." He went on to add, after a pause, "This ashram is always open for you, Akshyay and for you too, Sarah. Come whenever you need to and whenever you want to. Best of luck. May God bless you."

Akshyay and Sarah went out of the room and walked towards the waiting Tonga. Avtar Singh and Allen loaded the luggage. The couple then climbed on to the back seat, facing the ashram. As Allen climbed up and sat in front, beside the indifferent tangawalla, the horse began to trot. The Tonga slowly moved out of the silent ashram. Akshyay and Sarah sat staring at Swami Ananda, Panchu, and Avtar Singh. They stared at the diminishing ashram gate, at the thinning, glittering river behind the rows of rooms and the wall, until the Tonga turned into a bend of the narrow lane to blinker their vision.

Chapter - VII

The taxi crept along the high walls and stopped outside the iron gate, which showed through the iron bars, a driveway leading to a double-storied building. The over-spreading branches of a neem tree in the garden half-covered the porch. It also shaded the over-grown grass in the lawn and the flowering plants.

Akshyay got off as the honk of the taxi brought Abdul scurrying down the brick-lain drive.

"Salaam! Baba salaam!" He said, his right hand involuntarily rising to a salute and his face breaking into a wide smile. The smile turned to confused curiosity when he noticed the foreign woman in a red-bordered sari with the resplendent bindi on her forehead, like the sun setting on a wide horizon.

"How's everything going, Abdul?" Akshyay asked, and without waiting for a reply, ordered him to bring up the luggage. After Sarah came out of the taxi, following his signal, he led her to the teakwood door of the house and began to climb the staircase. Looking back all the while at Sarah as he went up the staircase, he could scarce notice his aunt standing on the landing.

"Who is this girl?" She charged, with an expression of disbelief in her face and eyes, even before Akshyay and Sarah had reached the landing.

"She's Sarah . . . Sati," Akshyay said, reacting to the sudden attack. He recovered himself and quickly added, "We got married in Rishikesh."

"You mean, you really married her and didn't bother to let us know," she said, showing her anger and the feeling of being outraged.

"There was no time to inform you . . . In any case, we are here, and now you know."

Sarah, whose eyes were downcast, slowly climbed on to the landing and bent to touch her aunt's feet.

This gesture from a white woman surprised Miss Monica. Instinctively, she stepped back saying, "No need for that", and after a moment's dithering, as she recouped herself from the cultural shock, said, "come into the house and get ready for lunch." Turning round, she walked across the drawing room, to her room on the right and closed the door.

"Come on in," Akshyay said apologetically, to Sarah. "Let's go to our room." Their room was opposite to Miss Monica's across the large drawing room. An old piano stood on one side and in the middle, a large twelve-seated dining table of black mahogany: tastefully carved legs and high-backed padded chairs. Adorning the walls, were photographs of Akshyay's ancestors: the most eye-catching one being the one of his great grandfather, who was a great social reformer. The luminous eyes seemed to stare out from the past.

Akshyay led Sarah, to a large bedroom cum study. An old-fashioned double bed stood on one side. Floor-length heavy curtains covered the windows. A big glass bookcase stored a rich collection of books ranging from Encyclopaedia Britannica, Sigmund Freud, and Karl Marx to Rabindranath Tagore, Max Mueller and Zimmer. A writing desk and chair were beside it.

Sarah sat on the bed and sighed. The long train journey and the taxi ride through the congested city roads had been tiring. The sound of clanking trams and the honk of impatient cars racked her nerves. Finally, the assault on her nerves at the staircase landing was too much to bear, after the peaceful life at the ashram. The haughty, intemperate, imperious, unfulfilled personality of Akshyay's aunt, with her greying shoulder-length hair, around a face wrinkled by a thousand grimaces, were in sharp contrast to the serene and cheerful face of Swami Ananda. It was his face, which had, among other things, endeared her to the ashram. For a moment, as she saw herself, sitting under the Banyan tree, she almost forgot her new role and longed to be back at the ashram. A sudden recollection of the telegram brought her back to her present predicament and to the bed on which she sat.

"What have you done with the telegram? Won't you check with your aunt?" She asked Akshyay, with an anxious look in her eyes.

"Oh shit! I forgot completely. I'll just go and find out, what's it all about. Meanwhile, why don't you wash yourself and get ready for lunch?" Akshyay raised his hand to indicate that he will be back soon and left the room in a huff.

"What's it?" Miss Monica asked, wrinkling her nose in disgust at Akshyay's hippie-type dress. His habit of wearing dirty clothes indicated his disinclination of having a bath every day like all good Indians.

"Well, you know better . . . about the telegram, don't you?"

"Oh! Do you want to know why I sent for you? You didn't want to come off that horrible place, where you jumped into the net of that hippie girl, did you?"

"Mind your words, Auntie. She is my wife now . . . And I didn't get trapped into anything. I'm mature enough to decide what is good for me, and what is not. You needn't interfere with my life. Now tell me: why you sent the telegram."

Miss Monica paused for a while, wondering how she should tackle Akshyay. She wanted to tell him about the family tradition, but decided to drop the idea. Instead, she said, "Abinash is coming over from London."

"So what do I do about him? Have you called me because Abinash is arriving?"

"Don't get impatient, Akshyay. Hear me out first and then talk. It's the will. Abinash is coming over only for that. You have to be present too because you are one of the inheritors."

"Couldn't you settle the matter without me? Why am I required at all?"

"Don't be a fool, Akshyay. Don't you realise: after your father's death, you have inherited his share of the property along with your mother. She is actually the real owner, but since she's in hospital and not in a normal state of mind, her share may be yours. "My mother! Where? In which hospital?" Akshyay asked becoming excited. He suddenly felt the urge to see her. "Do you know where she is? Right now I want to see her."

"I'm sorry. You cannot see her now. She's in a mental home: under treatment. Mr. Roy, the family lawyer, will give you all the details. He is the one who is looking after her treatment after your father's death. That's how your father wanted it to be. By the way, it was Mr. Roy, who had asked me to call both you and Abinash for settling some of the provisions of the will, in the changed circumstances."

Akshyay fell silent. His thoughts began to revolve round his mother. Faint images of his encounters with her, crept out of the deeps of his consciousness. He suddenly felt a longing for her: to see her, to talk to her, to be held in her arms, close, never separated again. He became aware of the gap between them. It has been a very long time since he had last seen her. He tried forming an image of her languishing in the mental home.

"What are you thinking about, Akshyay?" Miss Monica asked, seeing him lost in thoughts. "Are you worrying about your mother? No need to worry, she's in safe hands. You will get to see her soon, I suppose. Our lawyer will be able to tell you how and when. Now, don't you get upset? Go get ready for lunch. It's already late."

The discussion over lunch veered round the will and his mother's treatment. Akshyay had kept Sarah briefed about what had transpired between him and his aunt and therefore the conversation drew her attention. Akshyay wanted to extract more facts about his mother and so he began to ask his aunt one question after another. It was also a ploy to keep his aunt engaged so that she might not start a discussion either on his marriage to Sarah or on her background, which could be embarrassing.

Miss Monica, however, unaware of Akshyay's motive, felt happy answering his questions. She liked the idea of keeping Akshyay under her control. For those few moments at least, she held his attention. It was the only way she could belong to his life and scheme of thing. She was acutely aware that her world and Akshyay's world were moving apart. She could not allow that to happen, but she could only make vain attempts to keep them together. Already in their midst she felt like a complete stranger. There was a palpable generation gap between them: in their apparel, attitudes, thought processes, and culture. There was little in common save for the topics, on which they dwelt.

Miss Monica's personality flourished on the Indian version of the British tradition, which tended to hang on to the wrong end of it. Akshyay, on other hand, having been born in Independent India, and having seen in his youth that being Indian was the in-thing, had no difficulty in adapting to Indian ways and thought. There was no contradiction between the Western and the Indian in his mind, as it was in his aunt's. Akshyay could easily get himself to like Indian classical music or to wear kurta-pyjamas or even think of becoming a sadhu type. Miss Monica thought all these to be symptoms of irrational behaviour, which he had possibly inherited. She could not believe that a convent-educated Indian young man could even think of going to Rishikesh, let alone stay in an ashram.

The discussion about the will and his mother soon petered off, as no information was forthcoming. Miss Monica could not really open up before Sarah, who she still felt, was an intruder in their private and family affairs. Therefore, she made an attempt to arm-twist her with, "Sarah, I am sorry, we had been discussing something in which you are not directly concerned. You were getting bored, weren't you?"

"Not quite. After all, I am Akshyay's wife and I do have an interest in his affairs."

"Of course, you must. I have not yet got to know anything about you . . . Let me see where should I begin? Oh yes! Where are you from?"

"New York."

"Parents?"

"They are there. My papa runs a departmental store."

"Why did you think of coming to India of all places?"

"For peace. I left home in search of peace and freedom, when I was seventeen. I've been through Europe, Iran, Afghanistan . . . . I didn't find what I was looking for anywhere, but in Rishikesh. The police hounded me out of Hyde Park at night. I didn't have enough bread for a hotel. I raised funds singing in the streets of Paris along with a Greek, who played on a guitar. I ran along the deserted lane in Morocco: a rapist, close on my heels. I've had my bottom pinched by truck drivers in Afghanistan when I tried to hitchhike through that country. I've walked through broken glass, all over, till I reached Rishikesh. You know; the pure cold Ganges water here and the purity of the ashram healed my wounds. Then I met Akshyay and decided to marry him."

Akshyay felt surprise at the sudden flow of information; but he remained calm and unflustered. His experience with Rita crept into his mind . . . the night at the Astor Hotel, where he took her for a screw, and struggled to unhook the bra. Miss Monica, however, could not fully believe what she heard and did not know how to react or what to say. She was completely at a loss, unable to make any comment or pass judgement and to keep the conversation going, said "Were you alone in your trip through Europe and Central Asia?"

"Of course, I was alone. As I said I had left home at seventeen. The professor was teaching psychology and the subject was association. He was explaining how a chair conjures different images in people's minds depending on their past experiences. Someone may think of a classroom, someone else of a tree being cut, and yet another, of a lady teacher's bottoms getting pricked. Such inane, disjointed, half-truths, about the working of the mind: did not interest me. I wanted to know my own mind and the mind of the universe, and for that I had to get out of the classroom and live life close to nature. That afternoon, I stood outside the Professors' Lobby and the tall bespectacled professor in a grey suit stopped to ask me what was the matter. His face became red, when I told him why I was leaving.

"My old man felt outraged and said that he would not fend for me. I didn't care and told him so. I left home the same day and shifted to Jackie's place. He used to play the flute beautifully. I began to live with him until one day I heard Krishna's flute and since then I've been in search of that pure music. I went back and told my father that I needed money to go to India, en-route Europe. He agreed to pay me a lump sum of four thousand dollars. I landed in London, and then to Paris, Athens, hitch-hiking through Morocco, Istanbul and then to Kabul. I took a Kuwait Airlines flight to New Delhi and finally I reached Rishikesh, where I was staying at the Swiss Cottage."

Miss Monica listened to Sarah's words with rapt attention, her mind working backward to see fragmented images of her past: the convent school in Darjeeling, and later Loreto College, Calcutta. The handsome Anglo-Indian, Roland, the hotel manager, who offered to pay for her bills; their escapades in the afternoons to the lonely spots of the Botanical Gardens and the zoo; bunking classes. She remembered the feeling of being left behind, when she couldn't find her roll-number in the gazette. It only added to her misery when Mitali, her best friend, informed her that Roland was a married man. Her world had seemed to fall apart and be buried under a dark shroud. She began to see all men as deceitful and decided not to allow herself to fall in love again, even by mistake. Then one day, when she looked at herself hard and long in the mirror, she realised that she was too old for any suitor. Her brother, Akshyay's father, couldn't care less. He was too busy with his work and his drinking bouts into which, he drowned himself, to erase the memory of his responsibility in his wife's madness. Like him, she was doomed to pass her time in silent solitude, in that very house, where she was still living, and in that very room: the dry neem leaves strewn on the floor.

She saw that Sarah had been lonely too. She had decided to go it out all alone. She was raped on the cobbled streets of Morocco. She begged in the streets of Paris. She hitchhiked through . . . And yet she was one piece, as if nothing had happened.

She looked at Sarah and thought: how different she was from herself, as a young woman. How beautiful she looked in the red-bordered white sari! She wondered whether her ancestors, who had come to India centuries ago looked like her. Was free sex there, then? Why did she not allow Roland to make love to her and later the bank manager, whom she had met at the Windsor Bar? She saw herself lying in the back seat of the car and Mr. Dasgupta driving. He had escorted her out of the bar. She had not been able to stand on her feet, without his arms around her waist, supporting her. Her head had been swimming after the fourth round of whisky. She wondered whether Mr. Dasgupta had made love to her, while she had been unconscious. She had no means of knowing, but she recalled that he never made a pass at her though they had several meetings later in the bar. She wondered whether Sarah was a teetotaller.

"Why, Sarah, you're not eating? Isn't the food tasty?" A bowl of rice, a dish of fried potatoes; brinjal, dal, hilsa fish with mustard; puris, chutney, banana, grapes and sandesh—all laid on the table. Sarah's plate had barely some puris and fried potatoes. "Won't you take some fish or dal?" Miss Monica continued.

"I prefer to be a vegetarian for some days, you know. I've just come from a place, where I got used to that kind of food and I found it groovy," Sarah said, helping her appetite to some more puris and fried potatoes.

Miss Monica did not know what to say. She could not believe that an American could talk about vegetarian food, which she had always associated with widows, orthodox North and South Indian and Jains. She wondered now, whether her distaste for vegetarianism was correct, since even an American could turn out to be a vegetarian. However, she rationalised against the notion with the argument that Sarah was a rebel American. She did not represent the American tradition, or their eating habits. With that conclusion, she began to concentrate on finishing her meal. Sarah also fell silent and continued to eat her puris and fried potatoes.

After lunch, while they lay side by side on the bed, looking at the fan, hanging from the ceiling, its blade turning round and round, Akshyay began to think about the future. He had Sarah with him, as his wife, and he had not only to think about a regular income to attend to their basic needs, but also of ways and means to keep Sarah happy. He tried to think of objects and activities that could make her happy. He realised that he could not impress her with his house, the collection of books, the piano, and the wall paintings of his ancestors. His fair skin or blue eyes were also of no consequence. India interested her: oriental and ancient. He could not offer that Indian-ness in his personality. He was a Westerner by choice and upbringing, with no firm belief in the caste system or life after death or the law of karma, which permeates the mind of Hindu India from ancient times. He recalled that he had read some books on Yoga and some chapters of the Bhagabat Gita in translation. He had also read through the Tibetan Book of the Dead. This enabled him to talk about Indian Philosophy and Buddhism with some amount of authority. However, he knew that he did not believe in all that he talked about Indian philosophy and traditions. Not all that he read or learnt could penetrate the inner core of his being.

"Sarah!" He suddenly called out, "What would you like to do in the evening? Would you like to go to the Strand? We could walk along the river, you know. It's called by a different name here. We can talk about our future course of action in peace there."

"Of course! I'd like to see how the river looks down here," Sarah opined confidently and eagerly.

CHAPTER - VIII

Sarah felt strangely relieved at the sight of the river flowing between the concrete banks and the ships, steamers, jute-laden boats, and jetties that lined the strand. She recognised the same power in it, which she had seen at Rishikesh, a power that was beyond the control of man, effortlessly flowing towards the sea. She felt as if she saw in the shimmering waters a Broadway leading to eternity, to a timeless nowhere, where all humanity mingled into one undivided and unending mass of limit-less nothingness.

"You know", said Akshyay, as they walked along the strand, "I used to come to bathe in the river every Sunday. It was just far out. I always wondered how the muddy water could give such a feeling of cleanliness. I have not had a dip here, however, for quite some time now, after reading and hearing a lot about pollutants being fed into the Ganges. All the jute mills, thermal power plants and refineries have been injecting all their wastes into the river; at several points along its length, from Rishikesh to its mouth at Gangasagar."

"Are there any pollutants in the river here?"

"No, I'm sure there aren't. Many of the boatmen drink the river water and hundreds of people continue to bathe in the river everyday and carry the water to their homes for puja. The charanamrita[12] of all the temples in the city is nothing but Ganges water. The city-supplies are from the river. Is it not a wonder that in spite of so much of squalor, dirt and slums; and the violation of basic hygiene everywhere: there hasn't been any epidemic here?"

"I suppose man is able to adjust to his environment. You know, I've not fallen sick although I've had food several times at dhabas in Chadni Chawk, and all the cheap hotels and motels I've been to. I didn't have enough bread, you know. It's only in Rishikesh of all places, that I got good, clean, food to eat in the ashram. It was the food, I think, which gave me a new feeling of purity and illumination." Sarah said, raising her eyebrows, as if she had just discovered a truth.

"It's all there in the Shastras, and in the Bhagabat Gita too. You know, the vegetarianism, which you have adopted: will take you closer to the spiritual life, and reduce your physical needs."

"Why don't you become a vegetarian?"

"I don't give a damn to what I eat. I eat everything; I can be a vegetarian as well. No hassles; but I don't dig compulsions."

"But don't you think you would do better if you were a vegetarian?"

"I've not really thought about that. In fact, I have always felt it's a kind of deprivation. Our widows cannot have meat and fish. Several writers and social reformers, championing the cause of widow remarriage and female education, have opposed this."

"You mean the social reformers have objected to vegetarianism?"

"It's not so. They have propagated widow remarriage and opposed the cult of widowhood. In doing so they have actually gone against vegetarianism. Our widows could only take vegetarian food and wear black-bordered saris for the rest of their lives. That was what they went against. They saw in vegetarianism: a deprivation of basic human needs."

"There is a large chunk of population, who actively participate in vegetarianism, in North and South India. Can you explain that?" Sarah asked getting into the argument.

"Well, that is due to historical reasons. You know; the effect of Jainism and Buddhism. The Hindu counter-attack, absorbed the tenets of non-violence and vegetarianism, which was responsible for vegetarianism becoming a habit with Hindus."

"Did you mean to say that by adopting the tenets of Jainism and Buddhism; the Hindus stopped the trend of conversion to those religions?"

"You are right. Hinduism has been assimilating and adapting in this manner, even to this day, with the result that it is still a valid, practical, religion. I think our discussion is going too heavy. We have also reached the end of the strand. Let's go over to the jetty." Akshyay said, concluding his speech.

Sarah took Akshyay's hand and they walked over the creaky causeway to the jetty. It was already dark and the river was dotted with boat-lights, still in mid-stream, bobbing up and down in the waves. The breeze was soft and cool. Sarah felt it caressing and lapping up the sense of fatigue; unravelling the entangled thought-waves in her mind.

"How lovely it is here and peaceful. I remember the river at Rishikesh: the oil lamps on sal leaves, keeping afloat as long as they can in the turbulent waters."

"Yeah, it is beautiful, indeed. Let's go home now. I have to get on with my lessons and meet my Guru," he said, as he realised that what he just said was unplanned and spontaneous.

"Oh really! You never told me; about this?"

"I didn't. You know, I thought I'd give up music altogether, when I went to Rishikesh. I wanted to give up everything and not come back again. I became fed up with my scene and wanted to split. That's why I went to Rishikesh: to start a new life."

"But," Sarah interrupted, "you were not going to be a sadhu, were you?"

"No, not really a sadhu . . . renouncing the material world . . . But you know, I was on a spiritual trip, if that is the right word for it. I just wanted to split . . ."

They became silent. Akshyay heard the sound of the waves lapping the jetty and pulling back, repeatedly in rhythmic monotony and his mind joined in the pattern. They remained silent as if in a trance. After quite some time, Sarah experienced a strange feeling of emptiness, with the waves repeatedly pulling away. She suddenly gripped Akshyay's hand, rather firmly.

"Let's go home," she said to Akshyay, imploringly, with a strange look of fear in her eyes, "let's go."

Akshyay took a tram to drop Sarah home and then a bus to Jadavpur, where the classical music teacher, who had earlier given him sarode lessons, lived. Akshyay got off the bus on a road flanked by shops. Looking around, he wondered where the lane to his Guru's house was. It was almost a month, since his last visit. There were groups of people on the road hugging the bus-stand and shops. Hawkers and vegetable vendors occupied the footpaths. Consequently, pedestrians had to spill over to the road, too close to the slow moving, fuming, honking, traffic of buses, lorries, private vehicles and cycle rickshaws.

Akshyay moved away from the crowded bus stand and then he suddenly recognised the teashop on the opposite side of the road. He had once had tea in a bhar[13] there, while waiting for the rain to stop. The road to the music teacher's house was beside it. As he descended on the lane, the sounds of the road subsided. There were only residential houses in the area and a few dimly lit shops, which made up, to some extent, for the absence of streetlights. Soon the pond appeared in view. Akshyay lifted his pyjamas with both his hands, as he began to tread on the kutcha road that skirted a pond, full of croaking frogs and creaking crickets. His Guru's house was on the other end. The broken lights that fell off some of the half-open, pane-less, windows lit up in patches the otherwise dark passage. Mosquitoes hovered round his head and as he jerked his head to avoid them, he noticed a group of boys in their late teens, huddled under a porch. As he came near, one of them stepped out and blocked his way.

"Hello Sahib! Have not seen you for long?"

"Oh!" Akshyay said, recognising the voice. "You are the Naxalite; are you not?"

"Shoo! I am Shamir. There are informers all around. The police have powers to arrest anyone."

"Really, I didn't know," Akshyay said with concern, but the curious pairs of eyes staring at him, smothered his desire to keep on talking. "Is your father at home? I wish to meet him."

"Oh yes! He is at home. You can just walk in. He is sitting in the drawing room."

"Bye then!" Akshyay said with a measured smile and walked ahead towards the house. The Guru, Mr. Sanat Lahiri, was sitting on a divan, in the dimly lit room, on the right of a corridor, which had rooms on either side. His face lit up as he saw Akshyay.

"Oh Akshyay! Where were you away, all these days?"

"I was in Rishikesh. I came down this morning."

"Oh really? I was wondering whether you had given up Sarode and gone back to your Western Music."

"How can I do that, Guruji? I had to go to Rishikesh: in keeping with my father's wish."

"Oh I see! I hope there was no trouble coming here at this hour? Why are you standing? Come sit down here, beside me."

Akshyay sat down quietly on the chair in front of the divan. "I met Shamir on the road," he said.

"Oh that rascal! He is gone to dogs. His college closed due to union disturbances, and he spends the whole day on the streets with his friends, doing nothing but gossip. He doesn't even take any interest in learning to play the sarode. There is no use for it—he says. He just wants to destroy everything and bring in a new society where there will be work for all and education for all. I have failed to drive into his silly head, that such a dream cannot come true in this country: where people believe in God."

"There is nothing wrong in having an ideal. I also believe that there should be education for all and employment for all. In any case, I give top priority to freedom. No one should force me to work or prevent me from playing the sarode." As he was speaking, he noticed a mosquito at the back of his hand, sucking his blood. Mr. Lahiri, who was following his eyes also noticed it and at once slapped it dead. The mosquito stuck dead in a smear of blood on Akshyay's hand. Akshyay looked at it, the congealed blood and the smashed mosquito, and then at Mr. Lahiri's eyes. He thought whether he should relate this action to the discussion they were having, but he gave up the idea, as one too far-fetched, and flicked the drying paste off his hand. "How's the music scene in the city, Guruji?" He asked, changing the topic.

The Guru, happy to tread on familiar ground, said, "There are very few conferences nowadays because of Naxalite trouble in the city. During the past winter, I have performed only in one function and that too, inside a theatre hall."

"Which raga did you play? Was it the Bhairav rag?"

"Yes, the sarode brings out the raga very well, like the Kanchenjunga reflects the beauty of the sunrise. I'll teach you someday how to play this raga, but you will need to come to me in the morning around ten o'clock so that you have the entire day-light hours to practice. In the evening there are too many mosquitoes and it is unsafe to move about at night. Do you think you can give enough time to sarode? It is only with dogged devotion and inherent talent, which you have in abundance, that you can master the art of sarode."

"I am free all day, Guruji," Akshyay said, but while saying this he also thought: 'how will I pay the tuition fees? How will I look after Sarah?' He drove away the thoughts from his mind in his customary fashion of not caring for the future and said, "Guruji, I forgot to tell you, I'm a married man now."

Oh! That's wonderful news. Where are the sweets? How foolish of me not to have guessed it! There is a certain change in your personality. It is common to all married men. Of course, how could I guess? The pitfalls of my son's career carried me away. Well, who is she? How did it all happen?"

"It happened at Rishikesh. My father had a friend there, a Swamiji. In his ashram I met a good American girl: we got married in the Shiva temple."

"Oh! How beautiful and romantic! Does Indian music interest her? I have heard that many Westerners are going for Indian music, nowadays. That's after one of the Beatles, George Harrison, showed interest in the sitar and tabla, and sang a number called 'Jai Guru deva'. When are you bringing her?" He turned his head towards the doorway and raising his voice, called out for his wife, "Are you listening? Akshyay has married. Why don't you send in some sweets?"

Akshyay heard a familiar shrill voice replying, "I'm bringing in tea. Don't allow Akshyay to go."

When Akshyay had finally left, Mrs. Lahiri turned to her husband. "How is it that Akshyay married within two months of his father's death? One can only marry after a year, isn't that the rule?"

"Yes that's the tradition, which all Hindus follow. These rigid rules are all for people like us. For those people, of such rich families, as his, there aren't any rules. Those who make the rules: they are the first to break them."

Chapter - IX

The next morning Abinash arrived as scheduled from London, through New Delhi. He had a job in a Chartered Accountants' firm in London. Married and with two children, he had adopted the western lifestyle. He dressed smartly: full-sleeve shirt and tie, shampooed hair. There was a certain glow in his complexion. He spoke with an accent and his eyes twinkled. One could easily make out that he had achieved a major degree of success in the West.

Abinash arrived in a hired car at eight o'clock and joined Miss Monica for breakfast. After the initial inquiries about the journey and family, when Abinash wanted to know about Akshyay, Miss Monica said with a sigh, "I wonder what will happen to him. He has not completed his studies. He has not qualified for any job. Now he has mixed with those fake sadhus; and he's married a hippie girl."

"Oh really? Where is he?"

"He must be still sleeping. He came home late last night from his music teacher's place; and I could hear them talking over their dinner; when I was in my bedroom, preparing to go off to sleep."

"His wife is also here, then? What's her name? Where is she from?"

"She's from America. Her name is Sarah; changed to Sati."

"Well, Akshyay has done a wise thing; I must say; in marrying an American girl. He could easily become an American citizen and go to the US, where he could earn a good living without much difficulty. There are many opportunities in America for a young guy like him to make it in life . . . facilities, which are just not available here, in India."

"I don't think America would accept him and his hippie wife. You have not seen him lately: he wears a kurta and pyjama that's not even clean. He has long hair. He wears rubber slippers . . . Do you think the immigration office would give him a visa? I am quite sure that they would turn him out. Why don't you try, now that you have come? You can put some good sense into his thick head; or at least get him to wear proper clothes."

"Well I'd have loved to do that if I could, but I don't have time. I have to go to Bombay this evening on official work; and on Saturday, I'll have to fly back to London. I can't spend time here doing nothing. Nonetheless, I'll give Akshyay a piece of my mind and . . ." he stopped abruptly seeing Akshyay enter. "Hi! I was just talking about you. I was telling Aunt Monica; I could give you a few tips on what you could do for a bright future."

"We'll talk about my future later," Akshyay said, as he walked in, followed by Sarah. "First, let me introduce you to my wife." Turning to Sarah he continued, in a theatrical stance, "This is Abinash my cousin. He lives in London; happily married with two kids. He also has an equal share, of my great-grandfather's property. And this is Sarah."

After an initial reluctance, Abinash extended his hand towards Sarah with a smile on his face. As they shook hands, Abinash said, "Hello, Sarah, welcome to our family. I wish you a happy, prosperous, life."

"Thank you for your good wishes. For how long, have you been living in England?"

"Oh! I have left this God-forsaken country five years back. I passed out from IIT with electrical engineering. Thereafter for two years, I worked in a multinational company in Calcutta. They sent me to London on assignment, and I saw first-hand, the vast differences between our country and theirs. You know, between Calcutta and London, and I chose to stay back. This country, and particularly this city, has no future. Don't you agree with me?"

"Well I don't quite subscribe to your view-point. I find a lot of love and innocence here and a yearning for the spiritual life. In England, I suppose, in the entire West; materialism governs everything." Sarah said.

"I agree there is much love in the home front here. That is between parents and children, between brothers and sisters and even between relatives, but when it comes to love for the Nation, or love for the people of India there is a void. People would cheat the Government and loot public money for the benefit of their family members. This is not something you would find in the West and that is why they have progressed much faster than India. This country is full of thieves."

"That is an extreme view. The backwardness of India is due to historical factors like exploitation and subjugation. Even today, the super powers would not like to see India progress faster or be self-reliant. They would like to sell their products, here."

"Isn't that natural business instinct? Who would not like to sell his products?" Abinash retorted.

"Yes, but that does not give them a right to meddle in another country's internal affairs to suit their business interests."

"I don't understand what you are saying. You mean; Western countries would like to keep India backward?"

"Perhaps, if that would help in their business interest." Sarah said promptly.

"But how could you explain a Government having all the powers, not making any attempt to solve the basic problems. The problems of unemployment, poverty, black money, rural backwardness, lack of educational facilities; are there for ages and ages?" Abinash said.

"Now let's give it up, Abinash. Why do you have to worry, about these problems?" Akshyay intervened, and turning to Sarah, said, "There is no end to this discussion."

"I agree with you, but I don't like this blind admiration of the West and that too by an Indian. I think; this country is far-out." Sarah said firmly.

Sarah's words seemed to strike Abinash dumb. He had not expected to hear her speak in the manner that she did. He wondered whether Akshyay had taught her all that; and if he had, how could he possibly influence her so much, and how long it took him doing that. All of a sudden, he blurted out, "Have you been practising the discipline of being a Hindu wife? Your views are; those of Akshyay's, I presume?"

Akshyay, with annoyance marking his speech, said, "What makes you think she's been repeating my views? They are entirely hers. I don't believe in forcing my views on anyone, not even on my wife." He controlled himself and said: "Why don't you join us, for another round of coffee?" Turning to his aunt, in an accusing voice, he continued, "Why couldn't you call us for breakfast? With Abinash around; we wouldn't have refused."

Miss Monica was not ready for the question and took some time to answer Akshyay: "I did not think you'd be ready for breakfast at eight o'clock. It's good to hear that you'd have been ready."

Akshyay felt like telling her to go to Hell with her British traditions, but he restrained himself and walked towards the dining table holding Sarah's hand.

"Let's get to the main issue," said Akshyay. "What do you have to say about the will? Why was it so important that you sent a telegram, to call me back? Is there some bread, coming from the property?"

"Well," Abinash began, sitting opposite Akshyay at the large dining table. "I received a letter from the trustees. A large sum of money, around rupees twenty lakhs[14], will have to get transferred to our names, now that uncle has passed away. The money is from the rent of buildings in Calcutta and Bhubaneswar. Now Auntie, you, your mother, and I, are the joint owners of the property; and of the rent collected from the tenants."

"I never knew there was so much money in the bank just from collected rent," said Akshyay, somewhat surprised. The emotive content in his voice could not hide a certain degree of pleasure at the prospect of owning a few lakhs of liquid cash. It could at least solve the major problem of earning a living, if not anything else. "I had known all along that our family owned some buildings in the city, which were quite old and the rent was low."

"You were not very much off the mark. Our trustees have informed that recently the American Consulate has agreed to a raise in the rent. They have also paid a substantial amount for carrying out some modifications. Our lawyer is likely to arrive at ten o'clock, today. We'll have to sign certain documents and bank papers. That's why I rang Auntie, and asked her to call you back."

Sarah, all along, listened nonchalantly to the conversation about the will, money and rents, and wondered what lay in store for her. She recollected her life in the ashram, where she was like a free bird in the midst of nature, in an atmosphere of peace and tranquillity. She remembered her life in her father's house. The discussions over the dining table were on the sale proceeds of her father's departmental store; the falling price of shares; and the rising cost of grocery. She wondered whether she had returned to the world she had left behind or whether this was a different world, on which she had set foot. However, it was too soon to have doubts. Rather, it would be better to go through the whole hog and see first-hand, before coming to any conclusion.

CHAPTER - X

At ten o'clock sharp Lakshman ushered into the drawing room, a middle-aged man of average height and build. He was wearing a black coat and black tie, typical of lawyers. Miss Monica got up to receive him and after that began to formally introduce him to Abinash.

"This is Mr. Kamal Roy. He is our family lawyer. He is one of the owners of the firm 'Imperial Lawyers and Chartered Accountants', who are our Trustees." She turned to the lawyer and pointing at Abinash, said, "This is Abinash, my nephew. He lives, in London."

The lawyer, beaming with admiration, and in a high-pitched voice that was almost comically discordant to his figure, said, as he shook Abinash's hand, "You really live there? My father did his bar-at-law in London. How long will you be in India? How do you feel, back home?"

"Well, I have to go back on Friday. I came only because of your letter. I have no attachments here—this hell of a place."

The lawyer, who had a habit of adjusting his glasses every now and then, released Abinash's hand, a little shocked at Abinash's brash style and began to adjust his glasses, looking away. He preferred not to continue the discussion any further, certain that it would only hurt his feelings. He turned to Miss Monica for further introductions.

"Oh! This is Akshyay; my other nephew and this is his wife," Miss Monica said quickly. She guessed that she had purposely stopped at Abinash, leaving out Akshyay and his wife.

Akshyay folded his hands in the traditional namaskar posture, before the portly lawyer could extend his hand for a handshake, and said, "Namaste."

Sarah followed suit and said, "Namaste."

The lawyer's round-rimmed glasses almost fell off the bridge of his nose, as he confronted Akshyay's striking but rather quaint appearance and demeanour. His dress of kurta-pyjama, his unexpected use of the Indian form of address, his foreign wife's red-bordered sari . . . all seemed strange and outlandish. "I used to know your father," he began slowly, adjusting his glasses. We played cards together in the Calcutta Club. He was a very well behaved man: very educated, traditional, and patriotic in his way. He told me once about how you had left North Point without notice and how the whole town went on a spin.

"I left North Point to find out where my mother was. I had to leave without notice, because the school authorities decided to disallow her from seeing me."

"You see, your father didn't want you to come to any harm. Your mother wasn't well and you were in a tender age. He decided that it was in your interest, that you do not meet each other. I am sure you don't know where your mother is, even today," the lawyer said, adjusting his glasses.

Sarah, who had been listening casually, suddenly became interested.

"No, I don't. Could you tell me?" Akshyay said.

"Yes, I'll tell you. Your father has made out his will; and therein, he has left instructions that we could tell you about your mother's whereabouts. Further, we could make her treatment, your responsibility. However, there are certain conditions, to be fulfilled."

"What are these conditions?" Akshyay asked with interest.

"Well, I'll come to that," the lawyer said as he adjusted his glasses. "Are you ready? Shall I begin, Miss Monica?"

"Wait a minute. Let me get you something to eat. What would you like with snacks; tea or coffee?"

Miss Monica rang the bell and Abdul appeared. "Get us some tea and some samosas[15], will you? Now you may begin, Mr. Roy."

The lawyer took out his notebook; flipped through the pages. He adjusted his glasses and began to speak, "The purpose of this meeting is to advise you about the changes in the ownership and income, about the state of the foundation money and about other conditions of the Trust. This has become necessary after the sad demise of Mr. Ramen Chaudhuri. We have prepared a special, detailed, report. You can go through it later." He took out three envelopes from his briefcase and handed them over to Miss Monica for distribution.

"To give you the main points, I should begin with the property at your disposal and in our Trust. There are five houses: one with the American Consulate; two in Bhubaneswar; and two residential blocks in Calcutta, rented out to tenants. We had sought to revise the rent, payable by the American Consulate and by the tenants of the two houses. While the American Consulate has agreed to pay a substantially higher rent, most of the tenants in the two houses have not. Concerning the two houses in Bhubaneswar: a private party has taken one on rent; and the other, the state government, there. While the private tenant has agreed to a raise in rentals, the state government has not. The rent from all the five houses has increased from twenty thousand rupees to thirty-five thousand rupees per month. This means, thirty thousand rupees for distribution amongst you, after deductions for municipal taxes, maintenance cost, salaries of chowkidars and other incidental charges. There is also the accumulated rent in the bank, to be shared."

Besides all this, there is a sum of fifteen lakhs rupees in the Nalini Devi Foundation, for the benefit of meritorious, but poor students, for pursuing higher studies. We have received the applications. We will screen them. Then you will have to unanimously decide about the recipients. You may just sign for approval or prefer to call for fresh applications or screen the applications yourselves."

"No! No! Mr. Roy. We trust our Trustees to do all that. We'll just sign for approval. Don't you agree, Abinash?" Miss Monica said.

"Yes! Who has the time for all that? I wonder why so much money is there for these social activities, while we have so little?"

"Your forefathers never expected such a steep rise in prices or any legislation ceiling the rent payable by tenants and protecting them from eviction," the lawyer explained, adjusting his glasses.

"I suppose so. In any case, of what use is the money to me? How can I get pounds in London?"

"You can't. You could however, convert the money to gold; and take it out of the country, after declaring it as your wife's jewellery."

"I'll have to think of doing something like that."

"Well, shall I continue? There is another fund of twelve lakhs rupees, which is for annual assistance to philanthropic organisations. The name of the fund is Mrinalini Devi Fund. As of now, R.K.Mission, Bharat Sevashram and Sivananda Ashram have been getting grants. You may now choose to give a percentage, to some other organisations, such as Mother Teresa's Sisters of Charity, or even, an organisation like Kasi Viswanath Seva Pratisthan. The money from the fund is for distribution, amongst different organisations, and on this; you have to decide. In case of any disagreement among the owners; the final decision lies with the Trustees."

All along, Akshyay heard the lawyer with rapt attention. Sarah also heard him with interest. She had begun to get a feel of the family tradition and could see vague images of a glorious past, which had resulted in the accumulation of so much wealth. She noted that Akshyay's forefathers had protected the wealth. Future generations could not fritter it away. Nevertheless, it looked after the well being of descendants, as well.

Akshyay wondered what lay in store for him. He had never known that his family owned such a big estate. He became conscious of the fact that a sizeable income from the family property could mean freedom from the hassles of earning a living. It would mean fulfilment of a dream and solve all his problems, as would a magic wand. A sense of the irony of the situation rebuked his conscience. He was now turning to the family from which he had turned away. Nevertheless, he waited in bated breath for the words of the lawyer that would set him free. He could again hear his words.

"There are three owners, today, even as it was earlier, Miss Monica, when your two brothers were alive. Now in place of Mr. Arun Choudhuri, Mr. Abinash Choudhuri, his only son is the rightful owner and you too. You have your share of one third; and finally, in place of the late Mr. Ramen Choudhuri, his wife, Mrs. Diana Chaudhuri is the rightful owner. However, since she is a mental patient and staying at a mental home in Ranchi, her share of one-third is with the trustees for the last two months." He looked at Akshyay as he said these words. We have spent five thousand rupees, out of a total of twenty, for her treatment at Ranchi and kept the balance of fifteen thousand, in the bank.

At the words of the lawyer, announcing his mother's whereabouts, a vague longing filled Akshyay's mind. The waves of emotions connected with his childhood separation from his mother surged back. He recalled his boyhood yearning for her during the school vacations and his arguments with his father and Aunt. The world had appeared lonely and loveless. He would feel utterly bored. He searched for his mother, in the face of every middle-aged woman, on the streets of Calcutta, in trams, in crowded buses and in trains. As would a lost child in a fair, looking for his mother, he caught hold of the lawyer's hand and imploringly asked, "Is she really in Ranchi? How is she? Can she remember me?"

The lawyer suddenly felt uncomfortable as he saw that he had unwittingly pricked a hidden wound and in a repentant and sympathetic manner began, "I am sorry Akshyay about what I said. I wanted to tell you the truth. She is fine and recovering. The doctors have informed that she is progressing very fast. She heard the news of your father's death. She was sad to hear it and cried like a normal woman. She has almost immediately begun inquiring about you. Some day, very soon, we will arrange your meeting with her, with the permission of the doctors. Right now, the doctors won't allow anyone to meet her, not even you, as it may retard her progress towards normalcy."

The sympathetic yet practical words of the lawyer brought Akshyay back to a state of calm and self-assurance. He could see the logic in the lawyer's statement about the need for his mother's isolation and treatment and controlled himself. He quickly readied himself to hear the further modalities of the will.

The lawyer continued after looking around at the faces of Miss Monica, Abinash and Sarah. The sudden burst of emotion bewildered them. "As part of the share of rents, both Miss Monica and Mr. Abinash would each get rupees ten thousand per month. Mr. Ramen Choudhuri has willed that his wife's share should be with the trustees and the trustees in turn should look after his wife. He has also mentioned that in case Akshyay takes the responsibility of looking after his mother he would get fifty per cent of his mother's share or rupees five thousand per month. However, the balance of rupees five thousand, is for her treatment. In case there is need for more funds for her treatment, all the owners will have to meet and decide to divert a part of the interest from the Nalini Devi Foundation Fund. Now, Miss Monica and Mr. Abinash, you will have to decide. The will proclaims it. You have to decide whether Akshyay can take charge of his mother, or should it remain with the trustees. I want to remind you that allowing Akshyay to take charge means that he will get five thousand rupees per month as his share. In case you don't, Mrs. Diana Choudhuri's share will not get split for Akshyay." The lawyer looked at Akshyay apologetically. "I cannot do anything about it. This is all there is for you at the moment. However, your father's bank account is available for you. Around fifteen thousand rupees should be available there. You could withdraw it with a succession certificate, which we will arrange for you."

The lawyer's statement surprised Akshyay. He quickly referred to his words about his mother. He would have happily agreed to have his mother back, but as a mother. He could not savour the idea of taking charge of her treatment since the trustees can do it better. At the same time, however, he would lose five thousand rupees per month, in case he decides against taking her charge. He turned to the lawyer with a confused look on his face. "That means I get five thousand rupees, if I take charge of my mother, right."

"Yes, that's right. The correspondence with doctors, the payment of fees, arranging her further treatment, if necessary—you will have bear all this, if you take charge of her treatment. The decision, whether her care will be with you, lies on your Aunt and Abinash."

"I know; you have already said that. I should also like to decide for myself. Please give me five minutes for it." He looked at his aunt for acquiescence.

"Yes, your decision is obviously important. You may consult your wife or aunt before giving your opinion." The lawyer intervened.

"No, no, let him take his decision," Miss Monica said. "Come Abinash; we must talk about it. Mr. Roy, do you mind if we go to the other room and discuss amongst ourselves, while Abdul brings you tea?"

"No, not at all."

Miss Monica and Abinash walked out of the room. Akshyay and Sarah also left for their bedroom.

"Sarah, what do you think? Do I agree to taking charge of my mother?" Akshyay asked, when they entered their bedroom.

"Why do you have to? She's already in safe hands, isn't she?"

"No doubt she is and she is progressing fast as the lawyer himself said. Our trustees are better experienced in these matters. Perhaps they are able to maintain good relations with the doctors treating her. In any case, we would not be allowed to meet her. Therefore, taking charge of her treatment would be an unnecessary burden. Won't it?"

"I don't think it would be a burden. You'd get a tidy sum of money for your upkeep; don't forget that. Further, we need it, don't we?" Sarah said.

"I am not hung up about money. The lawyer said that my father's got fifteen thousand in the bank, which, could be transferred to us. That would last us for three or four months, at least, and by that time my mother might recover and then we would take her charge and get the money as well."

"I think you are right, Akshyay. It's better not to take an emotional decision or one generated by greed for money. A mental patient needs proper treatment and professional handling. Certainly, the Trustees are more qualified to look after your mother. You'd really be useful when your presence would be needed for her recovery. We could then approach the Trustees and seek your aunt's permission for taking charge of our mother."

"Yes that will be the right course of action." Akshyay concluded.

Meanwhile, in Miss Monica's bedroom the discussion began with Miss Monica's statement that Akshyay had been a spoilt child. "He has somehow completed his schooling with average marks in the final exam and then he has dropped out of college. He's got, mixed up with a rock band, and taken to drugs, perhaps. He's been disobedient to his father and also to me. He is utterly irresponsible and wayward: he is a hippie."

Abinash thought for a while and said, "Auntie, I don't think Akshyay is responsible for what he has been doing. You know he's had a rough childhood; his mother became insane when he was only nine years of age. A child, who loses his mother at such an early age, is not like everybody else. He is also the only child of his parents and his father was neither available to perform the mother's functions, nor did he arrange for a governess, to look after him as a child."

"How could you think of a governess looking after Akshyay? Don't you know our family background? Can a governess bring up a child of our family in the proper way? Won't the child's growth be warped?"

Abinash thought for a while and then began; "Perhaps you are right. No one can substitute a mother. But the result has been that Akshyay has become bitter. Remember how he used to rave and rant about meeting his mother and my uncle would tell him that he couldn't see her. I remember hearing that on some days he would refuse to eat and just cry all day in his bedroom. He wouldn't go out to play with other children out of fear and shame. They had their mothers and fathers to love them. He had only his angry old father drinking the evenings away. He preferred to remain lost in his own sorrows, with no time for his son; and his wife kept captive, beyond the walls of a Mental Hospital. I can well understand Akshyay's plight and I'm not surprised that he has become a hippie. Countless people in the West, are leaving home, mainly due to lack of parental love in a mechanised society."

"What do you think then? Do we agree to give him charge of this woman, who has ruined my brother's life?"

"Dear Auntie, don't be so unkind to her. After all, she's insane and I am inclined to believe that it was a case of maladjustment to our family traditions that had led to her mental agony and depression."

"That's true. She was an Anglo Indian Christian, working as a nurse in a hospital, when my brother first met her. They fell in love and wanted to marry. My indignant father flatly refused, and so all our other relatives, not only because she was not of our standard, but also because his marriage had already been arranged, with the daughter of the Maharaja of Cooch Behar. As fate would have it, he defied everyone and married Diana. The result was constant warfare with our family members. My father refused to accept her and denied any financial assistance to him. My brother was pushed into earning his own living, working for a reputed publishing house as a manager. That, however, kept him going, but our family was affected adversely. We were socially ostracised for failing to keep the commitment of marriage and then, the prospects of my own marriage were doomed forever. After my father's death, my brother moved into the house with his wife, but she was a complete misfit. Our servants knew better table manners than she did. We used to hear the couple quarrelling every night and then he started drinking heavily. He began to accuse her for his fate, for his father's death, for my marriage getting scuttled. He even removed Akshyay to your place to keep him away from her influence. Poor girl, she became insane out of an acute sense of inferiority, guilt consciousness and deprivation. I still remember the day she was locked up in her bedroom. Akshyay was then ten or eleven years old. We brought him to the house to see his mother for the last time, before her journey to the hospital. I remember seeing him crying at the door, banging his head, for his mother."

"Don't you think Aunt, we should now give his mother back to him, now that he is grown up. He is educated. He is married. I'm sure he would be responsible enough to look after her, Perhaps, her recovery would be faster, if she got her son back."

"I wonder whether his wife would accept her. You know the type these hippie girls are. She told me how she's had numerous affairs before her marriage to Akshyay. Would she be able to tolerate her? Didn't she leave her own mother and father back home and left for India? Can we expect her to look after Akshyay's mother?"

What I saw of her, I think she has a lot of love in her. I don't know why she left her parent's home. Perhaps it's a fashion nowadays to leave home. It doesn't prove that she's uncaring and selfish."

"You don't know these women. They are all alike. I won't be surprised if she discards Akshyay and finds another man to fool around with."

"No, no, Aunt. I hope that doesn't happen. Give them responsibility and they'll be tied to it and gradually they'll learn to take on more of it. They'll mature and become responsible persons. For their good, Aunt, I think he should take charge of his mother. He will also get five thousand a month. That should keep him happy."

Well then, I'll agree, but I still have my doubts. Let us go to the lawyer and tell him."

Akshyay and Sarah were already in the drawing room talking to Mr. Roy, when Aunt Monica and Abinash re-entered.

"So what's Akshyay's opinion, Mr. Roy?" Miss Monica asked, sarcastically.

Mr. Roy guessed that his words would cause a clash of conflicting minds. Nevertheless, he decided that he should behave like a professional lawyer and perform his job. "Akshyay says that he is not willing to take his mother's charge. He considers his mother safe in our hands."

"That's very strange, Akshyay," Miss Monica said. She raised her eyebrows. "How could you come to that conclusion? It is most unbecoming of you, especially after all the raving and ranting for your mother."

"That was a long time back, wasn't it, when I was just a child? My reaction a little while ago was more in the nature of an emotional outburst," Akshyay said, feeling ashamed.

"You mean, you don't need her now? Is it because you have got a wife that you've forgotten your mother?"

Akshyay felt his anger getting the better of him. "Why do you have to drag in Sarah into everything? I have tried to take a pragmatic decision. After all, my mother is in one of the best mental hospitals and she's well looked after. Mr. Roy also mentioned that she's progressing well and . . ."

"Pragmatic decision?" Miss Monica interrupted with scorn. "Where was your pragmatism in dropping out of college and ganging up with the rock band? Where was your pragmatism in becoming a hippie and wearing long hair and dirty pyjamas? Where was your pragmatism in falling into the trap of a hippie girl? Has she taught you pragmatism?"

"Aunt!" Akshyay screamed, in surprise. "Why do you have to get after me in this fashion? Have I done you any harm? I want to lead life my way; how does it affect you? Your world is different from mine. You won't understand why I dropped out of college or why I've given up wearing the suit and tie, or why I went for rock music. I want to be free, you know; freedom is what I want. I don't want to hurt nobody. I just want to be free and no one's going to stop me from my trip. Now I'm going. You do what you want with the will." Saying this, he got up and caught hold of Sarah's hand and proceeded to walk out of the drawing room. Halfway through, he turned and addressed the dumbstruck lawyer in a controlled voice. "I'd like to meet you tomorrow to discuss about my mother, and my father's bank account. Where's your office; what time will be suitable?"

The lawyer, Mr. Roy, adjusted his glasses, and after a moment's silence said, slowly, "You can meet me at ten o'clock in our office at 109, Lower Circular Road, near Park Street okay?"

"Don't forget to meet us Abinash, before you leave for Bombay," Akshyay said, after nodding at the lawyer, and left the room, followed by Sarah.

CHAPTER - XI

They spent the following week in hectic activity. He needed a succession certificate from Alipore Court for transferring the cash in his father's account to his name. Akshyay and Sarah accompanied Mr. Roy to the court twice, to get it. They also went through the correspondence in the lawyer's office, with the mental hospital, on his mother's treatment. The lawyer had sent a letter to the hospital authorities asking for Diana's photograph, which they were to frame and hang on the wall of their bedroom. Sarah sent a letter to the bank in Rishikesh seeking transfer of five thousand rupees that she expected from her father, to her account in Calcutta. Akshyay reported back to Swami Ananda, giving an account of their life in Calcutta: the meeting with the lawyer, his cousin from London and most important about his mother, recuperating in a mental hospital. He added little anecdotes on their spate of parties, and finally about his new found love for sarode.

The week also saw them attending luncheons and dinner parties, entertaining guests and well-wishers, who turned up at their home to meet them. The members of the rock band belonged to well-to-do families. They offered their cars by turns to them for visiting the Kali Temple, Belur Math and Dakshineshwar. However, acceptance of invitations to dinner and luncheons could not be one-sided. They were soon left with a feeling of being takers and not givers. While they did not have the means to invite others, some of their friends even called them up, wanting to be invited. Some people even bought them gifts. The love showered on them through these gifts and invitations seemed to tie them to the city. Akshyay felt and Sarah also reasoned, that they should stay on for some time. The link to their mother was in the city, and so was the lawyer's office.

By the weekend, they received a letter from the lawyer. It enclosed a photo of his mother. Her face was pale and the sad blue eyes slightly shrunken. Akshyay could hardly recognise her, but for the colour of her eyes. They were like his. The letter informed them that she was progressing fast. She had learnt to eat her food at the dinning table. She had begun to read the newspapers, but she still had bouts of depression and sometimes she turned violent and murmured in her sleep. In the doctor's opinion, hers was a case of psychosis, which could be cured. The letter further advised Akshyay to be around, so that they could call him over at short notice. His presence could be useful in the treatment process. It all meant that they would have to stay on in Calcutta.

In another visit to the lawyer's office, the latter informed that she had suffered her third attack of acute depression. She has been under treatment for the last four months, which meant that she was ill even two months prior to his father's death. Prior to that, she had been living in an orphanage in Darjeeling, looking after children. She had been living there, after her release from a hospital after her first attack of psychosis. She had wanted to be of service to the community there and did not want to go back to Calcutta: to her husband's house, which had been the cause of her mental disease. She had preferred to stay on at the orphanage. She had found that she was more acceptable there. She was herself brought up by the Church and had been a nurse by profession. Therefore, she could easily adjust to the simple and pure environment of the orphanage.

The doctors at the mental home at Srirampur, where she was interned, after her first attack, had recommended that she should not return to her husband's house. Akshyay's father, on his part, did not want her to live there, because she was a potential threat to his son's fragile mental state. To him, Akshyay was the torchbearer of the family tradition, in the words of the lawyer. Akshyay's father had often accused himself of not having lived up to the family traditions and hence he assiduously worked for Akshyay's development along the preferred lines.

"He had sent you to North point, a very elitist school in Darjeeling and, as you know, he wanted you to study English literature at Oxford. He wanted to make amends through you. But that didn't work out because you dropped out of college."

"I didn't drop out of college. I just didn't sit for the Part II exams," Akshyay said quickly. I had attended most of the classes, though. I can appear for the exam at any later date. You know; I'd joined a rock band and we had to play in concerts and then, we also won the all-India championship in 1970. You know, I just couldn't be ready for the exam."

"Why didn't you tell your father that you'd appear for the next year's exam?"

"I tried to explain to him. But he wouldn't listen. He thought I had deserted him and had gone wayward.

He had heard I'd taken drugs. He wanted me to go to Rishikesh to a Swami, whom he knew, for my recovery. I protested, but finally, I relented, because I learnt that Rishikesh was the destination of all the young people, who were seeking freedom and peace. However, before I could leave he had a massive heart attack and died."

"It was all very sad. He died out of grief and a sense of defeat: his wife lost; his family traditions lost; his son lost." The lawyer concluded philosophically.

That day, while walking out of the lawyer's office, with Sarah, Akshyay had felt cheated. He wondered why they kept his mother separated from him. He couldn't understand how she would have spoilt him. After all, was not it true that all that he had learnt, were from his school and his teachers? "I didn't even follow my father's footsteps, so how could my mother affect me. My idea of life was different from my father's. Parents can't influence their children much, you know; that's how you have the generation gap. What do you think?" He asked Sarah, hoping she would corroborate.

"Well, parents do affect their children, especially in their emotional build-up. I think your father worried about your mental balance. Meeting your mother would have disturbed your mental equilibrium. Therefore, he kept her away from you and the family. Gradually, the prolonged separation became a way of life. It took her farther away from you and your father. There was no bringing her back. It appears that Mr. Roy had been looking after your mother's treatment from the very beginning, otherwise, how could he know so much?"

"I wonder whether my mother was a Christian." Akshyay asked Sarah. "The lawyer was mentioning about her being brought up by the Church."

"It seems likely."

"I can understand now why she couldn't adjust to our family. She was a Christian; she was an Anglo-Indian; she was poor. We were devout Hindus; we were high-caste Brahmins; we were traditionally rich landlords. It's the differences of culture and social status that wrecked the marriage. I wonder how human beings can be so incompatible. After all, God is in everyone, and why should anyone be put down and set apart because of a different culture, race, or class. You know; all the problems in the past have been due to this sense of separation. God! When will they see all human beings as equal and love everyone?" Akshyay looked through Sarah at the distance hoping to find and answer to the problem, but soon he looked away as he realised that there was no answer.

"You're right, the world needs to change: all these separations into nations, states, classes and races have to go, if peace and love are to prevail."

"Are you suggesting a world government?" Akshyay asked, with a trace of sarcasm in his voice.

"Yes that's the only solution to all these problems." Sarah said confidently.

"But don't you think the disparities amongst classes of people, among regions, would cause problems? Would the stronger people make sacrifices for the weaker? Would the areas that are richer, forego their luxuries to provide essential supplies to the poorer regions?"

"Why not? Won't you forego something for your brother?" Sarah remarked.

"Ah ha! So first of all you have to love everyone and that is something that has been sadly missing from the world. People can't understand this simple, single, truth that love can solve all problems? Did not Christ say two thousand years ago: "Love your enemy?"

"People know; everyone knows; love is the only salvation. It is the greed for power, greed for comfort, greed for sex and money that has come in the way. These have separated people into warring groups: generating hatred, violence, and lust."

They became silent, wondering at their own words.

They suddenly felt uplifted into a higher plain and above the crowded street. The dust, the fumes of cars and buses, the oppressive heat, all, seemed to be the effect of, greed and lust. Akshyay wondered whether they could change the world; spread the message of love. He would have liked to work for an environment, where every individual was free—free from economic hardships, free from the shackles of race, language, caste, class, and types. Every human being should be essentially a free individual, with the least of social compulsions. What would he have to do to achieve all that? Will it be enough to try to achieve these ideals in his own life or would he like to sacrifice his own needs to make it possible for others to achieve these goals? He did not find an immediate answer, but felt that he would not be able to give up his own freedom, to achieve freedom for others. In any case, he needed to be free first.

At the present, however, he had to think of earning a living. The five thousand rupees from the rent collection were not his. He had preferred not to take it. There was now only his father's money on which he could fall back. The bank would have to transfer it to his name. Sarah had only five thousand rupees in her account at Rishikesh. This would sooner or later be spent. Though they did not have to worry about food, if they lived in Calcutta, because their aunt would foot the bill, they had other expenses to bear. Toiletries, saris for Sarah, transport costs, the music teacher's fee, cost of a new sarode and tabla, and other miscellaneous items. He would have to give Sarah a good life, in lieu of the peaceful ambience of Rishikesh. He was sure that she would find Indian culture and tradition interesting. With his lessons in Sarode, his ways and his personality, he could provide a slice of the quintessential Indian civilisation. However, it would be quite difficult to match her requirements. Would he be able to satisfy her mind? Hindu philosophical ideas, yoga, meditation, the purity and simplicity of Indian life-style had enthralled her. Would he be able to provide all that to her?

Sarah, for her part wondered, as they walked along, whether she would be able to stay on in Calcutta. In Akshyay, she has just seen a rare quality of lack of greed and a fine sense of reason. He was full of love for people and for a good life. His idealism was attractive. His words were wonderfully elating. She thought she could live in Calcutta for sometime with Akshyay to support her. She would adapt to him, love him and meditate on him. She would try to be a Hindu wife, as Swami Ananda had told her. It would be her yogic trip. She would accept life with Akshyay as it befell her without protest, and would not allow anything to tilt her mental balance and happiness. She would not allow anything to disrupt her peaceful mental state: her steadfastness in her yogic role of Hindu wife.

CHAPTER - XII

The spectre of financial constraints began to loom large over their lives. It became more pronounced as the days progressed and soon became a problem that they could not leave unattended. They spent fifteen thousand rupees in a week's time, with all the taxi rides to various parts of the city to attend to dinner invitations and luncheons. The cost of a new sarode was one thousand one hundred rupees and the tabla two hundred rupees. The music teacher's fee was three hundred rupees per month. Sarah had to buy a couple of saris and then they had to entertain a number of guests every day, who dropped by to say 'hello' or to see his American wife.

That morning, a fortnight after their arrival in Calcutta, Akshyay woke up from sleep with a start. He had had a bad dream. He had seen himself and Sarah in a boat on a narrow stream of clear water, flowing between grassy banks, lined with shady trees. He had been playing the guitar and singing "Picture yourself in a boat on a river" and they had dozed off in the cold evening breeze. Suddenly, the soft breeze became a storm and at once their boat was in the midst of a violent sea. There was no sign of the grassy bank and trees. He woke Sarah up and realised they were frantically holding on to their sides of the boat, as it tossed about in the waves. Now sliding down a wave, which could break at any moment over them: then, going up another. All of a sudden, there was a sound of cracking wood and within moments their boat was separated in two, leaving their feet in the tearing water, while their bodies clung to the severed halves of the boat. Akshyay began to shout, frantically ordering Sarah to hold on tightly to the sides of the severed boat, but she was unable to hear him in the din all around. He could see her body sliding into the powerful waves as they pulled at her feet.

"Sarah! Sarah!" He called again and again, but she could not hear him above the roar of the waves. Her face, calm and serene, unnerved him, as if nothing had happened even as her body was sliding into the waves.

Akshyay called again, "Sarah! Be careful! Hold on tight, pull yourself up!" As they rose up the side of a big wave, the crest at her end curled and broke over her. It dragged her along and her part of the boat, while he slid down safely on the other side. He could not see Sarah anywhere. The swelling waves blocked his vision.

"Sarah! Sarah!" He cried hopelessly into the deafening waves till a big wave curled over him. He woke up with a start to see Sarah's calm and serene face wrapped in sleep.

"Sarah, Sarah," he called after some time, when his heartbeat had become inaudible again and his mind, calm. "Won't you get up? It's eight o'clock."

"Oh! Why don't you let me sleep a little longer? I'd been dreaming of Rishikesh and the cold clear water of the Ganges."

"You must get up. I have to tell you something."

"What is it?" Sarah said, rubbing her eyes, almost in exasperation.

"I've had a bad dream. It's about us in a small boat in the middle of the sea. I don't know how we got there, but the result was" . . . Akshyay stopped suddenly, realising that he should not tell her about the separating boat and began, "You know, we must do something about earning some money. I've been thinking that I'll pick up a job in some hotel in town. I'll play the guitar and sing, as well."

"You really mean to go back to the guitar?" Sarah asked incredulously. "What would happen to your sarode lessons?"

"That could go on, uninterrupted. The hotel sessions would only take my evenings. I'll be free the whole day to do whatever I please, and of course, whatever you want me to do. We could as well make love all day long." Akshyay encircled Sarah with his arms and pulled her close to him and kissed her on her cheeks.

Sarah smiled coquettish manner and cuddled close to him. "Why should you work in a hotel, love. I'd much rather pick up a job and sustain ourselves as long as we are in Calcutta. By that time, I mean in two or three month's time, your mother may recover and then you'll get enough money to blow up. There'd be no need to work then. A few months of work somewhere would also keep me engaged, during the day. What do I do all day, when you're out for your music lessons?"

"Well, I don't mind at all, if you feel like doing a job, but I can't live off you. It'll not be the right thing to do. I'll have to earn something for ourselves."

At the breakfast table Akshyay broached the subject of picking up a job.

Aunt Monica immediately reacted: "That's really good news, Akshyay. It shows that you have some sense of responsibility, I must say. Where do you propose to work? You must have to go to work in proper clothes. I'm sure you won't be allowed anywhere with your kurta-pyjamas."

"Well, I'm going to work for a hotel as a guitarist. They'd have to allow me in kurta-pyjama. No one is going to make me wear a suit and a tie," Akshyay asserted.

"I don't know why you have to be so dogmatic. Don't you have any respect for our family traditions? Have you not seen the framed pictures of your ancestors? Have you not seen how they are dressed? After all, people expect our family members to behave in a certain fashion; wear clothes of a certain type; talk in a particular way. You can't be like a man of the street, you know."

"I'm different from . . . don't you see that, Auntie? I'm on quite a different trip."

Miss Monica squirmed, as she became conscious of her own inadequacy. If she went on talking on the subject, she would only expose herself. She would feel belittled. Her thoughts however kept hovering around Akshyay's dress and attitudes. In contrast, the images of the smartly dressed Roland with his fitting trousers, shining belt, striped shirt and bow tie came to her mind. She remembered how she would stand out in a crowd, on her heels, as he would walk down the corridor to greet her. "Auntie, are you listening?" Miss Monica heard Akshyay saying, and her eyes turned to him, as her mind still held on to Roland's image.

"We are going out for lunch, today," Akshyay said.

"Which restaurant?" She asked, thinking of Roland, behind the hotel manager's table.

"Oh no! We don't go to restaurants," Akshyay said. "We have been invited to a friend's place. Do you remember Satya? He used to play the drum."

"Oh yes! He is the son of Mr. Biswas, isn't he? I knew his father at the Calcutta club. He was good at badminton and bridge, but . . ." Miss Monica stopped, as another thought came into her mind. "You have not had lunch in the house at all, for the last five days . . . not even suppers," she said with concern.

"What to do? There's been a spate of invitations to cope with," Akshyay said, evincing a feeling of helplessness in the face of the inevitable.

"I hope you've not been trying to avoid me. You know; this is as much, your home as mine. Looking at Sarah, she continued, "You have a right to have food, here. Traditionally, we've been living together; Akshyay's father and myself; and hence it is your right, whether your contribution is there, or not."

"Thanks a lot for that," Sarah said, with a smile. "I'll remember that." Inwardly, she wondered whether she sincerely meant what she said. Free food and lodging would be of great help. Would her aunt allow her to invite guests for dinner, without contributing? Would she accept any contribution? She wanted to ask Miss Monica, but she restrained herself, deciding that it would be better to leave it to Akshyay to organise things.

After lunch that day at Satya's place, Akshyay dropped Sarah home and went to a hotel-cum-restaurant in Park Street to meet the manager, Mr.Bassi. At the reception, he referred to the advertisement in the newspaper, which specified the need for a lead guitarist. A bellboy ushered him into the Manager's chamber.

Mr. Bassi was a well-dressed, suave, gentleman. Talking bout himself, when Akshyay mentioned that he was from North Point, Mr.Bassi was immediately interested. He was from the same school. Akshyay also impressed him with his credentials as a musician. Their Group "Amazon" had achieved a certain degree of fame in the music circles of the city and the popular belief was that their band broke up copying the Beatles.

"I know you are a good guitarist but would you be able to play Blues or Cliff Richard songs or Elvis'. You know, the sort of crowd, who come here, want love songs."

"Well, I'd started with Jimmy Hendricks, Bob Dylan, Elvis and Cliff Richard . . ."

"Oh yes, I suppose rock music was not there when you got started," Mr. Basis interrupted, a little impatient.

"It was there all right, much before the Beatles began to popularise it."

"Of course, I forgot, Beatles were not the founders of rock. There were others." Mr.Bassi tried to cover up his ignorance.

"Yes there were . . ." Akshyay began, but held his tongue as Mr. Basis interrupted him again.

"Your appointment is confirmed, Mr. Akshyay Choudhuri. You can start from tomorrow. We'll give seven hundred rupees for three hours everyday, except Monday, from 7.00 p.m. to 10.00 p.m. You'll have to come an hour earlier for a few days to practice with the other members of the group. There are three others including Miss Julian—the singer. You must have heard of her."

Akshyay nodded, "Thank you very much, Mr. Bassi. You have really pulled me out of the rut. I'm grateful to you. Good day, then. See you tomorrow." He raised his hands and brought his palms together in a namaskar.

Akshyay's manner irritated Mr.Bassi. He recollected that he had forgotten to mention about dress regulations. "Wait a minute, Mr. Akshyay," he said, moving menacingly towards him. "You can't put on these lousy clothes, while you perform."

"Why? What's wrong in these clothes? I like to wear kurta and pyjama."

"You can wear what you like at home, but if you join us, you will have to wear proper clothes. In fact, while you perform, you'll have to wear a suit and bow tie. Your shoes must be polished. No rubber slippers. Once you become part of us, you'll be known as part of us. You'll have to wear the right clothes even when you move about in society. You know what I mean. We can't allow our corporate image to come down because someone likes to wear lousy clothes."

"Have you finished Mr. Bassi, fu . . . I don't want to wear a suit and tie. I feel suffocated in them. There's nothing wrong in kurta-pyjama. It's the in-thing with the hep crowd."

"You will not teach me what are the fashions of my customers. They certainly don't dig kurta-Pyjama . . . And, let me tell you, I'm not concerned with your conception of what they like or dislike. There is a dress regulation for the musicians in the restaurant and you've got to follow it."

"Why can't you relax the rules for me? My quaint dress would only add to the variety. I'm sure you wouldn't insist on my clothes, after you've heard my guitar. You couldn't have dress regulations for artists, could you?"

"Yes, why not? Don't you have the army band in uniform and have you forgotten-the choir in school? Were they not in school uniform? You know, let's not argue on this. I wouldn't have even talked to you in the dress you're in. It's just that you are a good musician and then I empathised with you because we were in the same school and obviously you're from a good family. I'm surprised at your attitude. You must be crazy."

"I'm sorry Mr. Basis to have argued with you. I was only expecting you to respond to the changing times."

"Well, I am. And many people I know, are."

"Thank you once again for the offer of appointment, Mr. Bassi. I'm sorry I can't accept it because of your conditions," Akshyay said. He concluded the argument and walked out of the Manager's chamber with another 'namaskar'.

That evening, while Akshyay and Sarah were sitting in the drawing room sipping tea and discussing about how he could not get the job of a musician in the hotel, the telephone rang.

"Hello, can I speak to Akshyay?" Akshyay heard the voice as he picked up the receiver.

"Yes, may I know who's calling?"

"I'm Pradip Agarwal. I heard that you are a good guitar player. Satya told me about you. He was in school with you, wasn't he? I want to learn to play the guitar. Can you teach me?"

"Well, I don't play the guitar nowadays but..." Akshyay paused and looked at Sarah for approval.

"Go ahead, agree to it," Sarah said.

"Yes", Akshyay resumed, speaking over the mouthpiece, "I can teach you to play the guitar, but for three days in a week, and for three hundred rupees."

"No problem and thank you for agreeing. When can we get started?"

"You can come from day after tomorrow and I'll expect you to bring your own guitar," Akshyay said, and after saying good-bye, placed the receiver back.

"Don't you think, Sarah, that luck has been favouring us? Just as it seemed that there is no chance of making money, here comes Pradip, out of the blue, to help us. I wonder whether it is the law of karma or fate or sheer chance that has brought Pradip, for example, to our rescue."

"We were not really down and out, were we? We could have agreed to look after your mother and get five thousand rupees a month and surely you could get a job somewhere with the help of your connections."

"I could, you know, but I don't feel like asking people to help me out with a job. They won't believe in the first place that I need a job and secondly, it would be damaging for our family. It's really been lucky that Pradip has arrived on the scene. At least, we can pull on with this for some time. And I may get a few more students through him to supplement our income. For the next three months that we have to stay here in this city, we should be able to manage with this. Once, my mother is cured, we'll take her to Rishikesh and rent a place near the ashram. You know, on the banks of the river, and live peacefully."

"That would be wonderful. I could continue my lessons on yoga, philosophy and meditation and you could bathe in the cold, clear river every day and be on your own trip, with no hassles to bog you down. Your mother could either stay with us or we'll tell Swamiji to arrange for a place for her. She could also learn meditation and yoga. I'm sure that yoga can cure her mental problems for good. She would be able to find herself and work for her own salvation, with Swamiji's help."

"You mean you'd like my mother to stay in the ashram and not with us?" Akshyay looked at Sarah with concern.

"I've no objection at all to her staying with us, but the ashram could be better for her mind. I think we should leave the decision to Swamiji. Don't you think that'd be the right thing?"

"Yes, I think you're right. Swamiji could take the right decision. In fact, I'll write to him tomorrow about our plans and seek his advice."

That night, Akshyay and Sarah slept peacefully after talking about their plans. The idea of living in Rishikesh had come out of Akshyay's mind spontaneously and it appeared to them to be the right decision. There was no need for them to stay in the city of Calcutta, plagued by problems of over-population, slums, unemployment, load shedding, Naxalite violence, and pollution. With the support of a regular income, of as large an amount as, ten thousand rupees, per month, there would be no reason for them to stay in Calcutta. They knew that Calcutta could better provide music teachers and spiritual gurus, than those possibly available at Rishikesh. Nevertheless, Calcutta did not have anymore the holiness of Rishikesh. The city today is full of materialistic souls chasing their petty desires, even as they are bogged down by the problems of migrant labour and displaced population from Bangladesh. At the back of Akshyay's mind, however, a thought kept knocking. Would he be able to get a music teacher in Rishikesh of the calibre of his Guru?

Sarah could be in awe of Swami Ananda, but he wasn't. What would he do in Rishikesh? In Calcutta, at least, he could learn to play the sarode and the mastery of sarode was a long-drawn-out affair. 'One can learn it only through prolonged perseverance and practice' . . . A task, which could take up quite a few years of his life. He could also become a music teacher himself. With these thoughts he projected himself into the future. He soon retreated. Planning for the future had never been his forte. He had always lived life, spontaneously, doing what he liked to do and things, which gave him intellectual, spiritual, and sometimes emotional, pleasure. Right now, he saw Sarah lying half-awake beside him. His bones sank deep into her soft flesh. The thoughts of the future just evaporated and he found himself delving into the present, with his body, mind, heart, and soul.

Chapter - XIII

After the first day's guitar lessons, while Akshyay, Sarah and Pradip sat down in the drawing room for tea; Miss Monica walked in to join them.

"This is Pradip. He is taking guitar lessons from me." Akshyay said, introducing Pradip to his aunt.

Miss Monica looked at the well-dressed boy of about nineteen or twenty years, obviously from a well-to-do family and said, "Hello, how do you do? How did you get to know Akshyay?" It appeared unusual to her that Akshyay, who was almost like a hippie, could come into contact with someone, who was definitely on the straight path.

"I didn't know him, earlier. I heard about him from a common friend. He told me that Akshyay is the only one in the city, who not only knew the guitar, but also has the knowledge of the latest trends in Western music. That's why I decided that if I must learn to play the guitar, I must learn it from Akshyay."

"Why are you interested in the guitar? Is it just because you love music or there are other reasons?" Miss Monica asked, probing.

"Well, I do like music, and knowledge of Western music is very useful in our parties, where we have people coming over from African countries. There are even Englishmen and Americans."

"Do you have an export business?"

"No, not really. We have shares in a number of companies. There is a rolling mill at Howrah, an agency of air and ship cargo handling and two tea gardens in Assam, among several other smaller units."

"Yours must be a big concern? Where's your office."

"We've got our head-office at Camac Street."

Miss Monica was quiet for a while, and then looking at Akshyay, said, "Why don't you ask Pradip for a job, as an executive trainee in their company?"

"Why should I work for any company? I've got my music lessons. Don't you know?"

"My dear Akshyay, where would your sarode lessons lead you to? Your life is not just for playing the sarode. If you join a firm, especially a big business house like theirs, you could learn a lot about business and our wealth could be multiplied."

"Auntie, will you please stop it? It told you, I'm not interested in business gains. I want to lead my own life, in my own way."

Sarah, who had been listening to the conversation in silence, began, "Well, Akshyay, do you have any objection if I offer myself for work?"

"But where are the vacancies? Pradip hasn't talked about any places lying vacant, has he? I can't understand how he can provide a job. In the private sector, posts don't lie vacant. If they need people for the organisation they'd take them immediately." Looking at Pradip he continued, "Am I not correct?"

"Well, you are, but I don't think there'd be any problem in getting a post created. I'll have to talk to my father. I think we could find a place for Mrs. Choudhuri, in our office. I'll let you know tomorrow."

"There's no hurry, you know. My aunt's somewhat anxious about my career. I hope you don't mind this kind of persuasion." Akshyay looked at his aunt, as he said these words, and found her smiling in satisfaction.

The next day Pradip brought the news that his father had agreed to take in Mrs. Sati Chaudhuri.

"What kind of post do you think he'd have for her? What would be her pay?" Akshyay asked.

"I think my father would have to talk to her, first. In fact, he wants her to meet him in his office, tomorrow, at 11:30 a.m."

The news of Sarah's appointment appeared to be a like a boon for Akshyay. He would now have the mornings to himself to do his 'rewaz'[16]. In the afternoons, he would go to his Guru's place, for the sarode lessons. In the evenings, there would be time enough to give his pupil, lessons in guitar. He would now have more time to himself to live life his own way. He could now let go and lose himself in the ecstasy of riding with the ragas, clinging on to the fleeting feelings of order, in a sea of disorder.

Sarah was also happy about the job coming her way. It would certainly solve for the time being, their pecuniary problems until Akshyay's mother got cured, and they became entitled to fifty percent of her share of the estate's earnings. Even if she was to remain a patient, they could still take charge of her treatment and get the share. She also felt contended that she would be able to help in running the family. She was, however, a little apprehensive about the kind of reception she would get, and whether she would be acceptable in the office environment. She waived the thought aside with the sense of complaisance that came from her past experiences. Her father was owner of a departmental store in New York and she had often, on her return from school, sat at the sales counter. Further, her travels through Europe and Africa, and, among other things, her encounters in Delhi government offices, had opened her eyes. The atmosphere of a private company, in the prime area of Calcutta, even though daunting, could not take her completely by surprise. She could adjust to it. On the whole, she felt somewhat excited at the prospect of a new experience. It was her first job, after all.

"I don't think you'll have much of a problem," Akshyay assured her when they lay in bed, and the lights were switched off. "They work in English and they'll probably ask you to handle the correspondence and other secretarial jobs. By the way, I guess you know typing."

"Of course, I do. It's something, all educated girls must know."

"Well, I don't. In India, most people don't know typing. People by dint of habit avoid doing their jobs themselves. You can hire typists to do your jobs for you at reasonably cheap rates."

"Life here is really quite comfortable, I must say. You don't need to slog."

"Yes, it is really cool for certain sections. The upper classes are as comfortable or as well off, as their counterparts in the West. In fact, the quality of life of the rich in India is more luxurious, mainly because of the availability cheap labour. The condition of the poor and middle-classes, however, is bad. In the West, I suppose, the quality of life, on the whole, is much better."

"They may be better off, but I don't dig their systems. There's just no mind. In India, people may be poor. They may be backward in terms of material amenities. Even then, I've seen in them a rare human quality, which beats the West, with all their technology and living standards.

The people here seem to understand life better and they have accepted their fate."

"You may be right, Sarah. But I've got my doubts. It's a subject on which you can talk endlessly. We'd better go to sleep. There's a lot to do tomorrow. You'll have to go for your interview and you need to look fresh. I suppose; you'll wear a sari."

"Of course! I don't wear skirts!"

"But I think you've only red-bordered white saris and your marriage Benarasi."

"What's wrong with 'em?"

"You can't wear a red-bordered sari to office; not even a Benarasi. You must wear a cotton or a silk sari."

"Oh God! Why didn't you tell me about all this earlier?"

"It didn't occur to me until now. But don't worry; you could get a sari from my aunt. She would feel happy to have contributed in your getting the job."

"I don't like asking her, for a sari," Sarah said, feeling irritated.

"But what can you do? You'll have to wear a proper sari," Akshyay said, rather gravely.

"You don't give a damn to dresses, do you? So why are you now insisting on me wearing a proper sari?" Sara said in exasperation.

"Now let's not raise a controversy. You need a silk sari and you must get it from my aunt," Akshyay said slowly and firmly, looking straight into her eyes.

Sarah remained silent for some time and then she said, "Okay, since you are insisting, I'll get a sari from your aunt. For heaven's sake! Don't expect me to repeat this kind of thing again."

Akshyay realised that he should not drag the matter any further. He had tread on unknown territory and it would be better to keep within the precinct of his own world. As he lay in bed beside Sarah, he had begun to see that his knowledge of her was hopelessly inadequate. He only knew the exteriors of her personality. He knew about her lackadaisical attitude to dress. He had a fair knowledge of her behaviour and mannerisms, her way of smiling and talking, her attitude to certain aspects of the Indian environment. However, he had no idea of her behavioural patterns in a different environment, for instance, the environment of female relationships. He became aware that his own self knowledge was inadequate: he could not find reasons for his own contradictory attitudes to dress. On the one hand, he had refused to take up a much-needed job because of his aversion to dress regulations. On the other, he had just told his wife to wear proper clothes for the interview. He knew that both points of view were right, but Sarah did not think so. He began to ponder on what Sarah had said, but could not immediately reconcile the two viewpoints as emanating from a single mind.

As he lay with his eyes half-closed; he tried to solve the problem. He began to systematically try several viewpoints to explain the contradictions. Was it because he was secretly a male chauvinist, laying down separate standards of behaviour for a woman? Was he basically a traditional Indian trying to protect his wife? Was it simply his fear of the world outside, taking advantage of a simple woman, who could appear to be a hippie? He could not decide, which was the correct answer, but any one of these could be true. However, he surmised that it was primarily, his sub-conscious fear of her security that pricked his conscience. He had heard stories of how people exploit women in the business circles: how they could become victims of an unscrupulous greedy society. A thought suddenly came to his mind: had he begun to love his wife, during the three weeks they had been together? She had indeed been able to provide some direction to his life. Her practical, yet loving nature, had drawn him towards her. He had not expected her personality to be as affectionate and mature as she had proved it to be. He quickly summarised her position. She had come to India on a mission of peace and freedom. She married him in an ashram, and now she was putting herself back into the same society, which she had discarded. She was willing to do all this for his welfare. He had never met someone, who had offered to do so much for him.

He turned to Sarah and found her eyes closed. He wondered of what she could be dreaming. Would she call her and explain the reasons behind his suggestions? He thought for a while, looking at her beautiful serene face; her golden hair lined her wide forehead. She had a perfectly chiselled nose and perfectly shaped eyebrows. A closer look revealed a thin line of hair over the closed, pink lips, and a faint tinge of red on her smooth cheeks. He saw, as if for the first time, that she was really beautiful. How lucky he was to have her as his wife! He wanted to kiss her on her cheeks, on her lips, all over her face. As he looked on at her, a strong carnal sensation engulfed him. It started welling up from the base of his spinal cord and abdomen. His consciousness began to sink into it.

All of a sudden, in an impulsive motion, he brought himself over Sarah and began to kiss her violently. Sarah woke up with a start and tried to push him off but he forced his kisses on her lips and face and pinned her down with his hands and body. Sarah, finding herself smothered by the kisses, his pounding chest on her, and her limp hands pinned down, felt as if she was on the verge of being suffocated. Almost by reflex action she began to return the kisses passionately, and much to her relief found herself regaining her breath. As she continued to kiss him, Akshyay loosened his hold on her. He felt as though the kisses were drawing out the strength from his body. He began to involuntarily murmur, "I love you Sarah. I will never leave you Sarah. I love you, Sarah."

The two of them then clumsily shook off their clothes and their naked bodies merged into a oneness, which took them into an unknown pinnacle of ecstasy.

CHAPTER - XIV

The next morning, Sarah got up early, and found Akshyay still sleeping. It was dawn and she became conscious of the chirping of birds, as she walked across the drawing room to the veranda. She noticed the dewdrops sparkling on the lawn. Someone had left his footprints on the grass. She drew in the fresh air by the yogic sitali method, by curling up the sides of her tongue against her lips to form a cylindrical shape. She closed her eyes and felt the air cleaning her insides. After a few moments she released the impure air through her nose, slowly. She repeated the process three times and felt fresh and light, ready to face the city and the people with whom she would have to interact. She paused for a moment, as she visualised for a fleeting moment, the road near house and the traffic. She could hear the trams clanking along about a hundred and fifty metres away from their house. For a moment she imagined the sound mingling with the chaotic sounds produced by the traffic mix of buses, taxis, handcarts, rickshaws, as the day progressed into the busy office hours. She recollected the river at Rishikesh. The deep, rumbling, sound of the river would become louder as they would approach its bank over the cobbled lanes. She would often sit for hours in the evening on the round stones, absorbing the chorus of the flowing stream.

The image of the city scene came back to her mind. She wondered what would happen to her in this place, over-crowded with people and their problems. Would she be able to sustain herself in her mission and her chosen role of being a dutiful, self-sacrificing, wife? She remembered the words of Swami Ananda; "You sacrifice yourself to gain yourself."

Recharged with the idea of sacrifice she began to get ready for a new chapter in her life.

According to the program, Pradip would come along with their office car for her. As suggested, Sarah had asked Miss Monica for a sari and she had willingly given one of her Madrasi silk ones.

"You can take this one. It'll suit you. The light green colour and the designs in black along the borders are well-matched."

"Thanks a lot, Aunt Monica," Sarah had said.

"No need to thank me. You know I owe you a marriage gift. You can keep the sari. It is a gift."

When Sarah had put on the sari and appeared at the dining table, where Akshyay and Miss Monica had been waiting for her, Akshyay exclaimed, "Wow! You are looking great!"

"The sari has brought out her hidden personality," Aunt Monica could not help but add. The dark colours of the sari instead of heightening her fairness had in fact mellowed it to an extent that Sarah looked more attractive and more like an Indian woman.

Sarah blushed and smiled. "Thank you for the compliment," she said to Miss Monica and shot a quick glance at Akshyay, who was still staring at her, in awe.

"I'm feeling a bit worried about what they're going to ask me," she said to Akshyay, as she took the seat opposite his, at the dining table.

"Don't worry. You know enough of business and about India. Above all, you are smart."

"I don't know anything about business beyond the pigmy-size experience at my father's departmental store."

"I think that should be enough," Akshyay said, smiling reassuringly at her and then turned to his Aunt. "What do you think? Isn't she capable?"

"Yes, I don't think she would have any problem adjusting, but she should be careful in projecting her image correctly. If she's able to project herself as a smart, punctual, efficient, strict woman, she's going to earn respect in the organisation. By force of habit, Indians are respectful towards the white man. Of course, that's a hangover of over two hundred years of British rule. It is for this reason also that they would not respect the white man or woman, who distorts that image," Miss Monica cautioned.

"Do you mean that in order to be respected in Indian society she should wear a skirt and top and high-heel shoes?" Akshyay asked, with a look of disagreement on his face.

"No, I don't mean that," Miss Monica said, cheerfully, finding herself on a superior logical plane. I mean that people would accept a silk sari, but any other type of sari, you know, the red-bordered ones, for instance, would brand the wearer eccentric and game. It's one thing for you to dress in peculiar clothes, but the same principles are not applicable to women in an unequal society as in India."

"I think you are correct," Akshyay said, and turned to Sarah to see what her reaction was to the views just expressed.

Sarah had sat quietly through the conversation between Akshyay and his aunt. She knew that Miss Monica wanted her to protect the image of the family. Probably she feared that people would exploit her sexually. Her mind browsed through the numerous adventures she had in her teens, in Jackie's place, in Morocco, in Greece, and even in New Delhi. She was still one piece. She did not give much thought to those experiences. It was in this same spirit of detachment that she took up the role of being a Hindu wife or at least that was what she was trying to be. In this, she would be sacrificing, not only her body, but her mind and self, as well.

"I think what you have said is not without sense," Sarah said, finding Akshyay looking at her, as if trying to read her mind. She turned towards Aunt Monica. "So it's because of this fear that you've given me the green silk sari?"

"You may say so," Miss Monica said. "I thought it my duty to caution you. People out there are bad. They'd do anything for money. You must take care."

"I will," Sarah said, softly, as if trying to convince herself.

Soon after, they had had breakfast and were sitting quietly in the drawing room, reading their own thoughts; the bell rang followed by the announcement of Pradip's arrival.

"So, is everything ready?" Pradip asked, as he entered.

"Yes, would you have a cup of tea?" Akshyay asked.

"No, I've just had tea. There's not much time left for the interview."

"You must carry on then", said Akshyay turning to Sarah and added, "take care of yourself."

Sarah got up and proceeded to walk towards the doorway. She turned as she reached it and waved her hand bidding good-bye to Akshyay and Miss Monica with a smile on her face, before walking down the staircase with Pradip. Akshyay got up and also went after her. The car, which was waiting under the porch, started as Sarah and Pradip got into the back seat and moved out of the open gates on its way to Camac Street. That was the location of the office.

Akshyay saw fearful images spring up in his mind, but he pushed them down and proceeded to reorganise his thoughts to constructive action. He had to get down to plan his life and the long hours at his disposal: to suitably place his music lessons, practice sessions, giving guitar lessons, and the occasional visits to the lawyer. A visit to the mental hospital to see his mother was also on the cards. He would have to go there alone, in all probability, since her job would keep Sarah engaged. He knew that his future depended on the sarode and his mother. While, sarode could provide him with an acceptable career, his mother could bring him into the finance required to sustain himself and his wife. He believed that his life with Sarah would have to be different from the lives of the social types. They were both on a trip as it were. She had come to India expecting something different from what one could expect from American society. He had also wanted to be different from others and especially, his father and aunt. His world-view and reactions did not match theirs. The wavelengths were different.

Akshyay and Sarah were both rebels, against their social environment, which could not satisfy their basic needs, which, ironically, they had picked up from the same environment. Akshyay knew that learning to play the sarode was not what his society expected of him. He also knew that he would not be able to live up to the aspirations of the same society to see him as an executive of a multinational company. They expected him to increase the wealth of the family and to do things that would bring back the glory of the past.

Akshyay knew that he loved music and through music he could somewhat achieve what he wanted foremost: to be able to contribute to society. He wanted to teach Indian classical music to Western enthusiasts. Secondly, he would be promoting the ancient Indian culture. Thirdly, he could have a peaceful life of his own on the banks of the River Ganges, at Rishikesh, and this was also acceptable to his wife. Fourthly, he could live away from Calcutta, a city: highly polluted, beset with problems of over-population, unemployment, and poverty. A fifth reason was that he could achieve both name and fame by playing sarode. A sixth was that through music he could hope to achieve nirvana. A seventh reason was that as music teacher no place should tie him. He could go to USA and England, or even Germany and Canada to teach Indian classical music. Indian music and culture drew many people of his age group and he could use this to his advantage. An eighth reason was that he could, through music, be in the company of good people. That means the artistic types among the young crowd were wanting to break away from the chains of a mechanised Western society that could not absorb any more the stirrings of the soul.

Charged with enthusiasm, Akshyay set out, soon after, for the music teacher's house, in Jadavpur. He had to learn sarode. It was his only salvation. He had already picked up the basic notes of sa-re-ga, and some of the ragas, as well. Due to his practice, he could play some tunes quite well. The familiarity with the guitar had been quite an impediment at first, but at a later stage it gave him an edge, in acquiring the skills of playing the sarode.

As he dropped into the lane, which led to the music teacher's house, Akshyay became aware of an eerie silence all around. The windows of most of the houses were shut. The shops on the road had their shutters half-closed. There were no cars or cycle-rickshaws and very few people at that busy hour on a weekday. Akshyay thought that most of the office-goers must have left and the shopkeepers might have taken a break, as there were no customers.

No sooner than he reached the house and pressed the bell, the music teacher opened the door and pulled him in, quickly closing the door after him.

"There has been a bomb blast in the neighbourhood," the music teacher said, in a hushed voice.

"Where . . . When was it?" Akshyay asked, sensing his curiosity mounting.

"Oh! It happened about an hour back. At ten-thirty precisely, in front of the school building."

"Were there any casualties?"

"No, fortunately no one was injured, or that's what John told me. You have not met John, have you?"

"No, I haven't."

"Oh no! Why are we standing here? Let's go in." They walked back to the room. John was sitting on a mat on the floor, the sarode before him. He got up, as the music teacher entered with Akshyay.

"This is Akshyay", the music teacher announced, introducing Akshyay to John and this is John."

"Hi!" Akshyay said, and smiled. He noticed John's height, his strong muscles, golden hair and blue eyes.

"Hi! Where do you come from?" John enquired politely.

Akshyay smiled again and said, "I come from Ballygunge Phari. I'm Indian . . . Bengali."

"Well, you don't look Indian, at all," John said.

"Yeah, but I am."

"You don't know, where he comes from. He's from a great family of Bengal", the music teacher intervened, and turning to Akshyay, "John is from Australia. He's come to learn to play the sarode, too. He's also staying near your place. I was wondering whether you could play the tabla for him, while he practices the basic tunes on his sarode. You know the teen tal, don't you? You will have to play it for him. He'll pay you for it."

"I would like to do that," Akshyay said. He turned to John and said, "Could you come over to my house in the evenings, with your sarode? It won't be a problem. You could come in a rickshaw."

I don't like the idea of a man pulling another sitting on his rickshaw. I'll come on foot if the distance is not too much. I'm staying as a paying guest, but I have a full room to myself on Cornfield Road."

"That's near my place," Akshyay said. Then, seeing the music teacher seated on the divan; he abruptly ended the conversation.

"Let's begin our music lessons now. We'll talk later," the music teacher said.

Akshyay sat on the mat, next to John and took out a notebook from his kurta pocket.

"Well, last time, Akshyay, I told you about some of the ragas. Today, we will again discuss about the Bhairab raga. This is for you too, John. The music teacher closed his eyes and began to emit a low guttural sound. He raised his hands and began to make the motions of waves coming towards the shore as his voice rose in pitch. He stopped the guttural sounds and lowered his hands. "That was Bhairab. Imagine the sun rising from under the sea and you are standing on the shore, the waves rushing towards you, their crests, incandescent, in the light of the red sun. The music teacher took the sarode, which was lying beside him and played the Bhairab tune once. "Now you can play it, John."

"Yes, I'll try." He took his sarode and began to repeat the Bhairab tune.

"Not so fast. Do it slowly, step by step. Just use your forefingers to hold down the string over the gut."

John began to play the sarode, as instructed, repeating the process again and again. Akshyay watched John play, critically, frowning whenever the tune was not correct. Engrossed in the Bhairab tune, Akshyay was not quite aware of voices in the next room. As a tune died down to give way to another and in the silence in between, he became aware of the intruding sounds of human voices. He strained to hear and soon he could recognise the voice of the music teacher's son, Shamir. He made an effort to listen, even through the music. There was a notable excitement in the pitch. They were speaking in Bengali.

He could hear Shamir say, "You have not done the right thing. We might all be arrested."

Someone else said, "No, we will not be arrested. No one's injured. How will the police know of the person, who's thrown the bomb?"

"Surely, someone might've seen you. He might report the matter to the police."

"No one will dare report to the police. These bombs will not only make them aware of our movement; they will also cause panic among the people. Haven't you seen all the window-shutters and doors being closed, just after the blast?"

"But do you think these bombs will make the people sympathetic to our cause?"

"Oh yes! We have no means of preaching our doctrines to the masses except through slogans on walls and leaflets. Lately, the strong police action has made these methods ineffective. The police have obliterated the slogans. They have also raided the clandestine presses. We've no other means of arousing public consciousness except through these bombs, which we can make ourselves. It's safe too. A bomb can kill a jeep-load of policemen and you can still go Scott free."

"No, no, that's not the way. Do you think that by throwing bombs; you can overthrow the Government?"

"I don't know about that. These are the instruction from our headquarters. The advice is to mobilise action on these lines."

"Who has given these instructions?"

"I cannot tell."

"Why don't you trust us?"

"It is not a question of trust. It's a question of discipline. I have instructions; not to disclose the source."

"What is going to be the next step?"

"We'll have to kill a policeman."

"Oh no! We cannot do that

"You'll have to do that."

"But let's get out of here now," someone else said. "There are no policemen around. The shops have also opened and . . . . Let's get out."

He heard the sound of the opening door and of people trooping out into the street. Akshyay could see that John was still playing the Bhairab tune on his sarode, unaware of the proceedings. He looked up at the music teacher's face, which wore an expression of fear and anxiety. The music teacher was looking apologetically at him. He was embarrassed at being caught in the act, and his eyes pleaded helplessness. He did not know what to tell Akshyay. He could not also open his mouth on the subject of his son, in front of John. This was all the more because John was not aware, and rightly so, of his son's political activities. John might cease to have any respect for him. He might even give up taking lessons from him. What would be the fate of his son? Would he get to murder a policeman? Could he survive the reaction of such a silly and mindless action? The administration was all-powerful. They would not even require a warrant to arrest him . . . The sarode had suddenly stopped and the music teacher blurted out mechanically, "I think, we should continue in the next session. I'm not feeling well, today."

Akshyay got up and so did John. He was ready to leave and therefore, exchanged the parting gestures and moved into the corridor. The music teacher still seated on the divan called out, "Akshyay, could you come in for a minute?"

Akshyay felt ill at ease because of the proceedings that he had witnessed, involving the music teacher's son. He came back into the room from the corridor and stood before his distraught guru. The music teacher's eyes were downcast and he appeared to be in deep thought. Slowly, he raised his head and looked into Akshyay's serene blue eyes and fair face and recovered himself.

"What can I do, Akshyay?"

Akshyay thought for a moment and said, "He has to be spoken to. He has to give up associating with these people and he has to get out of this place for some time. This might mean; surrendering to the police."

"I don't know. I can't think. Can you help me to do something? I've tried to speak to him. I have explained to him that he should not get involved . . . but it's no use . . . He wouldn't listen to me. He has told me to mind my own business, of teaching tabla and sarode. He has advised me to stay away, from his revolutionary activities."

"Well," said Akshyay. "I'll talk it over with your son. I'll persuade him, to give up politics."

The music teacher's face lit up as the adrenaline drained. A faint smile played on his curled lips. "Could you come back—this evening and have a word with my son? I'll tell him that you want to meet him. I know he will not disagree. He respects you."

"Okay," said Akshyay, after a moment's delay. "I'll come over this evening. Tell him to wait for me. See you, Guruji."

"Yes, yes, good-bye," the music teacher said thankfully, as Akshyay turned and went out of the room and joined John, who was waiting in the corridor, with his sarode on his shoulder. Soon they were on their way out and on to the main road. It was already 11:45 a.m., and the peak hour rush was over. Within a short while, they got into a state transport bus and were on their way to Gariahat.

Chapter - XV

That evening, after the guitar lessons to Pradip Agarwal were over; Akshyay sat in the veranda, waiting for Sarah to return from her office. He considered himself lucky to get an offer to play the tabla for the Australian, John, for three days a week and for the two hundred and fifty rupees. His monthly income would jump to five hundred and fifty rupees, which was at least enough for survival with dignity. No one could point at him and say that he was living off his wife,

He wondered how much salary they would pay her. Would they pay her well enough? Would she be able to cope with the job and all the stress and strain that it could bring on her? How would they treat her in office? Would they exploit her because she was a woman? Would they . . . The cheerful face of Sarah floated in his mind and seemed to drive away all his fears. Soon he noticed Sarah coming up the road.

"How was it in office?" Akshyay asked, as Sarah walked in.

"Oh, it was okay. I have to work as secretary to the proprietor and also as a liaison executive. The job involves writing some letters, following up realisation of outstanding dues, and receiving and connecting telephone calls, as well.

"Will they pay you a salary?"

"The company has not yet decided it. The accounts manager, Mr. Bose told me that they would pay me around seven hundred."

"Didn't they give an appointment letter . . . That should show the pay?"

"No, but someone told me that it was getting ready. They'll give it to me in a day or two."

"So what did you do all day?"

"I went through some of the files. The company deals in non-ferrous metals and they manufacture various items in conformity with firms' orders. I have to make a visit to the factory soon, to get a first-hand knowledge of the working processes," Sarah said, putting down her bag on the sofa in the drawing room. "So what were you up to, during the day? Did you go to the music teacher's house?"

"Yeah, I went there. It was quite an experience."

"Why, what happened?"

"I met an Australian there, John Bernard, and it's arranged that I'll play the tabla for him thrice a week for two hundred and fifty rupees. Isn't that good?" Akshyay paused for a while, and then in a rather hushed voice said, "There is also a little problem that I have to sort out. The music teacher's son has got himself involved with Naxalites." He avoided Sarah's eyes and continued: "They are planning to murder a policeman. Guruji told me to drive some sense into his silly head and dissuade him from that dangerous path. The music teacher feels that Shamir—that's his son, will listen to me. "He quickened his speech, "I've promised to go back this evening to talk to him and try to persuade him to give up this foolish venture."

"Will it be safe for you to do that? What about the other members? If they come to know that you have brain-washed someone, in their group, they might harm you." The intonations in her voice betrayed her anxiety.

"No way! I know a lot of those guys. I'm one of them in many ways. I'm not against them, nor I'm for them. But I know they are on a wrong trip. This country's ethos is different. The people believe in God and consider things to be preordained. That's most of North and South India, where the caste system, which is fundamental in Hinduism, is still strong," Akshyay said, trying to instil confidence in her.

"How do you say, you are one of them? You are deeply religious, aren't you?"

"Well, I'm on a trip and they are also on their trip. My trip is for spiritual freedom: their trip is for material freedom. I am, in a way, unable to adjust to this society and they are also revolting against the same social system."

"But they are Communists, aren't they?" Sarah intervened, as if she was uttering a grave truth.

"Yeah, they do believe in some communist doctrines. But basically, these misguided youth can't see any future before their eyes. They are dreaming of a revolution, which they think will solve all their problems. I've just to explain to them, I mean to Shamir; that nothing's going to come off the trip they are in. They are not ready to fight against the all-powerful government, and that, too, with the masses, not in their support. The culture and age-old traditions of this country, are against the basic tenets of Communism."

"No, no, I don't think you can convince them. Communists cannot be talked out of their beliefs," Sarah said, in a manner that gave away the fear in her mind, aroused at the very mention of 'Communists'. "No, no, Akshyay, I think you shouldn't go," she repeated.

Akshyay could not help smiling as he could see through the cause of her fear. He thought he knew what made her so uptight . . . So much against communists. As for himself, he did not quite have anything against them as human beings, but he didn't subscribe to their views, which were, if not anything else, materialistic. To share food with someone was all right. He could also think of a society where everyone was equally wealthy or equally poor. However, he could not think of making it a cause or dogmatic belief. He could not accept it. To him life was for different things. Life was too big and abstract. It does not have a definite form or shape. It is beyond anybody's control. He suddenly spied that Sarah was staring at him and he felt she was reading his mind.

"There is no need to feel afraid. I've already told you that these people are not against me. They will not harm me. What will they gain from it? I'm neither a capitalist, nor an exploiter of the poor. In fact, I'm like one of them: without a job; without a career to look forward to." He had an uncanny feeling that what he had just said could make Sarah misunderstand him. So he quickly added, "But I do have a life to look forward to with you."

"Then you will go?" Sarah asked, resigned to the outcome of the discussion. She felt that she could not continue the argument any longer: she felt tired. "All right, but do come back by dinner time. I'll wait for you."

"I'll just go and come back. I'll not be long. But before I go, let me order a cup of tea for you. You look tired. Why don't you have a wash, while I tell Abdul to set the table?"

After Akshyay left, Sarah suddenly began to feel lonely. She knew that Aunt Monica was in the house and so were the servants, but she was alienated from them.

She could not communicate with them and she felt that they did not understand her. The fact that Akshyay too could not get along with his aunt reinforced her feeling of isolation from the household. Having nothing to do, no one to talk to, and unused to the pastime of reading, even newspapers, she decided to lie down in 'sabasan'[17] and wait for Akshyay to return.

She retired to her bedroom, changed into her night-gown and reclined on the bed. She lay on her back and stared at the ceiling, in a blank state of mind. She removed the pillow from under her head and soon relapsed into the posture of sabasan. She had been practising the asan during her stay at the ashram in Rishikesh, under the direct tutelage of Swami Ananda. Thoughts of the ashram flowed into her mind and like a mild electric shock sent a splurge of blood coursing through her tired calf muscles and the soles of her feet. She heard the familiar voice of the Swami, as she lay on the mat, on the ground under the mango tree.

"Let your mind go free. Don't think of anything. Let the thoughts flow unanchored in your emotions and feelings. Just let your body lie on the bank of a stream, on the soft grass and under the shade of a tree." The sound of the curling and swishing water seemed to dull her sensibilities, putting her to sleep and yet she was floating above her body. Her world experiences: of guilt, violence, anxiety, and the whole gamut of feelings related to social living, seemed to have moved away. Looking down at herself, she saw all those experiences like one sees a play on Broadway. One identifies with the main character, but remains detached. It was as if all those experiences did not effect her. She was beyond their reach. In the distance she saw the girl lying on the cobbled stone recuperating from the clutches of a frenzied rapist. She heard the frantic screaming as she ran down the deserted street, and then the fall with the Moor on top of her. Suddenly, she felt engulfed by the waves that followed, in a spasmodic rhythm that left her gasping for breath. Then suddenly, it was calm again like the sea receding from the beach leaving the battered sand dry, in its own form, as if untouched by it.

The waves suddenly came back again and she was now riding on their crests as they rolled below her in all their fury. The buoyancy that she experienced was ecstatic. There was no sense of guilt or anger or hurt pride in it. She felt that the Moor's attack was of little consequence, as was the act of leaving home to live with Jackie. In the same light, her marriage to Akshyay and the threat of Akshyay getting involved with extremists and coming to harm was of little or no consequence. Nothing affected her anymore.

The thought of Akshyay brought into sharp focus his serene face, the blue eyes: innocent, yet all-knowing. She was neither all-knowing, like Akshyay, nor innocent. However, she had left her experiences far behind. The traces on the sand had dried up in the hot sun and were about to blow away. There were more waves of experiences coming but she would be able to leave them behind again and again. The image of the ashram was now in her consciousness. The calm and serene atmosphere, the Banyan tree with the cemented seat around its trunk, where she had meditated every morning and evening, came to her mind. Did she yearn for it? Did she prefer this life with Akshyay with all its problems? The new associations in her office: was she not going back to the life she had left behind in the US? The life of chasing money and desires. Here, she was a Hindu wife, as Sita[18] or Draupadi[19]. That's what Swamiji had told her, would be her yogic trip. It was suitable for her too. There would be no need to starve her sexual appetite, as Swamiji had stated with a mischievous smile.

She got up from the sabasan posture and began to pace up and down, lost in thought. The memories of the ashram came back to her again and again. She recalled the silence of the mornings and the afternoons, broken only by the birdcalls and the sound of the river rolling over the round stones. Images of Rishikesh flowed into her mind: the peaceful ashram life, the river bursting, lurching, and speeding along. She recalled the prayer meetings in the courtyard and Swami Ananda explaining the stanzas of the Shastras and Vedas. There were also fleeting flashes of the city life, in between. Occasionally, the face of Akshyay appeared in her mind and now, as she saw him once again, she saw him being chased by a violent mob. All on a sudden, the train of thoughts passing through her mind abruptly ended.

A new thought like the full moon shone on her, as she lay down on the bed again. She had been performing the role assigned to her. The problems of a married life in the city were her creations. These were all part of the marriage trip. She would have to endure them and overcome them. Therein lay her nirvana. She felt reassured at the thought and closed her eyes to a relaxed and benumbed sleep.

CHAPTER - XVI

When Akshyay reached the music teacher's house, Shamir, his son, was not at home. Akshyay had seen him standing with a group of teenagers, under the portico of one of the houses that lined the road. Akshyay remembered seeing a man among the fresh-faced boys, whose harsh appearance and cold look gave him up as a hard-core extremist. Akshyay had felt like an alien as the pairs of eyes scoured his person. They had not taken him lightly that day. Perhaps the vicious looking man's visit had something to do with it. It was definitely not like the other days, when they had casually looked at him with harmless curiosity. The people in the locality knew his face, as one of Mr. Lahiri's foreign students, and in short, as one of the hippie types. The image was a comfortable camouflage of his real personality and background. It was especially useful in these localities, not particularly cosmopolitan in character, and inhabited mostly by immigrants from East Bengal, of whom many had settled there before the partition of the country. He had nothing to fear from them. He was certain of that.

"Come on in, Akshyay", the music teacher said, as he entered the room, where they had their music lessons, "my son will be coming in any time now."

"I saw him on the road. He was in the group by the roadside; as I was coming here."

"Didn't he seen you?"

"No, I think he didn't. He had his back turned towards me. A serious discussion was on or so it seemed."

The music teacher's face turned pale as he heard Akshyay's words "Oh my God!" He raised his hand to his bent head, in anguish, and said, "What will I do? How can I save him, from this?"

Akshyay knew what made the music teacher so anxious, but he feigned ignorance. "What is worrying you? Shamir was only talking to some of the young people like him. As long as he doesn't do anything illegal, there's no harm. I'll talk him out of whatever brainwashing he's been through. You may rest assured. After all, he's your son. How can he opt for a violent life?"

"No, no, Akshyay", the music teacher intervened, "you don't know. There are so many young men, who have taken to this kind of politics of hatred, and many have ended up in jail and quite a few have lost their lives, as well. I've heard of a young man, hardly past his teens. The police shot him dead in broad daylight, and in another case, someone was beaten with rods till the joints of his limbs ceased to work. There are stories of inhuman torture in police lock-ups and of fake encounters. How can I remain indifferent when my son, is treading a dangerous path? I cannot understand why he should go for such a life. We've got a house of our own and he is our only son. It's all his: all that I have. I don't know how he can talk about a bleak future."

"Young people tend to get carried away by ideologies, with which they can identify themselves. Look what's happening in the West. There too, young people are rebelling against a mechanised society, where human values and nature have become subservient, to materialism and consumerism. That's how they are looking to the East for guidance and solace."

"You are right, but that's a good movement; there's neither hate in it nor violence and," the music teacher stopped as Shamir came into the room.

"Hi!" Akshyay greeted Shamir.

"When did you come?" Shamir asked, smiling.

"I came in about ten minutes back. I passed by you on the road, but your were so engrossed in your 'adda'[20], that you didn't even notice me."

"Oh yes! I was. We were planning a major operation."

"Shamir!" The music teacher burst out, "What are you saying? Are you mad? Do you not know that the police will crack down on you and your group and finish all of you? Are you all fools to go against the police forces and don't you know that there is the army behind the police. Are you mad to fight against them?"

"My fight, our fight, is not against the police or the army. We are revolutionaries. We want to change the social and economic order."

"Now, now, wait a minute," Akshyay intervened, raising both his hands to stop the music teacher and Shamir from going at each other. After a pause, he began: "Shamir, I'd like to talk to you about this. You know, I am also one with you about correcting the social order. But I'd not go into the group that you've joined, simply because I know that I can't change the social order. Either you adapt to it or you get away from it—like I've been trying to do. I don't dig the society I was born into and so I've broken away. I could have gone for a cushy job and lived up to the expectations of that society, but I've spurned it for good and I feel happy about it. I don't have to eliminate anybody or for that matter, fight to change society. I've just to get away. I think you can do the same thing by being self-sufficient and independent, like, for example, your father."

"You mean, I should become a musician. No, no, I'm no good at music," Shamir retorted immediately, and looking at his father, continued, "My father has told me that I don't have any music sense and that I cannot become a musician. It's not that I don't want to. I want to be useful to society. I want a job just as hundreds of others, like me, who want jobs. This society cannot give us these jobs and hence we've to change it. It's as simple as that. It's a question of our survival. If we don't fight against this society, we will continue to be deprived. There is no alternative."

"You know, it is a question of adjustments. How do you say there are no jobs? There are thousands of people from other States, who keep coming to the city for jobs. There is a continuous migration to all the urban centres from rural areas, spurred by the belief that there are many ways to survive in a city. To come to your case: true, there aren't many jobs or enough offices for all the people passing out of the colleges with knowledge of history, politics and literature—they do not know any work. I mean if you ask anyone of them what work he can do, he'll say he does not know any. There is an unending demand for work-knowing people in our society and even of teachers. I'm quite sure those who know automobile mechanics, electrical jobs, or are simply plumbers, carpenters, or motorcar drivers, are never without work. Why, a stenographer or even a typist can find a job easily. Even if you sit with a typewriter on the footpath under a tree, near any of our law courts or employment exchanges, you can earn a living. The trouble is our young men are against manual labour. Most of them would like to be doctors or engineers. In case these categories are beyond reach, one settles for a clerical post in the government, banking sector, or in the private firms: in that order of priority. Now, because these jobs are in short supply, you are talking of a revolution? Is it at all justified?"

"Do you know of any political and social system, better than independence? Don't you cherish the freedom that we have achieved after a long struggle, that had left so many people dead, to whom we are forever indebted? Don't you realise that they have bestowed on all the citizens the responsibility of keeping our country free? Do you think it will be right to bind everyone with the chains of Communism? I don't deny that your aim is good: assuring food for all and employment for all. But what about freedom? Would you have allowed the British to continue to rule over us if they had promised food for all and employment for all?"

"No, certainly not," Shamir said, falling into the trap, into which Akshyay had led him.

"So you admit that freedom is of paramount importance?" Akshyay asked quickly, with a disarming smile.

Shamir smiled back at Akshyay, quietly accepting his logic as right. He suddenly felt as if his earlier ideas were tumbling down like a pack of cards, in the clear light of Akshyay's words. He had heard of class enemies and about Capitalists and Proletariats; about the rich and the poor; about the landowners and the land-less. He had heard that a handful of people at the top had been exploiting the masses with their power over capital. He had to understand and someone explained to him that annihilation of the handful of exploiters would change everything. It was in his own interest that he should join the party because every other person in his college was joining it and almost all the young people in his locality. Many of them were in the same college as his. The political discussions in the canteen had spilled over to teashops and street-corner meetings. He could suddenly see that these words had changed his way of thinking, made him believe in certain things and talk of other things. In the light of Akshyay's words now, these thought-control clusters seemed to burn away and get replaced by the warmth of his genuine feelings, which seemed to ignite the thoughts of love, compassion and freedom, arousing a covenant of acquiescence.

He began, "Akshyay, I can see the truth of your words. Your understanding of life is better, because it is based on love, unlike mine, which was based on hate and jealousy. I am sure I'll be able to explain to others to give up this path and to think of positive ways of solving our problems. I think I will learn some mechanic's job, so that I can earn a living."

"Why do you have to be a mechanic?" A look of irritation came over Mr.Lahiri's face, which had so far been cheerful. He had witnessed the change in his son's thought processes and his readiness to give up the political yoke, which had sapped his power of independent thinking. An old adage came to his mind and he could not hold his tongue:

"Those of us, who will study hard,

Will ride horses and cars."

"Father, now why don't you realise that there are no jobs waiting for all the graduates. Haven't you heard Akshyay saying just now, that one has to learn to do that work, which will be useful to society? A graduate's utility, when there are so many around, is zero."

"No, no!" The music teacher continued, "You must be a graduate and try to get a job. Only then you can uphold the family tradition. How will I show my face if you become a mechanic?"

Akshyay felt uneasy at his Guru's words. They appeared to strum a discordant note in his mind. He knew that he too could not have taken up any job that came his way. In the context of Shamir's predicament, however, where people like him needed jobs for their survival, as Shamir had said, there was no question of any choice. He felt his respect for his Guru being tarnished by the latter's penchant for white-collar jobs. He decided to intervene and correct his Guru's ideas on manual labour.

"Gurudev, why do you think a mechanic's job is unworthy? Isn't a manual labourer an equally important member of our society? Does it not involve a reasonably good intellect, to become a good mechanic? Didn't Gandhiji talk about the dignity of manual labour?"

The sudden reference to Gandhiji left the music teacher speechless. He kept his gaze on the ground, avoiding a reply. He knew that Akshyay would not understand him. He was a Bengali Brahmin from a middle class family, while Akshyay belonged to a family, where traditions were different. He believed in the caste system and he felt proud of being a Brahmin. He knew that Akshyay had no faith in the caste system and that he had a mixed parentage. His attitude to life would be quite different from his. Becoming aware that his continued silence would be tantamount to rudeness, he began to slowly nod his head and said, "I think you are right, Akshyay. I hope Shamir accepts your logic and gives up the wrong path, that he had chosen for himself." He looked at Shamir and then at Akshyay, to elicit a favourable reply, a faint smile playing on his lips.

Shamir was the first to speak; "I've not accepted all of it. But I agree that with Akshyay's guidance, I may be able to make it in life. But what is there for all the others? There's no hope for the common man. They don't have a person like Akshyay to show them the way or parental property to fall back upon. It would not be easy to convince them and many of them are the hard-core types."

"Thank God, that you are convinced that the path of violence will not lead you anywhere," the music teacher blurted out in emotion. Looking at Akshyay, he continued, "I am really grateful to you for having come over today to convince my son."

"It was only my duty to help him and then you are my Guru and he is your son. I was trying to follow the old 'guru-shisya'[21] tradition."

"I know that, but who takes risks these days? Does anyone have any respect for our old traditions? They have been allowed to be forgotten, due to disuse and the impact of Western education and thought. Even this Naxalite movement, which is going on . . . Isn't it also a Western idea? And . . ." The music teacher suddenly stopped, realising that he was treading a territory that was dangerous for more reasons than one. His son's safety was at stake. "Let's have some snacks and tea before you go. It's not safe out there these days. Anything may happen on the roads." In a louder pitch, for his wife to hear, he continued, "Are you listening? Akshyay is here and he has to leave. Get us some tea and something to eat. Shamir, why don't you go and help your mother?"

They could hear Mrs. Lahiri's voice, "Don't let Akshyay go. I am getting tea."

Akshyay looked at the old wall clock and saw that it was already eight o'clock. It was quite late and Sarah would be waiting for him. He began apologetically, "No, no, Guruji. I'll not have anything now. I've to get going."

"Oh yes! I forgot that you are newly married?" The music teacher said, and got up to accompany Akshyay to the doorway. "Be careful, Akshyay. Don't get into trouble."

"Don't worry. I will make it safely. I am neither a Naxalite, nor am I against them. You may rest assured there won't be any danger."

"You never know, Akshyay. The times are bad. You must make a move. Now, take this." The music teacher picked up a torch from a shelf and handed it over to Akshyay. "The way to the main road is quite dark. You may also need it to scare away the dogs."

"Thanks," said Akshyay, as he took the torch and walked out of the house, following the spotlight in the darkness. In the silence he could still hear the voice of Mrs. Lahiri, "Why did you let him go?"

Chapter - XVII

When Akshyay left the music teacher's house, it was past eight o'clock. The lane was strangely bare by then, though he could hear the sound of occasional buses and other vehicles on the main road and frogs croaking in the pond, breaking the silence all around. An eerie feeling filled his mind of danger lurking beyond the spotlight in the darkness. He brushed aside the thought from his mind and with an image of a marching column, floating before his eyes, kept moving on.

He had already covered half of the length of the road skirting the pond, when he suddenly heard a sound of moaning. He felt his heart beating fast and his thoughts and feelings getting entangled. With an effort he controlled himself and readied himself to help whoever was in need of it. No sooner he had taken thirty steps, he found a person, in dhoti and shirt, lying on the ground writhing and cringing in pain. The spotlight revealed patches of blood on the ground and gaping wounds on the person's back. Someone had repeatedly stabbed the man from behind. Quickly and spontaneously, Akshyay knelt down and lifted the man's head with one hand, trying to see his face. The man's had closed his eyes and the strong lines of his face were limp and drawn in the struggle with the painful stab wounds, which were drawing out the life from his body. The moaning soon ceased and the speechless quivering of his lips and the muscular contractions were no more than inert and irregular twitches of the skin and reflex movement of hands and feet. Akshyay couldn't help imagining the slaughtered goats at the meat shop, soon after the butcher skins and hangs the animals on the hook before the eyes of waiting customers.

He saw that the man was in the throes of death and unless he could rush him to the hospital, there would be no chance of his survival. He looked around for help but there were still no one around or approaching. The croaking of frogs in the pond was all that he could hear. The doors and windows of the houses lining the road were all closed, shutting in their dim interiors.

Akshyay did not know what to do. Should he shout for help; knock at people's doors; go back to the music teacher's house and call Shamir? No, not Shamir! It must be one of his gang members, who had done this. Was it the brutish-looking person, who had appeared to be the ringleader? Had they not been discussing about a murder in the afternoon? 'I'm wasting my time thinking about who's done this,' he heard himself saying, and started to walk towards the main road at a brisk pace to see if he could get help from there. 'Perhaps a doctor's chamber would be there; or a Policeman . . .'

When he reached the road intersection, he saw the rows of shops, which one can generally find at all such locations. His immediate impulse was to approach one of the shopkeepers for help. He was still in the process of making up his mind when he saw a police jeep approaching at high speed and stopping with its brakes screeching, about ten yards away. A police inspector was sitting upright on the front seat and behind him were four armed policemen. The driver leaned out and asked a 'pan-walla'[22] where Ram Kinker Mitra Street was. The latter pointed to the road, from which Akshyay had emerged, and soon the jeep accelerated towards the site of murder.

Akshyay became aware that he was unnecessarily waiting there. The policemen would take charge of the fatally injured man and they should not see him standing around the place. He quickly began to walk to the bus stop, which was about thirty metres away and stood waiting for one to appear.

Almost all the buses that plied on that route passed through Gariahat, an important road junction near his home. Akshyay wished dearly that a bus should appear and take him away from that place. He feared that the jeep would come back and stop in front of him, at any moment, and the stern-faced police inspector would start reading his mind with inquisitive eyes. He detested the very thought of having to talk to a policeman, let alone being interrogated by one. He kept looking in the direction from which the bus was to come but his mind was on Ram Kinker Mitra Street. Feelings of fear, associated with the police jeep's reappearance and those of hope, associated with the bus's arrival so clouded his vision that he was almost hallucinating. Whenever he imagined the jeep appearing, he would see it stopping right in front of him, the feet of the dead man protruding from its rear. The image of the jeep hurtling down the hillside on its way down from Darjeeling came to his mind. He is sitting sandwiched between his drunken father and the rash driver. In the middle of his reverie, the police jeep came rushing out of the lane on to the main road. Much to his relief, it did not stop as he had feared; but he could see the dead policeman's feet sticking out, as it sped away.

Akshyay tried in vain to drive away the image of the dying man on the road and the jeep-load of policemen. He was afraid that they would be after him. Once again, the sequence of events revolved in his mind. He could see the missing links in them; some questions, that were crying for the answers.

Was the dying person really a plain-dressed policeman? How could the police jeep arrive at the spot soon after the murder? Who had informed them about the murder? There had been no one at sight, when he had encountered the dying man on the road and, if anyone had chanced to be there before him, could he have informed the police? How could he possibly have left the person to die on the roadside? He could not find the answers to these pressing questions. He felt too tired to think clearly. The feelings of pity, fear, and horror, raised their heads in his mind, along with their bizarre images, which caused his fogged his thoughts.

Presently, as the bus came along, Akshyay found his eagerness to get away from the place coming back. He quickly boarded it even before the near-empty bus had come to a stop. A feeling of relief seeped into his mind as it began to move and sped off towards Gariahat.

Sarah was in the drawing room, reading a book on yogic philosophy, when Akshyay entered the house. She lifted her serene face to look at him, and immediately noticed that there was something wrong.

"What's the matter? You look so pale?"

"Oh, it's nothing," replied Akshyay, trying to compose himself.

"No, no, you're hiding something," Sarah persisted, as if she could read his thoughts.

Akshyay felt like blurting out the whole episode to her, but at the same time he wanted to forget it. The whole thing was like a lurking tempest about to lash at the shore. On the one hand, was his urge to get away from it, and on the other, his desire to tell everything about it, to share the feelings of agony and pain.

"Let's have a glass of water first," Akshyay finally said to Sarah as he sat on the sofa. After he had had his fill, he felt the strong feelings gradually ebbing. He began to recount the episode of his chance encounter with a dying policeman on the road. He spoke of the possible conspirators, who could be behind the murder and the policemen, who had arrived at the site, out of the blue.

"I'm sure that guy, who's the ringleader of the Naxalites, must have done it," said Sarah, after hearing the story. "Who else could it be?"

"Well, I'm not so sure. I've not seen anybody in the act. I'd only seen the injured man on the road and no one else. There was no time to look around. I saw the man; I went for help; and then, the police arrived."

Just then, Miss Monica walked into the drawing room, rubbing her eyes. "What are you talking about? Weren't you saying something about the police?"

"Well, yes," Akshyay blurted out, without noticing Sarah's signal to stop. "I saw a murdered policeman on the road."

"My God! What have you done Akshyay? Why did you have to witness a murder and that too, of a policeman? Didn't you know what it could mean? They'll be looking for you now."

"Why should they look for me? I've done nothing wrong. It was only a coincidence that I saw a man dying on the road and all I did was my duty—I tried to help."

"I'm not saying that you have done anything wrong, but you've somehow got them on your trail. I'd like to know the full facts. Could you tell me exactly what happened?"

Akshyay retold the story, leaving out the parts concerning the music teacher's son and his associates. He also avoided revealing the real reason for his visit.

After he had finished the story once again, Miss Monica sat thinking awhile and then asked, "Are you sure you didn't leave any clues behind?"

Akshyay could not reply immediately. He began to visualise the whole scene part by part and this time he remembered the torch that his Guru had given him. "Did I give you the torch?" He looked at Sarah foolishly hoping that it would be with her, but knowing that it wouldn't.

"No, you haven't. There wasn't any torch in your hand when you walked in, was there?"

Akshyay could not remember what had happened to it. A thought knocked his mind. Was he trying not to remember? Was it fear, which clouded his memory or was it simply a case of forgetfulness? He tried to recollect the scene again; the one, in which, he had raised the man's head to have a look at his face. The torch was in his right hand then, and while he had lowered the man's head—did he use both his hands? Did he keep the torch on the ground, so that he could use both his hands? Had the torch still been in his hand? He was not sure. He must have switched off the light and kept the torch on the ground, so that he could gently lower the man's head. Did he pick up the torch, before going ahead to seek the shopkeepers' help? It would have been unnatural to leave the torch behind, on the ground. In any case, the shops were not very far off. There was no need for it. His mind sought to recapitulate the details but he could not retrieve the position of the torch after he had used it to focus on the man's face.

"I can't figure out where I'd left the torch. Maybe in the bus."

"I think it could be in the bus. You must have left it on the seat. You couldn't have left it beside the dying man. Nobody would do that." Sarah said, a mixed stamp of hope and anxiety marking her face.

"You don't know Sarah. Akshyay's capable of doing the most unusual things." Miss Monica interposed. "It's inherited, you know," she continued, addressing Sarah. "I don't blame him."

"Why do you have to drag in my mother?" Akshyay retorted, flaring up.

"You won't understand, Akshyay. You're not to blame for what's happened to our family. It's she."

The billowing anger suddenly died down, as he quickly concluded that talking about his mother was best avoided. The feelings of compassion and sadness, which came rushing into his mind, like a river in flood, quenched the angry flames. Miss Monica was aware of Akshyay's weakness for his mother. He often reacted like a child. Akshyay loved his mother and he could not bear to hear anything against her, especially now that she was in a mental hospital. It was cruel to hit at someone who is weak and unable to hit back. A mind-drugging sadness closed in on him and with it, a feeling of fear. He could not bear the thought of seeing his aunt mocking his father or mother in front of Sarah. He sensed that he should change the subject and began, "Well, Auntie, let's not go into the past, let's think of the imminent future. What do you think I should do now? Should I not go to the police and record my statement?"

"Don't be a fool, Akshyay," Miss Monica said, "Do you think the police will believe you? They will promptly arrest you. By God, don't you know that some days back the police arrested a Naxalite and his English wife in Midnapore under the MISA? They could as well take you in and Sarah too."

"Why should they do that?" Sarah asked, irritably. "I'm not a Naxalite, and even Akshyay's anything but one. I could prove it to them."

"They are not looking for proofs these days, you know. They don't have to produce you before a judge. They can just arrest you and keep you in jail for six months."

"Yeah; you're right; they are not to be trusted. I can't put Sarah, like myself, into trouble. I'll not go to the police. We can go back to Rishikesh and then let the police find me. We'll be in the Ashram and Swami Ananda will certify what we are. He's also got connections with the DM and SP of Dehra Doon."

"Don't think you can escape the police. They will trace you down if they have any reason to suspect you. The right thing to do is to find out whom we can bank on to help you: someone in the police, for example. Your father had a few friends in the Government. I also know some people. We'll have to find out who can help you, should the police create a problem."

"Are you sure, you know the right people? Is there someone you know in the police force?"

"Well, I'll have to check my diary for the names. But I do know some people in the income tax and customs departments."

"Can they help in case there's a problem?"

"It all depends on whether they can wield enough influence in the police circles."

"Would you find a way to help me out?" Akshyay finally asked submissively.

"Oh yes. Isn't it my duty?" Miss Monica shot back. "But you must give me a chance to help you."

"What do you mean?" Akshyay asked, suspecting something and retracting back to his aggressive stance. Miss Monica looked at Sarah and then at Akshyay and said nothing. She appeared to be lost in thought. She browsed through the various options of reacting to Akshyay's effrontery. However, she chose to take a conciliatory stand and composed herself, saying, "No, no it's nothing, I meant that you should do as I tell you, so that I can help you."

"There's no reason why I shouldn't, especially if it concerns my safety."

"You haven't been really concerned about your safety, have you?"

Akshyay could feel that he was once again going in for a long, drawn-out argument and decided to cut it short. He was also feeling tired and wanted to forget everything in the cosy comfort of Sarah's arms. "I guess, you are right," he conceded and quickly added, "I'm feeling tired and hungry. We might as well get ready for dinner."

"Oh yes, its time for dinner. It's good to be reminded by you about dinnertime, for once. It's a sign of your coming back to reality," Miss Monica said, in a manner that revealed her feelings of disdain.

"In a way, it's . . ." Akshyay began and stopped, giving up. He beckoned to Sarah to follow him and raised a hand to show he has had enough. He turned round and walked out of the drawing room, Sarah following, leaving Miss Monica in the middle of an incomplete argument.

At the dining table, there was hardly any conversation. Abdul, the cook, had prepared soup, chappatis, chicken curry, a cauliflower potato curry, dal, and curd. The vegetarian dish was for Sarah, but she shared it with Aunt Monica and Akshyay. Apart from answering each other in monosyllables, they only exchanged cursory glances.

Akshyay felt relieved that he was not again the target of Miss Monica's verbal attack. He could never make her understand his predicament, but he could very well understand that with her Victorian ideas and 'materialism with a finesse', it was, obvious that she could not approve of his ways. He wondered what was her precondition to her helping him. Was it something to do with Sarah? He knew that she did not approve of the marriage at all. To her it was a repugnant affair. She was also in a way, jealous of Sarah and all her escapades. Such a girl as she, had tied the wedlock and was apparently consummating. Her own life had been incomplete. She had nothing to look forward to; she could only cling to an elusive family status. Akshyay was the symbol of the family tree and it pained her to see him squandering away his life; destroying the heritage, on which she sought to thrive.

The dinner over, Akshyay and Sarah went to their bedroom, after saying 'goodnight' to Aunt Monica. They were both tired: Sarah from her first day in office, and Akshyay from his misadventures. When they were in the privacy of their bedroom, there was no energy left to discuss the subject any further. They just clasped each other and lay still, looking blankly at the ceiling, until they fell asleep.

Chapter - XVIII

The next morning, Akshyay, decided to call on John, after Sarah had left for her office. The purpose was to send a message to his Guru about the incident. He had decided, before setting out that he should not go to the music teacher's house during the next few days and accordingly had made out a note giving the reasons for his absence. He would ask John to deliver it to the music teacher. As he passed out of the iron gates of his houses, he looked again at the pad sheet, to check whether he had covered all the points.

"Respected Guruji,

"Last night, on my way from your house, I encountered a wounded policeman, lying in a pool of blood. He had been brutally stabbed. There was no one on the road at that time, and I had knelt down to pick up his head to see if he was alive or could talk. Finding him close to death, I rushed to the main road to see if I could get some help. As soon as I reached the highway, a police jeep arrived and turned towards that very lane from which I had emerged.

I could not wait there any longer and left by the first available bus. I am not sure, but I think, I left the torch, which I had picked up from your place, beside the dying policeman. The police must have found it. It would be desirable for me, or so I feel, to keep away from the area, for a while. I will, in the meantime, as agreed, play the tabla for John and also practice the ragas on my sarode. In case you should like to communicate with me, I should feel obliged if you do so through John. He will be visiting my place every evening. I do hope that Maaji and Shamir are in good health and spirits.

Please accept my pronam.

You're faithful disciple,

Akshyay

On the way to John's one-room flat, he kept debating on the efficacy of sending the note through John, against explaining the whole situation personally to Guruji. A feeling of insecurity knocked at his complacent ignorance of what the police were up to. As if to fill the vacuum, he wanted to see for himself the situation prevailing there: whether there were any inquiries made; whether Shamir knew anything about the murder or about the torch? He feared that the torch, like Theseus' thread in the labyrinth, would lead the police to him. Surely, fingerprints would be available and the policemen would trace the torch to the music teacher's house and link him to the murder. He desperately tried to drive away the depressing thoughts of being arrested, but they kept coming back like waves returning to the shore. He tried to divert his attention to the traffic on the road. There were the beautiful young women, to look at, in saris and salwar kameez, in the latest fashions copied from Hindi films, walking past, or, ahead of him. Somehow, he did not feel any interest in them: his thoughts hovered around the murder-arrest syndrome.

It took him half-an-hour's time to reach John's flat. It was on Cornfield Road, near Gariahat. The room was on the mezzanine floor, above a garage, in a double-storied house. The landlord lived on the first, and there were other tenants on the ground floor. John's room had an attached bath and a small antechamber, which he used, as a kitchen. When he was not eating out, he cooked his own meals. The landlord had offered him the facility of dining with the family like most paying guests. However, he preferred to have his own arrangements, ever since he discovered the cheap and tasty food of Punjabi dhabas. The dhaba at Ballygunge Phari was indeed close by for an easy walk down to a sumptuous dinner of nan, tarka, and coffee.

"Hi Akshyay!" John exclaimed, as he opened the door to let him in. "Come on in. It's nice to see you. What's the matter? You look a bit worried." There was a sudden change in the pitch of his voice, to one of concern, as he looked quizzically at Akshyay's eyes to see if he could read what was amiss.

"It's nothing," Akshyay reacted, suddenly recoiling within himself, not sure whether he should tell John the truth. "I didn't sleep well last night. I've had a bad dream," Akshyay said, avoiding the truth. He hesitated for a while, in telling John about the incident but something told him he should. The image of John's sombre face appeared in his mind, assuring the police about his innocence. "I've actually had a bad experience last night, while I was returning from Guruji's house . . ." Akshyay began. He then narrated the incident and on completing it, took out the envelope from his side bag. "Can you deliver this letter to Guruji?"

"Oh sure!" John said. "But aren't you going there?"

"No, not for about seven days. You may read the letter and see for yourself, why."

John took the letter out of the envelope and then put it back again. "I might as well hear from you; what you've written." He recollected that it was rank bad manners, reading someone else's letter.

Akshyay recounted its contents and noticed John listening attentively.

"Why don't you report this to the police?" John said. "I'm sure they'll believe you and take necessary steps to arrest the real culprits."

"I'm afraid it's not so easy. There's a lot of politics involved in these things. In all probability, it's a case of political murder and it's well known who are the persons behind the scene, and this makes the situation very complex. If I've actually left the torch there; they could as well prove that I'm the murderer."

"You mean, they would arrest you even though you haven't committed the murder . . . By the way, I've read about a policeman's murder in the newspaper. Let me see where I saw it." John picked up the newspaper, as Akshyay felt amazement at not having considered it for whatever it was worth. He had to admit to himself that it was the result of giving up the habit of reading the morning newspaper. He turned his attention on John. His eyes were glued to the page. The news was staring out.

"Here, it's given here. I'll read out . . ." In yet another gruesome murder a policeman was found stabbed to death in the Jadavpur Thana area last night. According to police sources, the murder was committed around 8 p.m., in Ram Kinkar Mitra Lane, where the policeman had been on surveillance duty. The police, in course of a routine patrolling of the area, found the forty-five year old Ratan Mondal, in a pool of blood. He was rushed to the civil hospital in Jadavpur, where attending doctors pronounced him dead.

"Ratan Mondal leaves behind his wife and two school-going children. The Association of Serving Policemen has demanded payment of compensation to his wife from the State Government. All the major political parties have condemned the attack on the policeman as yet another example of mindless, brutal, murder for political gain.

"This is the third case of a policeman being killed this year." It goes on about Naxalites being the probable suspects, responsible for the murder and steps being taken to prevent them and so on."

"Let's have a look," said Akshyay. He picked up the newspaper and reread the report, comparing it with what he had seen, and looking for concealed clues that could implicate him. While the report was quite factual, there was, much to his relief, no mention about the torch. He felt a sense of relief. After all, there was nothing pointing at him. He read on looking for other differences with his perception of the incident. The account, of the jeep being on a routine patrol, appeared concocted. He felt that the jeep had come to pick up the injured man, on receipt of definite information. He could not be sure. It could as well be on a routine patrolling duty. He wondered how he could ascertain the facts. Did the speed of the jeep mean anything? He recalled that some of the police jeeps had to face bomb attacks recently. As a precautionary measure, wire meshes had to been provided to cover the glass front, the cloth roof, and sides. Surely, no jeep could go at a slow speed in a Naxalite-infested area. However, he was not able to conclude definitely, and surrendered. How did it concern him? His only concern was that no one should harass him.

"So that's that. There's nothing so far against me, as I can see in the report. But, I still feel I should stay clear for a few days."

"Well it's up to you, really. You know better. I still feel you should report to the police."

"Why don't you understand? I can't go to the police and keep mum about Guruji's house. It would be like leading the police to his house and his son, you know."

"Yeah, I remember you had mentioned about his son being involved with extremists. I don't see why you should protect him, especially when your own safety is involved."

"I know, but Guruji's son is like my own brother; I mean that's the relationship. It has been a tradition from the Vedic ages. I can't deviate from it. I can't betray him either. It would mean severing relationships with Guruji and that's not right, you know."

"I get your feelings. You can't go to the police. But then, you should be ready to face the consequences. I hope you are prepared for that."

"I guess so," Akshyay said. He realised that he was committing himself to a path; to an ideal, which may have lost its relevance in the modern self-centred world of consumerism.

There was a brief silence between them as they both sat pondering over the dug up issues. Akshyay had never thought of the guru-disciple relationship before. He wondered how he could commit himself to such an old tradition. Did it come to him naturally, from the sub-conscious mind?"

John surmised that Akshyay was unnecessarily inviting trouble. He wondered whether he could have done the same thing or thought the same way. Perhaps he could. He remembered how he had taken on punishment on himself in school to save a friend, who had stolen a book from the library. Weren't there countless other people, who had sacrificed their narrow self-interests for a cause? He admitted, however, that Akshyay's case was unique. He could easily surrender to the police and save himself. His was a well-known family and obviously well-connected. It would not be easy for the police to take him in their custody. There was an obvious choice involved—getting himself absolved would mean fixing the music teacher's son. The guru-disciple relationship would get fired. In any case, there was hardly any chance of avoiding arrest, if he did not report. Perhaps, Akshyay was banking on that faint hope of the police missing his trail.

"How long did you say you would stay away?" John finally asked, as they came out of their reverie.

"Well, about a week, I suppose. There'd be another murder, by then to divert their attention."

"I doubt that very much. Murder cases are known to remain unsolved for a long period, but the investigation goes on."

"I have to get my aunt to find out someone who can help. She has told me she's got someone in a position of authority in the bureaucracy."

"I see, you'd better get going then, It's time for me to go to Guruji's place. See you in the evening."

Akshyay rose to leave. "Find out, if you can, from Shamir or Guruji about the situation—whether anyone has been arrested. Don't worry about meeting, Shamir. I've already talked him out of the political game he was in. He had seemed to admit his mistake. Just check if he's turned a new leaf and explain my position to Guruji. I hope you will."

"I'll see to it that there is no misunderstanding. I'll come in the evening and tell you all about it. Till then, cheer up, and get your tabla ready. I'll come for practice."

That evening, John came as scheduled, at 5:30 p.m., with his sarode. They went to the music room. Akshyay's tablas and sarode were there and also his guitar. They sat down on the carpet that covered the entire floor.

"I met Guruji and Shamir," John said, as he sat down with his sarode. There have been no inquiries so far, but most of the young men in that area have fled, anticipating a police raid."

"You mean, Shamir didn't go with them?"

"No, he didn't. Guruji said that he wasn't a Naxalite any more and so there was nothing, really, to hide from."

"But isn't that a weird way of seeing things? I mean, he should've realised that in associating with those extremists, he had become like one; it's only now that he's suddenly changed. True, I did some talking last night, and he's also accepted my arguments, but that does not free him from the past. The police would get on his trail, sooner or later. They won't give a damn to his turning a new leaf."

A deep concern clouded John's blue eyes and handsome face. "You are right, I told Guruji that Shamir should watch out, but Guruji seemed strangely nonchalant. Even the murder, of the policeman, seemed not to have perturbed him. He is ecstatic that his son has come over at last. I actually found him slightly off-balance, drunk, as it were with the feelings of relief and joy at getting his son back. He was expressing his gratitude to you. 'It's only for Akshyay that my son has been saved. Tell him to come for the lessons. I don't think there is any danger for him. I'll explain to the police, in case the need arises, and tell them he's innocent. How can they arrest Akshyay! He has saved my son from being an extremist.' This is what he said."

Akshyay listened to John's words with rapt attention picking up each line or phrase for their inner meanings, when suddenly his thoughts seemed to do a somersault. His Guruji wants him to come back for the lessons. He would have to obey him. Would it not be dangerous? He felt another problem raising its head. On the one hand was obedience to his Guruji's instructions and on the other was the impending arrest. He would have to take a decision, keeping in mind the condition that disobedience of his Guru's instruction could be bad for his music lessons.

"Well, I'll make up my mind after talking to Sarah. I think there'd not be any problem. You didn't find anything, did you?"

"No, I didn't. I only saw that there was something bare about the area; like you feel on entering a familiar room and find the furniture removed. The young groups of teenagers, who used to hang on around teashops and street corners, have all disappeared. Whom would the police catch there anyway?"

After a pause, Akshyay said, "Yeah, I think I'll go. By the way, did you learn any lessons today or shall we practice on that khambaj[23] tune?"

"Let's get going!" John positioned his sarode and Akshyay his tabla and soon they began to play. The soft notes of the sarode melted into the rhythmic sounds of the tabla like water pouring into a moving assembly line of pots of equal size. The sarode's tunes and the tabla's beats seemed to mingle and mix into each other and form into patterns of sounds, which filled the room and their minds. Akshyay closed his eyes as the sounds leapt out of the tabla. He continued to play with his eyes closed and gradually the patterns of tabla-sarode sounds engulfed his consciousness. He was playing almost mechanically now as a strange feeling of detachment overtook him. He lost sense of time and place and floated in a space of light and sound waves. Then suddenly he felt he was under water weaving through the seaweed. He was unaware of how long he must have been hallucinating, but a sudden fear of drowning overtook him and he opened his eyes to find Sarah sitting in front of him. Her eyes were closed and John's too, as he played on with concentration.

"When did you come?" Akshyay began without stopping his tabla, as she opened her eyes.

"Oh! A few minutes back. I took half a day off thinking about you. The music attracted me, as I came up the stairs and I just sat on the mat. Isn't it far out?"

"It is. By the way, this is John. I had told you about him, didn't I?" We'll have the music sessions every evening now." Akshyay looked at John, who had opened his eyes by then.

"Hi!" Sarah greeted him.

"Hi!" John replied, as he continued on the sarode,

"You are from Australia, aren't you?"

"Yeah, Sydney. What about you?"

"New York," Sarah said. "How long have you been here?"

"About a year now. I came to learn the sarode. How about you?"

"I left home, you know, because I felt claustrophobic out there and right now I am a Hindu wife."

"I see. My good wishes," John smiled, and stopped playing the sarode. "I think we've had enough. Let's call it a day."

Akshyay looked at John inquisitively for a moment and then recollected what John had said about visiting Guruji's place. He quickly saw that he needed time to talk to Sarah about the developments and plan his course of action "I think you are right. We'll continue tomorrow."

After a bath and change, Sarah joined Akshyay in the drawing room. Just then Miss Monica emerged from hers.

"So how was your office, today, Sarah?" She asked her directly, ignoring Akshyay.

"It was okay. I started working as Secretary to the Chairman. I typed out a few letters and went through the filing system. I think, I'll be able to pick up."

"What about you, Akshyay? What have you been up to?"

"I was playing the tabla for John in the evening and I also made some inquiries about possible police actions."

"Has anyone been arrested?"

"No. John went there, today. He's been telling that all the young men in the area have fled."

"That means you have to watch out. You stay clear of that place till you are sure that all the culprits are arrested."

"But my teacher has told me to come for the lessons. He's said that there's no problem. His son, who is in his late teens, is very much around. He has not fled, and our Guruji feels that there's no danger." Akshyay looked towards Sarah and said, "What do you say? Should I go for the lessons to my Guru's place?"

Sarah was apparently unprepared for the question. She could just say, "I don't know, really. It's very confusing. I feel you should use your own judgement and do what's right."

"The right thing to do is to follow my Guru, isn't it?" Akshyay said, looking rather foolishly at Sarah.

"Well, I can understand what you are aiming at. But this case is not within your Guru's domain. I don't think he should have asked you to go there, since there is a world of a chance of getting arrested," Sarah said emphatically.

Miss Monica, who sat through the conversation between Akshyay and Sarah and had begun to boil with irritation like a pot of water on a stove, suddenly felt relief in spilling over. She began, "That's what I have been telling him but he keeps talking about his Guru. Would you jump into the well if your Guru tells you to do so? He is just a music teacher. How can you allow him to rule your life?"

"Why can't you understand my predicament? I have to listen to my Guru. He is a good man. I have respect for him. He loves me like his son. How can I disobey him? And then, coming to ground reality, what do I gain by not going? I'll only be joining the group which has fled."

Miss Monica did not know what to say. Akshyay had made a valid point. There was complete silence for a while and then she began, "I guess you are destined to do as you must. There's no stopping you. It's the family tradition. How can I blame you?"

Akshyay felt his anger brewing, but he kept quiet. He knew that reacting would lead to a protracted argument and that was his aunt's pet subject. He decided not to give her the opportunity and remained unresponsive. Sarah also remained silent. She felt sad that she was not able to accept Akshyay's point of view, and at the same time, could not dissuade him. She felt that things were out of control, as if moved by fate or some unknown hand. She tried to remember Swamiji's teachings and her own reading. What should be her attitude? Should she step aside and allow the course of events to flow on or should she try damming it? She did not get a clear answer. Conflicting thoughts criss-crossed her mind and then suddenly she felt that she understood the pattern. It was like the patterns of sounds she had heard. The image of Akshyay's face appeared in her thoughts, serene and confident, unruffled by the threat of contrary consequences. She now saw his logic of obeying his Guru. It was a decision that tagged his moral responsibility to tradition.

Chapter - XIX

———✦———

The next few days passed without any unusual happening. Sarah went off for work every morning, but on her own. She preferred it that way. Akshyay went to the music teacher's house, as usual and, in the afternoons, gave guitar lessons. In the evenings he played tabla for John.

The threat of arrest, following his possible involvement in the murder of a policeman, lost itself in the rhythm of routine existence. The sarode lessons at the music teacher's house were more interesting with Guruji's cheerful mood taking the lid off his creative talent. His own guitar lessons and tabla beats also improved. It seemed that all his thoughts and feelings had got channelled into the creative process of music. The creation of ragas on his sarode, the strumming of the guitar and his fingers and palm reaping the metallic sounds from the table within the rules of the ragas, totally engrossed his mind. When he was not playing the sarode or tabla, he thought about the tunes and how he could make them more soulful. Most of his conversation with John or with Pradip, his guitar pupil, was on music. His discussions, even with his wife, were on the ragas and their meanings. He would keep saying that music meant freedom. He seemed to attach too much importance to music. It was with a purpose though. He tried to avoid thinking about the murder or the threat of arrest. Whenever those thoughts would raise their fearful heads, he would shove them away with the tunes of his ragas or the beats of his tabla.

The music teacher too, did not talk about the murder of the policeman, which had taken the locality by storm. It seemed to Akshyay that he purposely avoided the subject and was holding on to the happiness that came from his son's conversion. He was in the habit of talking about it at the slightest pretext. Especially, when he sought to express his gratitude to Akshyay, for his role in tackling his son, who would otherwise have gone astray.

"You have really saved him, Akshyay. You don't know what you have done for me. He is my only son. The police are going to crush these youngsters. Thank God, you made him realise that." This was what the music teacher repeated again and again.

Akshyay would listen silently and nod his head and look at John. They would read each other's thoughts, 'Was he really safe? Would the police accept the conversion story? Would it not have been better to run away like the others?' These were the questions that knocked at their heads, whenever the music teacher spoke about his son. The questions, however, remained unanswered, sinking into their mind's quicksand.

That night, Akshyay and Sarah had repaired to their bedroom, a little early. Their conversation at the dining table with Aunt Monica hovered around routine matters. Therefore, the dinner was over rather quickly. The humdrum of existence with Sarah's new office job, and Akshyay's complete immersion in his music lessons had quite sapped their energies. It seemed to both Akshyay and Sarah that they were giving more to life than they were taking from it. They were, as if, living at a loss. When they did lie down on the bed, they fell asleep, more out of a feeling of being drained out, than natural sleepiness.

The loud banging at the door, therefore, had appeared to Akshyay like a dream sequence, even when he had opened his eyes in the darkness of his bedroom. The continuous rapping and the rough voices accompanied by stomping on the wooden staircase brought into sharp focus the reality of the situation. The police were making a raid. Akshyay had heard of many such night raids, from his friends. Instinctively, he switched on the lights and pushed Sarah awake.

"I say, Sarah! Get up. The police have come to pick me up."

"What?" Sarah drawled, rubbing her eyes and then, as she heard the loud banging, "Did you say the police? You mean the police have really come for you?"

"Must be," said Akshyay, with a lost look on his pale face. His eyes were moist and he sought to dry them with the back of his hand, turning his face away from Sarah.

"Oh, don't worry, Akshyay. They'll soon find out that you are not involved and let you go. Hasn't Aunt Monica said she knows some people? Now let's open the door before they break it down."

Sarah's words seemed to remove the pallor of his face; he felt recharged. Nodding his head, he went out of the room, silently, his face downcast, to open the door. Aunt Monica had also come out of her room, by that time, and she stood in the drawing room, looking startled. Akshyay glanced at her and paused. Then, without saying anything, he switched on the lights and opened the old teak door.

There were at least five policemen standing outside, with torches in their hands; and one of them, who appeared to be an inspector, had a revolver cocked and pointing at him. The Inspector addressed Akshyay directly, in a deep voice. "Are you Akshyay Choudhuri?"

"Yes, I am. What do you want of me?"

"You are under arrest. You have to come with us immediately." The Inspector's voice was harsh.

Aunt Monica and Sarah had by then come forward and they stood behind Akshyay. Miss Monica was the first to speak. "Why do you want to arrest him? What's his offence?"

"There are orders from above. I'm only carrying them out."

"But without a warrant? Without any charges?"

"No, it's not that," the inspector replied. "We are to detain him under MISA."

Sarah, who had been watching the scene, expressionless and pale, while her mind made frantic efforts to find a reprieve, began saying; "I am his wife. I would request you to leave Akshyay now. We'll take him to the police station in the morning and you'll find out for yourself that he's not the kind of person you are looking for. You may be aware: this is a well-known family . . . You should treat him differently. I mean, we are not fleeing from this place. You can surely rely on us to come over to the police station tomorrow, can't you?"

Sarah's straightforward approach confused the fumbling police officer. He was speechless. His mind stopped working. As he heard Sarah speak, he noticed for the first time that she was a white woman, married to the family. Her tenor of her voice seemed unfamiliar and jarring, as if it was voice from another planet. He did not know how to react to it. A prodding on his back brought him back to his senses once again. It was his deputy reminding him of his duty. As if by reflex action, he got himself to wear a harsher look as he said in an unfaltering and steady voice, "I am afraid, he has to go with us right now."

Akshyay knew that there was no use requesting the Inspector to leave him, because he was acting on orders and could not possibly change them on his own. "I'm ready for it", he said, and then looking back at Sarah, "let it be. There's no use talking to them now. They have come to take me and I will go with them. I'm sure, they'll release me when they'll see that I'm neither a political person nor a criminal." He turned and faced the police inspector. "I am ready to go but can I take some clothes with me and a few books?"

"No! You are to go as you are, here and now. We can't wait any longer. If you don't come with us right away, we will have to use the handcuffs."

"There'll be no need for that," Akshyay said quickly, as the associated images of disgrace flashed across his mind. He turned to Sarah, who stood a little behind him. She appeared to be in a state of shock and disbelief. His eyes turned to Aunt Monica. She was staring at the ground and murmuring something to herself. Wrinkles of thought lined her forehead. A faint glimmer of hope lit up his spirits, as he remembered her connections and the family status. Her personality seemed to epitomise the society, which they belonged to. It could possibly relieve him from the clutches of the police and their impersonal laws. He caught his Aunt's eyes and for once he felt an affinity with her. He wanted to belong to her side, but it was too late and anyway he had other commitments to fulfil.

"Goodbye then, Pishi and Sarah. I'll be back soon."

Sarah, who was still in a trance, suddenly became conscious that Akshyay was actually leaving. For a moment, she did not know what to say or do. Just then, she remembered her role as Hindu wife and Swami Ananda's words. In a quick move that took everyone by surprise, she bent down and touched Akshyay's feet.

Akshyay, who did not follow this tradition of touching the feet of elders, was for a while confused. He controlled himself soon enough to placed his palm on Sarah's shoulders, in the characteristic manner in which a priest or an elderly person blesses someone. Sarah's example tempted him to touch his aunt's feet and seek her blessings, but he refrained from following it. He just looked at her, to say with his eyes that he was leaving and after putting on his rubber slippers, stepped out of the doorway. The policemen, who watched the scene in silence, followed him down the staircase. As he reached downstairs, he stopped to take a last look at Sarah, who stood limp and dumb, beside Aunt Monica, gazing dolefully in his direction. She raised her hand mechanically and stretched it towards him and then slowly waved a sad good-bye. Aunt Monica also raised her hand, but he had already turned his face away to walk out of the house with the policemen.

The next morning, Sarah felt the emptiness of her bedroom, when she got up. Akshyay's absence had completely changed the scenario. She almost felt as if a part of her self had gone away with him. She closed her eyes for a moment trying to figure out her position. It would require a lot of effort to get him back and in this she would have to depend heavily on Aunt Monica. She was not yet familiar with the people in her office. Therefore, the question of taking their help was out of bounds.

At the dining table, with Aunt Monica, she took up the subject of Akshyay's release. "May I know what would be the course of action now," she said after a moment of studied silence.

"Well, I'll have to see. I do know a number of people, who can help in this, but there are some problems in approaching them. First of all, Akshyay has alienated himself from many of them by his ways. Secondly, they would like to ask what he had been doing, and why the police are after him. Finally, I am not sure myself, whether he can be released, especially, with that torch episode remaining unsolved. I really don't know how I could tell anybody."

"But didn't you say that you'd help him out?"

"I did, but that was before his arrest. The situation is changed now. He is arrested under MISA, which means he is a political prisoner. It is not just a case of plain murder, that he's accused of."

"I don't see how you can brand him. He is neither having any political affiliations nor is he a murderer. Aren't you sure of that? He's not done anything wrong in going for music classes or in trying to help a dying policeman on the road, has he?"

"It's not that, you know. It is the way of life that's important. There is a fixed path that has to be followed. You can't afford to go astray."

"It's not necessary that everyone should follow a predetermined path. There are other ways of living, too. You know, for example, the sadhus . . ."

"Oh! Don't you tell me about sadhus? They are all . . . I just mean that Akshyay has a responsibility to fulfil. He's got property to look after and a tradition to uphold. You can't give up everything, and for nothing in return," Miss Monica said emphatically and fell silent wondering what to say next.

Sarah also felt that there was no use in conversing on the subject any further. She had got her reply and surmised that she'd have to seek help from her office contacts: an area, which she would have to explore. She had just joined and therefore the task would be difficult. It would be a challenge, no doubt, but she could do it. If necessary, she could also approach the police and seek Akshyay's release. She quickly prepared herself for the job, getting her mind to work on it, even as she sat at the dining table before the scrutinising eyes of her aunt.

"I'll have to go to office, now."

"Oh yes, you must. At least you are on the right track. I'll try to contact the right person, who can do something for Akshyay. In the meanwhile, a taste of reality might do him some good."

Sarah felt angry and frustrated at Aunt's Monica's words. She could fathom the reasons for her attitude though, and tried to accept it as it was. There was no use trying to change her thinking process. Their mental wavelengths were different. Without any comment, therefore, she got up from the dining table and made her way to her room to get herself ready to go out for work. She remembered the challenge in front of her. She'd have to get Akshyay released: on her own; through her own contacts: in this new city, yet unknown and mysterious.

CHAPTER - XX

The office she went to was small. There were ten clerks, one typist cum steno and an accountant. The hall accommodated all of them. However, a low-level partition of ply-board separated the accountant from the others. There were three chambers facing the hall. The owner, Pradip's father, and two other senior executives, one, an engineer, and the other, dealing with marketing, occupied these. The management had provided a spare desk for Sarah with the clerks. However, she had the option of sitting in one of the executives' rooms, if she felt any discomfiture, sitting with the clerks.

By her second week there, she had got to know the staff quite well. The curiosity and suspicion, associated with her sudden entry in their midst, had soon melted into a warm feeling of solidarity, and respect. It stemmed from her association with a well-known family and her own cheerful personality. The fact that she had to work for a living also drew her close to the staff-members. They were all from middle-class or lower middle-class families and quite a few from erstwhile East Bengal, and therefore, in a way, like her, immigrant.

The thought, that was uppermost in her mind, that morning, was how to approach her office colleagues for help. Her choice naturally fell on the Accountant, who had appeared to be a sensible old gentleman. The mere

GAUTAM SHANKAR BANERJEE

mention of police however put him off and he reacted by pointing to the Proprietor's chamber.

"Only he can help you. I don't know any policeman and I don't want to get involved with them. Please forgive me."

During the lunch break, when the other staff had left, Sarah knocked at the Proprietor's door.

"May I come in Mr. Agarwal?"

"Yes, please do. How do you find working here? I'm sorry, I've not been able to ask you so far."

"It's all new to me but I like the people here. They are simple and sincere."

"I've asked you about the work, not about the staff."

"There's not much work. I've only had to type out a few letters to some of the Government departments requesting them to pay our dues."

"Don't worry. There will be more work for you soon. Right now, you are to get acclimatised."

Sarah was silent. She did not know how to broach the subject of Akshyay's release and what kind of response it would evince. She braced herself to the task and began, "I have a problem. You can help me out," she blurted out, as she wrung her fingers.

Mr. Agarwal, who had been staring voluptuously at Sarah for the short while that she was silent, jolted back to his senses. "What problem? How can I help?"

Sarah said, in a matter of fact manner, "My husband's been arrested by the police last night, on a suspicion that he's a Naxalite."

"A Naxalite?" Mr. Agarwal raised his eyebrows. "How could your husband be a Naxalite? He is from a famous family . . . There must be a mistake somewhere. Was he mixing around with them? Was he caught in a combing operation?"

178

"No, he was picked up from the house at night. They did not even tell us the reason."

"You mean there was no warrant."

"They just came and took him away to the police station. You know, Akshyay's innocent. You can ask your son if you want to be sure. You must help me to get him out."

"I don't know . . . let me see what I can do." Mr. Agarwal began to scratch his head. He took off his spectacles and rubbed his eyes. "Oh yes!" He exclaimed, after a while. There are some people coming over to our guesthouse this evening. A couple of government officers, as well. It will be a good idea if you come along. I'll introduce you to them and I'm sure they will help you out."

"Where is the guest house? Is it far-off?"

"No, no! It is only a few houses away. You needn't worry. I will send the car for you just after the office hours. You could come there straight away and look after the reception of the guests . . . whether all the arrangements are okay."

Sarah felt inwardly happy that this chance had come her way. It was a coincidence that these people were coming over and she'll have a chance to meet them. In all probability they could help in securing Akshyay's release from the hands of the police. She couldn't really bank on Miss Monica. Her attitude was one of looking at the arrest as a lesson for him, as if it could bring him back to the straight road.

Sarah could hardly wait for the time to pass. She sat at her desk, with the other staff, but her mind was somewhere else. When finally, it was time for the office to close and the staff, ready to leave, she felt curious glances towards her desk. One of her colleagues, a married woman, with whom she was somewhat thick, approached to find out what was her problem. Sarah looked at her and said with a put-on smile that she had an assignment with the boss.

When all the staff-members left, and she was sitting alone in office, she suddenly recollected that she should have informed Aunt Monica, about her program. She should have told her that she would be returning late. She tried a number of times to ring, from the telephone on the accountant's table, but in vain. When she was in the midst of trying yet another time to get through, the security guard came up to inform that a car had arrived to take her to the guesthouse. She gave up trying to connect the line and put down the receiver, the errand before her completely filling her mind. Her thoughts hovered round; "Whom would she meet? How should she convince him? Would he really help? What price she would have to pay?"

The guesthouse was a five-minute drive away from the office. When she arrived, a chowkidar ran up and opened the car's door for her. It was a double-storied building in British style: high ceilings, thick walls, arched windows and teakwood doors with brass doorknobs.

The entrance was from a side passage. Sarah followed the chowkidar[24] and found herself in a large drawing room. Instead of colour-wash, wallpaper draped the walls in a design of black stripes and spots. An unlit chandelier hung from the ceiling. Four lamp-stands at the corners illuminated the room to a dull incandescence.

Sarah felt slightly unnerved as she sat on the sofa. She was alone and about to face an uncertain future. If the people she hoped to meet could help her get Akshyay's release, it would be a continuity of her state of being. If not, then she would have to think of something new. She had neither been able to inform Aunt Monica about her visit, nor about returning late. This could turn out to be another problem. She could visualise the posture of Aunt Monica and her accusing eyes, as she would blame her for ruining the family tradition. She could see Akshyay in jail huddled together with other Naxalites and for a moment, she felt she was in a way responsible for sending him there.

She was still ruminating on these possibilities, when Mr. Agarwal burst into the hall with five others, with boisterous chattering and laughter that seemed to reverberate in her unshielded sensibilities. Shaken up from her mood, she stood up as Mr. Agarwal addressed her. "Meet my friends here. This is Mr. Ghosh, our supplier; Mr. Grewal, a businessman; Mr. Mukherjee, a police officer; Mr. Talukdar, an advocate; and Mr. Biswas, a state government officer."

Sarah extended her hand to Mr. Ghosh, who was the first person in the queue. He hesitated for a moment, before shaking her hand. The others shook hands with her, without any qualms, though it was incorrect to shake hands with a married woman or for any woman for that matter. The right thing to do was a simple 'namaskar'. The feel of a woman's hand, especially that of a white woman's, was too tempting to resist, camouflaged as it was by a custom, albeit Western.

Mr. Ghosh, who was a bespectacled gentleman in his fifties, with bleary eyes and a paunch that didn't go with his lean structure, said, "So you are the new secretary of Mr. Agarwal?"

His knowledge took Sarah by surprise. Further, she didn't like the manner in which he pronounced the word 'secretary'. She promptly replied, "Yes I joined recently. I am looking after liaison with different firms and people . . ."

Mr. Grewal interrupted her with, "I hope Mr. Agarwal has kept you comfortably." There was a mischievous smile on his blushing face.

Sarah felt she could read a meaning in those words but she was not sure what he meant by 'comfortably'. "I get a reasonably good salary like all the others in our office. I have no complaints."

Mr. Grewal turned to Mr. Agarwal. "So you have done a good job by bringing her in the company. She has already spoken well about you and I hope she will do well for the company tonight."

"You will soon see," Mr. Agarwal said and Sarah could see Mr. Agarwal smile and wink at Mr. Grewal. "Get the glasses, Lakshman!" Mr. Agarwal called out, as he walked towards the door beside the entrance, which she guessed was the kitchen.

The waiter, Lakshman, soon pushed in a trolley, full of glasses and a jar of ice-cubes.

"No! No! Not you!" Mr. Grewal exclaimed, "She will serve the drinks. I hope you don't have any objections?" He first pointed at her and then turned to look at her.

"Why should I have any objection? Here, let me do it, Lakshman." Sarah said, hiding her tension behind her eagerness.

Lakshman went off, leaving her to serve the drinks. She took the trolley round to each of the guests, who were sitting on the three-piece sofas. There were bottles of Scotch whisky, rum and vodka. She served the drinks according to the choices of each of the guests. As she was finishing the first round, Lakshman brought in another trolley. There were bowls, of chilly chicken, fish fry, papad, and cashew nuts.

"What about your drink?" Mr. Biswas suddenly asked Sarah. "Don't your drink?"

"No, I don't drink. I only take hash," Sarah blurted out, and immediately bit her lips instinctively, feeling that she had made a throughly wrong statement. She felt that she should not have given out this bit of information. It was also true that for a long time she had not smoked hash. Swami Ananda had told her that it was not good for her.

"Well, well, that's wonderful," she could hear Mr. Grewal say, "Mr. Agarwal, you really have a great person as your secretary."

It was the police officer's turn to intervene; "Do you also have hash with her?" He asked Mr. Agarwal.

"No! Not at all!" Mr. Agarwal exclaimed, "Who told you?" He appeared flustered. "I didn't even know she has hash. Sarah, you never told me, did you?"

"Well, I didn't. I didn't think it was necessary. I don't have hash now. But at one time I used to. Please try to understand. I said it in the context of not 'having' drinks. People, who have hash, don't drink. I don't drink and that's how I said it. I hope, I've made myself clear, now."

"We will not let you go so easily, Miss Sarah," Mr. Grewal said, purposely forgetting that she was wearing white bangles, which signify a woman's marital status. "We will bring some hash for you. You will smoke some hash today and we'll see it. You know it will be something to see. I've never seen a woman smoking hashish. Can you believe it? Have you seen one Mr. Ghosh? You Mr. Mukherjee? Mr. Agarwal? He must have seen. What Mr. Agarwal, haven't you?"

"Oh come on, Mr. Grewal! Don't tease me. Don't you pull my leg? I know all about your escapades and all your private affairs. I'll tell every one about it," Mr. Agarwal said smiling.

"Go ahead, tell everyone about me. I have not done anything new. Everyone does it. Ask Mr. Mukherjee. He is a police officer. He knows about all of us. All our black deeds. But no one knew about your white deed. It was top secret, wasn't it? You wanted to surprise us all, didn't you?"

Sarah felt terribly nervous. She had never been in such a situation before. She felt like a lamb in a den of lions. She did not know how to get out of it, and she was far from turning this meeting to her advantage by getting a favour from them. Instead of gaining from the meeting as she had planned, she stood to lose. She had to find a way out of the tangle. She had to find a way out.

"Mr. Grewal," she suddenly said, interrupting the conversation between him and Mr. Agarwal, which all the others were thoroughly enjoying. "Can you get me a chullum and hash?" She took a chance to beat them in their own game.

The announcement surprised Mr. Grewal, as well as the others. Gaining control over himself, he said, "Why not? We will get you one, but first you will have to tell us who taught you to smoke hash."

"I have been in India for about five months now, and I had picked up smoking hash from hippies in Rishikesh."

"Were you a hippie?" Mr. Biswas asked.

"No, I wasn't. I came to India and stayed in an ashram in Rishikesh and today I am Hindu wife. I came here, to tell you the truth, to get my husband released from jail. Mr. Agarwal, my employer, had told me that some of you could help in this matter. I believe, Mr. Mukherjee is a police officer." She looked at Mr. Mukherjee with imploring eyes and continued, "You could help in releasing my husband. He is absolutely blameless. But he's been arrested by the police last night, for a policeman's murder, with which he had nothing to do."

"Are you talking about the murder at Jadavpur, some days back?" Mr. Mukherjee said, narrowing his eyes.

"Unfortunately, yes. My husband's been going there, learning to play the sarode from a gentleman named Mr. Lahiri. While returning home that evening he had seen the injured policeman lying on the road, and that's how he has been linked to the murder. They have arrested him on suspicion, not on any concrete proof. I am told there'll be no trial. He will just be kept in jail for six months without being produced in Court. Can you do something for him, Mr. Mukherjee? I shall, forever, be grateful."

"Well, I shall have to see the case and do the needful. It will take some time. But I can assure that I will help you. What's the name of . . ."

"Not so fast, Mr. Mukherjee," Mr. Grewal interrupted. "You can't have her alone. She is for all of us. She is like Draupadi tonight and we the Pancha Pandavas."

"But we are not five here; we are six," Mr. Ghosh said with a clever smile on his thin lips and his eyes twinkling behind his glasses.

There was a sudden silence as everyone thought of the problem. They were indeed six, and hence they could not enjoy the privilege of being Pandavas.

Mr. Mukherjee was the first to speak; "Mr. Agarwal is Karna. That makes us five, doesn't it?"

"Yes it does," observed Mr. Biswas. "But Karna was with the Kauravas, who were the arch enemies of the Pandavas. Mr. Agarwal is, on the other hand, with us. So the problem is not solved."

"Well, let me solve your problem, Mr. Biswas," Mr. Grewal said impatiently. "Let us all be Kauravas and go ahead. What's stopping us now."

"No, no, the Kauravas could not get Draupadi for themselves. Didn't they lose to Arjuna in the open contest?" Mr. Mukherjee said, showing off his argumentative skill. He looked at Sarah and smiled, as if to reassure her of her safety in the battle of wits. There was a momentary silence again, as the group sat wondering what to say. Mr. Mukherjee had taken them to a dead end. Sarah stood nonplussed, unable to participate in the arguments or defend herself. She stood there in the midst of the six men, defenceless and waiting for the attack, which could come at any moment. The passions that were waiting to pounce on her temporarily focused on an intellectual exercise. She only hoped that the deadlock would continue.

It was Mr. Grewal again. "Did you say that the Kauravas lost her? It was only in the archery contest that they lost her: not in the dice game. Didn't the Pandavas lose her to the Kauravas then? Didn't Dushashan pounce on her and pull her sari?" Mr. Grewal looked around him at all the stunned faces. They had not expected Mr. Grewal to come out with such an argument. Their bodies and minds stopped functioning, when Mr. Grewal suddenly jumped up and caught hold of Sarah's anchal.

"Let go of my sari, Mr. Grewal. There is no need to demonstrate your statement. Leave it, please ... Mr. Agarwal! What is this? Stop it Mr. Grewal. Stop it! Stop!" Sarah almost screamed out those last words. She tried to pull back the anchal of her sari as it slid off her shoulder. She looked around for help.

There was no help forthcoming from the men who were sitting round like statues without even batting their eyelids. Mr. Grewal held on to the anchal of her sari and tugged at it harder. Sarah's forearms, which held the anchal to her breast, were bent, as they gave way to the force. Mr. Grewal was around forty-five years of age and well built. The smile on his thin lips and the soft look of his green eyes turned to clenched teeth and glistening eyes, as he continued to tug at the sari. Sarah could not speak as she held on to the other end with all her might. She was quite strong for a woman and she felt she could hit out at Mr. Grewal or even kick at him in the groins. At that moment, however, the posture, of holding on to her sari, immobilised her.

The five others in the group remained glued to their seats, at the sudden action of Mr. Grewal. The transition from a war of words, to a tug of war over a sari anchal, was at once stunning as well as interesting. They were even waiting with bated breath, for the outcome of the contest, between Mr. Grewal and Sarah.

A sudden tearing of cloth startled the silent onlookers, as if something unusual had happened. Sarah also felt a sudden relaxation of her forearm muscles, as the sari anchal tore from the middle. Sarah found she could now close in on Mr. Grewal. As if by a reflex action, she quickly took a few steps towards him and before he could even guess what was happening, landed a resounding slap on his cheek with her left hand. By reflex, Mr. Grewal began to rub his cheek with his right hand, and the men sitting around, by a combined reflex action, began rubbing their cheeks too.

Mr. Grewal squirmed, smarting under the sting of the slap on his bearded cheek. He could taste blood inside his mouth. He let go of the sari and stood back licking the inside of his right cheek, his eyes rolling. Sarah threw the torn anchal over her shoulder and stood glaring at Mr. Grewal and the rest, one by one, breathing hard in exhaustion.

When she had regained her breath, she addressed Mr. Mukherjee, the police officer. "Mr. Mukherjee, I hope you have taken note of this incident. I am not going to spare anyone. I'll go to the High Commission and to all the newspaper offices and report against all of you."

"Please madam, please calm down. It was nothing. It was only a joke. Didn't you realise that? Now please don't think of reporting this to any one." There were the marks of fear and apology on his face, a peculiar combination indeed, like that of a father's, who has beaten up his grown up son and fears a reprisal.

Sarah calmed down, as an idea came to her mind. Here was an opportunity to bargain for Akshyay's release. She could tell the police officer that he should arrange to free Akshyay. She began slowly, "All right, I'll not report, but there's a condition: my husband will have to be released. And, I'll give you three day's time to organise it. I'll wait for three days and if he is not released by that time, I'll go to the Embassy and Press. By the way, you wanted to hear the name of my husband, didn't you? Well, he is Akshyay Choudhuri, great grandson of Radhakanta Choudhuri. Now I hope you know who you are dealing with."

Mr. Mukherjee stood up and with folded hands said apologetically, "Madam, I am sorry about what happened and, on behalf of everyone here, I beg your mercy." He looked around at Mr. Grewal who still stroking his right cheek, with his head bent in shock and shame. Mr. Mukherjee addressed Mr. Grewal, "I hope you are sorry for what you have done. You have to touch her feet and seek forgiveness. I will not spare you, if you don't."

Mr. Grewal, without a word of protest, his eyes downcast, bent down to touch Sarah's feet and said in a choked voice, "Please forgive me. I did not mean to harm you. This will not happen again." Sarah felt touched, but she did not utter a word. As Mr. Grewal got up, she turned round to face Mr. Agarwal. "I would request you to provide a transport for me. I'll go home."

"It's all yours. Take it madam. It will bring you to office everyday and take you back everyday."

"That will not be necessary, Mr. Agarwal." Sarah said and looking at Mr. Mukherjee once again, as if to remind him of the agreement, walked out of the hall.

CHAPTER - XXI

On her way home, Sarah wondered how much similar her experience was to the episode in the Mahabharata, of Draupadi's humiliation. While in the Mahabharata, it was Lord Krishna, who saved the day for Draupadi, tonight; it was her own will power that had saved her. Did she act like a Hindu wife or was it her Western personality, which had been in the forefront during the attempt to molest her? This was one thought that kept coming back to her mind. They had attacked her because she tried to be a Hindu wife, but she saved herself by her assertive personality. She recollected what her Aunt Monica had told her about wearing a sari. Was she right? Did Indians look differently at a Western woman, wearing a sari? She could not get an answer. She recalled how the moor attacked her on the streets of Morocco, and how she had to run to get away from his clutches.

"No! No! No!" She heard herself saying, "I must control my thoughts. I am Akshyay's wife and I have a definite role to play. I must see him released . . ." She could see Akshyay's blue eyes and flowing, long, hair, his innocent face, barred, behind a cell. She saw him bury his face between his knees, as he sat on the cold stone floor with others. They had forlorn looks on their haggard faces. A feeling of pity overtook her. It seemed to withdraw her mind from the external world. She woke up from her reverie as the car screeched to a halt, right in front of the iron gate of her house.

Sarah wondered how the driver knew the place, but then she recollected that he must be the one to have come to pick her up on her first trip.

Sarah got off the car and inspected the lock on the other side of the iron gate. She began to ponder on whether to call Abdul or Aunt Monica. Abdul lived in the servants' quarters, which were across the garden, while Aunt Monica's room was on the first floor and closer to where she was standing. However, she decided that it would be prudent to call Abdul. She could not predict Aunt Monica's reaction to her returning home at that hour of the night. It occurred to her that she should check the time. She didn't wear a watch and so she asked the driver and learnt it was eleven—thirty already and concluded that she couldn't risk calling out for Aunt Monica.

Advising the driver to wait till someone opened the door, she called out for Abdul. "Abdul! Abdul!" She called about six or seven times, her voice breaking the silence of the night and rebounding off the walls of the houses that lined the lane farther on. She noticed some of the dark windows spring to life and blurred faces pressed against the glass. There was, however, no sign of Abdul or anyone stirring in the house, which stood behind the iron gate almost like a ghostly mansion. Perhaps, Akshyay's absence made all the difference. She remembered that she had seen the house from that same spot for the first time when she had arrived from Rishikesh along with Akshyay. How different it was then! Much water had flowed down in the short intervening period!

She called out a few more times only to feel frustrated at not getting a response. She then decided to make use of the car horn. The driver was getting late and the neighbours' eyes were feasting on her predicament. She was fast beginning to lose her patience. Now she couldn't care less whether it was Abdul, who would wake up, or Aunt Monica.

The driver sounded the horn and the trumpet-like sound blasted the silence of the lane. At last, there was some stirring in the ghostly mansion and amid the branches of the trees in the garden, with the birds ruffling their wings and chirping irritably. Sarah saw the light in Aunt Monica's room, and then, a faint creaking and tapping on the wooden staircase.

"Who is it?" Miss Monica rapped, as she emerged on to the porch, in her night-gown, a black shawl covering her torso.

"It's me, Sarah."

"Why? Is this the time to come home?" She asked in a sharp voice aimed at hurting Sarah. Sarah could see her grimace. She preferred to keep quiet, feeling uncomfortable before the driver and in a bid to cut off her embarrassment, turned to face him, her back towards her tormentor.

"You'd better go back. It is all right now. Thank you."

The driver started his vehicle, switched on the headlights and drove off. Meanwhile, Miss Monica winced at her insolence as she charged at her.

"Do you know what the time is?"

"I don't wear a wrist watch. It is quite late, I suppose."

"It is nearly midnight. Where were you all this while?"

"I went on an official assignment, to meet some influential people. It was a chance that came my way, for arranging Akshyay's release."

"But why did you have to return at such an unearthly hour? Didn't you realise that there is a family tradition to uphold? You are a wife of this house and there are some codes of conduct, which are to be followed."

"I felt I was doing my duty." Sarah said, feeling angry and hurt. She could not understand why Aunt Monica behaved in the manner she did. Some of the lights at the windows of the neighbouring houses were still on, and so were the prying inquisitive ears and eyes. Sarah felt at a loss, bewildered, standing outside the closed gate of her husband's house, Aunt Monica spitting fire for no fault of hers. She felt that arguing would only aggravate the situation and decided to take a conciliatory stand and appeal to her good senses.

"Aunt Monica! Am I annoying you? Won't you open the gate? Won't you allow me in? Let's not make a scene out in the open! We'll talk it over indoors."

"How do you expect to be let in at this hour? You must first explain your conduct," Aunt Monica said, without relenting.

"Haven't I explained already?" Sarah implored. I was only trying to get Akshyay's release."

"Do you mean to say that you had to meet those influential people at this time of the night? Do you realise what you are saying... You sound as if you had gone whoring to save your husband," Miss Monica said, emphasising the word 'whoring'.

"What do you mean?" Sarah retorted. "Do you mean what you are saying? Do you think I had gone to sell my body in exchange for my husband's release? Well, it's not true, but you may be certain I'll not hesitate to do that, if it is necessary." Sarah added this in defiance. She wanted Aunt Monica to feel outraged.

Miss Monica could not believe her ears. Therefore, she repeated the unpalatable words. "What? What did you say? Could you really sell your body? You can be a prostitute? A whore?"

"I'm neither a prostitute nor a whore. I am a Hindu wife, loyal to my husband. The only man in my life is my husband. I have given my mind, soul, everything to my husband. How could you call a perfect Hindu wife a prostitute? Perhaps, you don't know the meaning of being a Hindu wife."

Miss Monica kept her eyes on Sarah as she spoke. There was a certain fire in her words, which seemed to mesmerise her for a few moments. She felt she saw in the face of Sarah, and in her words, apparitions of Parbati, Sita, Draupadi, and Sabitri. The same spirit of self-conviction and energy seemed to flow freely through her words like the flowing sari of Draupadi, with Dushashan pulling at it unceasingly and the sari flowing unceasingly. Her eyes fell on Sarah's sari. It was the one, which she had given her to wear. She noticed the torn anchal.

"What is this?" She said, pointing accusingly at the torn anchal. "How's it that it's torn?" She demanded.

"One of the men tried a go at me." Sarah said, truthfully. She felt unafraid. There was no way she could bring her to her side.

"Who was he?" Miss Monica asked excitedly. There was a ring of concern in her voice. "What's his name? How dare he try to do any such thing? Did he not know who you are?"

"Well, he didn't know who I was, but I gave it to him . . . A good slap on his face. I've warned them that unless Akshyay is released, I'll go to the US embassy and make a report." Sarah said this in a more lively fashion enacting the posture of slapping someone.

"No! No! No! You've not done the right thing. You should have gone to the police, to lodge an F.I.R."

Just as Miss Monica was uttering these words, the car returned. The driver stopped at the gate. There was an expression of surprise on his face to find Sarah still outside the closed gate. He said, "Memsaab, you had left your handbag in the car. Here it is."

"Hey! Wait a minute. I've an idea," Miss Monica said. "You can take this car to the police station, and make a diary right away."

"Can't it wait till tomorrow?" Sarah said, disappointed at the turn of events, against her. "I could as well do it in the morning."

"No! No! No one would believe you tomorrow. This has to be done tonight, while you are in your torn sari." Miss Monica said, concluding the discussion.

Sarah felt a choking sensation in her throat and an inability to think, as the irrationality of Aunt Monica infected her. She began to feel the harassment of not being allowed inside the house. The words of Aunt Monica reverberated in her mind, as she stood before it, suddenly appearing strange and different. She felt as if she was standing in a weird place, before a strange woman. For one fleeting moment she was Aunt Monica, transformed into a witch, menacingly advancing on her. Again, she was the cruel, unsympathetic Aunt Monica, telling her to get lost. She was holding her responsible for all that was amiss in the house . . . Taking revenge on her for all the misdeeds of Akshay and his mother. Sarah heard the jarring words of Aunt Monica. How different it was at Rishikesh! The soft-spoken Swami in the serene surroundings!

She suddenly felt that she would not be able to live in the house without Akshyay. She was an outsider for all practical purposes.

"Well then", she began, "if you think it is right, I'll have to go to the police. I'll go then." She turned and walked the few steps to the car and told the driver to take her to the police station.

The driver readily agreed, and Sarah left in the car, waving a perfunctory good-bye to Miss Monica, who stood like a rock, motionless and expressionless. Sarah found her mental faculties benumbed, as she sank into the cushioned seat, her head laid back. She was not able to control her thoughts. They were more in the form of questions, which arose in her mind one after another and remained unanswered. She was on her way to the police station to make a complaint. What would she gain from it? Would she not expose Akshyay's family? Would it be good for the family traditions? Did Aunt Monica really care for the family traditions or was it an excuse for turning her out? Had she not already reported the details to Mr. Mukherjee . . . or rather had he not seen it all with his own eyes? Wouldn't Mr. Mukherjee back out of the contract, if she went to the police? Wouldn't then Akshyay continue to languish in jail? The image of Akshyay's face behind the bars appeared in her mind once again. Now they were coming to take him for interrogation. Would they torture him; pull out his nails; make him lie down on a block of ice? Sarah sat up in the car, blinking away those thoughts. She had to do something to save him.

With an effort at conscious thinking, she recapitulated the day's incidents, culminating in her proposed visit to the police station. She saw at once that she was on the wrong path. There was no question of going to the police station, since she had already struck a deal with a police officer for Akshyay's release in three day's time. There was now no alternative, but to wait for three days. Also, she could not possibly return to the house, because Aunt Monica would create another scene. She had to stop the car, anyway, first, before she could choose the next course of action.

"Driver, please stop the car."

"Memsaab, did you say I should stop?" The driver brought his car to a halt even before he got her answer.

"Yes I told you to stop. We aren't going to the police station. We'll go to a friend's place for the night. You can drop me there. We have to go back to the crossing and take a right turn."

"Okay Memsaab," the driver said, turning his car. Sarah thought of John's house as the only place she could go to at this time of the night, without a hassle. She had been to John's place once only with Akshyay, and she considered him to be a gentleman. She pictured the room and John sleeping on the mattress on the floor. May be, he would have a spare mattress. If not, there would be his sleeping bag. She knew John would not ask her too many questions. He had already heard Akshyay's story and also had first-hand knowledge of their house. She was sure he would allow her to stay for a couple of days till Akshyay's release.

The car soon arrived at the doorstep of the house in which John lived. Sarah got down and after instructing the driver to wait, began to knock at the door. A darwan[26] opened it and with an expression of surprise, and asked her what she wanted. When she told him that she wanted to meet John Saab, he did not ask any more questions.

"John Saab is in the room above the garage. You can go up the stairs and knock at his door." He moved aside to allow her to pass.

When John opened the door, rubbing his eyes, he became, for a moment, motionless, to find Sarah outside. "Hi! Come in," he said recovering, somewhat embarrassed.

"I don't know whether I am putting you in trouble, but I need to stay here tonight, and for a couple of days," Sarah said clearly.

"No problem; I guess you are having problems with your aunt?"

"You're right! It's impossible to stay there without Akshyay."

"What? Has he been arrested or . . ."

"Last night the police came and picked him up."

"But he is innocent. Are you trying for his release?"

"Yes. I've been able to strike a deal with a police officer. He has promised to arrange Akshyay's release, in three day's time."

"That's good! Now let's get down to making a bed for you. Have you brought anything with you?"

"There's nothing at all. I'll have to use some of your clothes for the next few days I'm here. I am not going back till Akshyay comes and picks me up. Now, before I forget, let me go and spare the driver. It's the office car that I've brought along. I have to tell him that I'll be on leave for a week, at least." Sarah smiled, and went down the stairs to meet the driver. She found him chatting with the darwan.

"We are from the same village," the driver said, when he saw Sarah approaching.

"Oh really! How nice . . . It's already very late. You'd better go back."

"OK Memsaab. Shall I come to pick you up tomorrow?"

"No! That won't be necessary. Tell Mr. Agarwal. I'll be on leave for the next week. I will send my leave application later."

"OK Memsaab, I'll tell my Malik. He drove off and Sarah turned to the darwan.

"I hope you will bear with me. I'll stay for a few days here with my friend."

"No problem, Memsaab. If Saab is willing, I am also willing. The landlord will be willing too. They are very nice people; very fond of John Saab."

"By the way, what is your name?"

"Sitaram."

"Good night Sitaram," Sarah said, and walked up the flight of stairs to the mezzanine floor, where John's room was. The door was open.

"There you are. Your bed is ready," John said, as he saw her entering. Sarah surveyed the room and saw a mattress stretched out on the floor for her, against the wall opposite to John's.

"What about your pillow?" Sarah said, as she noticed John's pillow missing.

"Don't worry! I'll use some books for a pillow," John said with a smile. "You need rest. You've had a hectic day, I suppose. Do you need a change of clothes? I've got a lungi, which you could use, and a spare kurta."

Sarah looked at her sari and at the torn anchal. "I think I'll need your lungi and kurta for the night and for the next few days too."

John walked over to the wardrobe in the corner and brought out a lungi and kurta. He was himself dressed in pyjamas and kurta, as his sleeping dress. "Now, here it is. You could go to the bathroom and change, but the floor is wet. I'd better switch off the lights and close my eyes. You can change here itself and go to sleep. Good night! Have a good night's sleep."

"Good night John!"

Chapter - XXII

---◆---

It was his third day in jail. In Akshyay's cell there were three others. They were there with him for the last three days.

A small circular hole high up on the wall opposite to the cell door, was the only opening through which daylight filtered in. At night, the dull light from the corridor lamp seeped in meekly, dispelled at regular intervals by the flashing torchlight that dazzled their eyes whenever the sentry walked past their cell.

That night, after the removal of the thalis and glasses, following dinner Akshyay, along with the other three sat close to each other waiting for sleep to draw them apart. The three, who were there, had been there for longer periods. Arindam, who had been in the second year in Presidency College, when the police arrested him, had already served a year without trial. The police had picked him up from a student's hostel in College Street. They caught him red-handed making bombs.

Ritwick was the only son of his parents. They lived in Jadavpur, a hotbed of extremists. The police had picked him up in a raid following a bomb attack on a police jeep. When the police had entered his house, they had found a large number of pamphlets and booklets on revolutionary literature.

Tamal's arrest was from Darjipara, near Shyambazaar, after a resident complained against him for extortion. The job assigned to him was raising funds for the party.

Akshyay was already in a position of pre-eminence because his arrest was in connection with the murder of a policeman. The other three looked up to him as quite a hero; from the very first day, the sentries had pushed him into their cell.

"Don't you think the food was better today?" Ritwick asked Akshyay, in an attempt to pick up conversation.

"Yeah! It was all right," Akshyay said, without moving his head.

"Do you know any reason for it?"

"No! It must be because of some high official's visit, I suppose. There must have been some report in the newspapers about us, being badly fed and left to sleep on the bare floor without even mattresses," Arindam said, sarcastically. He grimaced.

"You are right. It could be a press report," said Tamal. "I wonder why they don't write about this detention of ours without trial, for days on end. I hope someone does. I cannot bear this any longer. It's already four months now. Do you know how much weight I have lost? I could not recognise myself in the mirror, that day, when they took me to the barber for a crew cut. I don't like this American hairstyle, you know, but they forced it. I feel the Americans are behind it, what do you think, Akshyay?"

"I think you are getting off the track," Akshyay said. "The reason why no journalist writes about our plight is that newspapers are pro-establishment, while we are anti-establishment."

"Do you think we'll ever get released?" Arindam asked anxiously.

"Well", Akshyay said, "you could expect it when you complete six months."

"True, they will release us after six months, but on paper only. We will be shown as re-arrested again," Arindam said, in dismay.

"You are right. There is no escape from this prison, except through a jailbreak or a revolution. You cannot expect the jail authorities to be humane. They are absolutely brutal, worse than animals." Tamal said these words in an unusually loud voice and soon they could hear the sound of approaching footsteps. A flash of light fell on their faces and then the harsh voice of the sentry. "Shut up, you bastards, not a word more."

A hushed silence descended on the precincts of the cell as the sentry switched off his torch. His heavy footfalls, however, continued to punctuate the eerie silence that seemed to engulf everything. With the sound of the footsteps waning, the only remaining sounds were those of their own breathing and heartbeats. They cowered together, quietly reading each other's thoughts. The police had branded all of them; they were all in the same plight; and they all wanted release. In the silence they sat, as if waiting for it.

The sound of boots and shuffling feet up the corridor awakened their minds. They could hear a voice now wailing now laughing, warbling and murmuring and every now and then, breaking into meaningful sounds. "I've killed all of you . . . No! No! No! No! I've not betrayed you . . . You must kill me. I am a traitor . . . Kill me . . . kill me . . . I have not killed you . . . They have betrayed me. They have cheated me . . . My friends . . . I have killed you all . . . My friends!" The sound of crying, wailing and laughter interspersed the monologue. The policemen's voices were strangely unheard. They were not trying to shoo him down. They could hear their footsteps, however, following the voice, up the corridor.

"Who's this man?" Akshyay asked, perplexed.

"He is a professor and he's gone mad."

"How?"

"That's a long story. I will tell you later."

"Where are they taking him now?"

"Oh! They are taking him to the clinic for an injection to put him to sleep. It's a ritual that's followed every third or fourth day."

"Does he frequently get mad?" Akshyay asked inquisitively.

"Yes he does," Tamal said. "Every now and then he becomes mad and then he's given a shot and he keeps quiet for the next few days. Then he starts again, shouting, crying, wailing and laughing hysterically."

"What is the reason for this kind of behaviour? If he's mad, why is he here?" Akshyay asked again, wanting to probe deeper.

"He's mad all right, but he was a Naxalite. He was a leader. Many of his students were Naxalites . . . let's wait for them to pass."

The shouting became louder and louder as they waited for him to come before the cell. He was still shouting incoherently accusing himself and then wailing at the loss of his dear students. Then suddenly they saw him before their cell door. He was a frail man, hardly above average height, with a beard and dishevelled hair that fell on his shoulders. There were round-rimmed glasses on the bridge of his nose that glistened in the reflecting lights of the policemen's torches.

"What's the matter with him?" Akshyay asked again, when the shouting had ceased, looking at the face of

Tamal, Ritwick and Arindam, by turn. Do you know how he became mad?"

There was a momentary silence, as each of the three waited for the other person to speak. "Let Ritwick tell the story," said Tamal to Arindam, when they had all begun to speak together. "He was the first to have heard of it, wasn't he?"

"So be it," Ritwick said, "I'll tell the story again. It's such a touching one: you'll feel sorry to hear it."

"Don't hesitate to tell every bit of it. I would like to hear the whole truth," Akshyay said with genuine concern, to Ritwick.

"Well then, let me begin." Ritwick remained silent as he recollected the sequences of the story, assuming a thoughtful posture. Akshyay, Tamal, and Arindam braced themselves to hear the travails of the man whom they had just seen, in his fit of insanity.

"He was a teacher in the college at Gobardanga," Ritwick started saying. "It's a small town near the Bongaon border. He taught economics to degree course students. He was very popular among his students. The students never bunked his classes because of his practical manner of teaching. He could make the subject relevant to each one of his students with examples from everyday life or comparing and relating the economic principles to everyday domestic chores and familial needs.

"His popularity in class, and his interest in teaching his students were both very high. Many of the students came over to his flat in the campus to discuss with him and to get more out of him. One of the reasons why the students found his teaching interesting was that he often deviated from the topic to other related fields. He also interpreted the subject, in terms of and in relation to, the current, socio-economic scenario. His views were quite radical and had a communistic bias and for this, he became known to all the students.

"It is said that some of the leaders of the Naxalite movement, contacted him and asked him to campaign for them, for the cause of the revolution. He agreed, and so, it happened that he began to hold meetings with his students and to some of them, he spoke of an armed revolution as the only salvation. Those students, who got interested, were specially called over to attend lectures on social and economic philosophy, and the goals of an egalitarian society. With his singular and consistent effort, he was soon able to muster the support of a group of fourteen students, who became hard-core Naxalites.

"In their first action, they attacked and beheaded a local landowner, who was also a political leader, after kidnapping him. A few days later, a policeman, who was on their trail, became their victim. They were able to kill two more policemen, before the latter got wind of their hideout and four of them were arrested. It is said that those who got arrested were severely tortured and the names of all the rest were soon extorted from them.

"No one however, gave out the name of their teacher and leader. The students were all tortured, but their shut mouths did not yield to the pressure or pain. Nevertheless, they confessed boldly to killing of the landlord, who was a class enemy, and the policemen, who were their protectors. In spite of the most severe torture for days on end, the fourteen young Naxalites valiantly refused to own up their leader's name.

"The police, however, were able to short-list the names of probable leaders and the needle of suspicion began to point at Mr. Chakraborty, the lecturer of radical views. He was arrested in a night raid of his quarters, where, we were told, they found some volumes of Das Kapital, purchased from College Street and some books on Mao's teachings. He was thrown into jail under MISA at Barrackpore and the same third degree methods of torture were applied on him. It is said that they pulled out his nails one by one. They plucked his beard with pliers and flogged him black and blue, but they were neither able to get from a confession, nor the names of his followers. He just told them that he was not a Naxalite at all. He was interested in the subject from an academic point of view. Having tried several forms of torture, but in vain, the police at last thought of a novel plan to teach him a lesson.

"On a wintry evening, towards dusk, he was taken out of the jail, blind-folded and driven in a police van to some deserted place, away from the town. He was brought down from the van and made to stand with his hands tied behind his back, his eyes still covered. He could sense something sinister lurking behind the folds that covered his eyes, as the sound of the police boots and cocking of rifles reached his ears.

"Suddenly, he heard the familiar voice of the police officer: "Here is the man who has betrayed you all. Each one of you. He gave your names to us after you killed the landlord and the two policemen, on the condition that he should be released. Yes, can you believe it? He wanted to be set free and see you all get killed. Now, what do you think of your leader? Can you not recognise him? Here, shall I remove the cover from his eyes so that you could see your beloved leader? Yes, the man who has betrayed you all so that he could be free.

"Mr. Chakraborty could feel the police officer's hand untying the blindfold, and he shuddered at the thought of seeing his followers lined up before him. All his valiant students, who had resolutely refused to name him before the police, as he had gathered from the other prisoners, would now be before him. It was almost a year since he saw them. He was probably sure that they would not believe the policeman. He would tell them that he had not . . . but then, he must have also thought that there was no way he could talk to anyone of the fourteen young men. He had to pretend he didn't know them. The police could he playing a trick on him. He would have to remain silent.

"When the blindfold was removed, he could barely open his eyes: the sight before him was unbearable—the students were lined up in front of a wall.

"He felt sick and dizzy: face to face with death. He had not expected to see his beloved students at the firing range. 'For what reason did the police bring them there?' He thought. But he did not dare get the answer. He could see the police officer smiling maliciously at him and at the students. He began again: 'Mr. Chakraborty, these students now know that you have betrayed them and they are going to die with that knowledge!'

"Mr. Chakraborty did not say anything to contradict the police officer, but he gave out a low exclamation of surprise and fear.

"The police officer's face, all of a sudden, became stern and within a moment, he ordered the firing squad to take position before the fourteen students, who were lined up. He ordered his men to fire.

"Fourteen deafening sounds of gunfire reverberated in the ears of Mr. Chakraborty, who was already distraught, and in a state of shock as a result of the proceedings that unfolded before his eyes. He could see as he stood watching powerless, his beloved students falling down, one by one, their accusing eyes fixed on him. Fourteen pairs of eyes eyed him with hatred, as they fell to their death. As long as their eyes were open; as long as they squirmed on the ground; their eyes were on him. The only feelings in those eyes were the feelings of betrayal and hate. They seemed to convey the feeling that their hopes were belied; their dreams shattered. They had not expected Mr. Chakraborty to betray them. Their eyes were unaware of the pain of bullets: they only stared at him with malice as long as they were open, and there was life in them.

"When the last of the young men had stopped squirming, a death-like stillness prevailed. The echoes of gunfire had died down save for what remained in the consciousness of those who stood their ground. They heard the sound of the wind and the rustle of leaves and the retreating chirping of the late evening birds. No one moved for a while, including the police officer, and the men of the firing squad, and then unexpectedly Mr. Chakraborty broke into an impassioned laughter. He laughed and laughed, throwing his head backward and forward till he gasped for breath. He stopped for a while and then began laughing again.

"It was a most unusual and incoherent reaction. The police officer looked at Mr. Chakraborty with surprise and fear as if he was looking at a ghost. He just laughed and laughed. Just as the staring policemen expected the laughter to stop, it began again, and finally, when it seemed to continue till doomsday, it began to get transformed into a loud sobbing. His face assumed strange contortions as he sobbed with an unintelligible warble accompanying. Perhaps, it was similar to what we have just heard ourselves. It is said that the laughing and sobbing continued for the whole evening and night and in the following morning he was taken to the health unit, for an injection, which put him to sleep.

"When he woke up, the laughter and sobbing by turns, began again. In the absence of any alternative, they brought him over to this jail, in the hope that a change of place may bring him back to normal. They were wrong. We have just seen how mad he was." Ritwick finished his narrative and looked at his comrades for their reaction. There was none from anyone. They all sat with head bent, looking at the floor of the cell. The tragic story seemed unbelievable and yet there were enough reasons to believe in it, especially when they had seen the plight of Mr. Chakraborty with their own eyes."

Akshyay was speechless for a while, thinking how similar the story was to Coleridge's poem, 'Ancient Mariner'. He debated within himself for and against its truth. While the possibility of such an incident, taking place, was there all right, the probability was in doubt. He couldn't recollect newspaper reports corroborating the story. He felt he should share his thought with the others and so he began; "I don't think the story is completely true. There has been no such report in the newspapers as far as I can remember on fourteen Naxalites getting killed."

"Of course not. Do you think newspapers will publish such a story?" Ritwick retorted.

"No, but surely there would be some report saying that fourteen Naxalites have been killed in an encounter." Tamal said.

"Well, I have been in jail for the last one year and therefore I couldn't tell whether there has been any newspaper reports." Arindam said in a sad voice and looking at Akshyay said, "Have you kept a watch on all newspapers?"

"I don't vouch for it, but a story of this magnitude would have come to my notice some way or other. In any case, I don't see how the police could be so brutal. They are also human beings, aren't they?"

"I do admit they are, but when they wear that uniform of theirs, they become something else. I won't feel surprised to hear of some more Naxalites getting shot in a similar way. Why! Could we also get shot?" Ritwick asked, making a point for others to ponder on.

"Oh no! No!" Arindam burst out; "You can't say that for sure, can you?"

"No I am not sure. I only said it could be." Ritwick said, to pacify Arindam.

"I wonder what they will do to us," Tamal said softly, his voice suggesting the feeling of resignation that seemed to envelop his mind. "It's long since I've had a good night's sleep. I am still not used to sleeping on the cold floor. I'd like to be free. I'd give anything to be free." He broke down as he said these words.

Akshyay in a compassionate gesture put his hand on his shoulder to comfort him. Don't worry. I don't see why they shouldn't release you. You are not a hard-core Naxalite, are you? It's only the hard-core ones they're after. Have faith in God. Pray to Him. You will find peace. Now let's all catch up with our sleep. It's already quite late."

The four prisoners got to lie down on the floor, beside each other, in a row. They lay on their backs, looking at the ceiling and at the faint light of the night sky that crept into the cell through the hole in the wall. All four thought for long of the fourteen pairs of eyes, full of hatred and scorn. They wondered what they would have done in similar circumstances. When they gave up trying to find a different reaction, they closed their eyes and fell into an uneasy sleep. But sleep it was and it soon switched off their thought-proc.

Chapter - XXIII

---◆◆◆---

The next morning there was a surprise caller at their cell. The warden himself stood right in front, as one of the accompanying sentries began unlocking the door. The four prisoners stood up, wide-eyed, anxiety writ large on their faces.

"Who is Akshyay Choudhuri?" the warden asked, as he walked in. He spoke, in an unusually soft voice, unlike a police officer.

"I am," Akshyay said, coming forward, with memories of school day actions flowing into his mind.

"You have to come with me to my office."

"What is it?"

"You will soon know. Now please come." The warden stepped aside and pointed to the open doorway. Akshyay looked at the faces of his three companions of three days and felt an overpowering sense of guilt at having to leave them behind. Somehow, he knew that he was getting released and he felt sorry for his three friends, who were not as lucky as he was. They looked at his face in expectation of something undefined. Akshyay could not meet their eyes. He only raised his right hand as if he wanted to say good-bye, and walked out of the door. The sentries locked the cell and followed the warden and Akshyay in cold rhythmic steps.

On reaching his office, the warden asked Akshyay to sit down. He brought out a printed form, from a file on his table. "You are being released; you can sign here to acknowledge receipt of your clothes."

Akshyay felt overjoyed at the thought of freedom. The heaviness in his mind melted away like sugar cubes in a cup of tea. The joy of meeting Sarah, to hear her voice, to feel her close, to gaze into her eyes, were thoughts that came in close succession. He could hardly see the paper and the pen, which the warden held in front of him.

"Where are you lost, Mr. Choudhuri?" The warden asked. "Here, take this pen and sign here."

"I'm sorry, I was thinking about people at home. Here, I will sign, right away."

"That's good," the warden said, "I'll give you your clothes. You can go in there and change." The warden walked to the wardrobe and brought out the pyjamas and kurta, washed and pressed, and handed these over. Akshyay looked at his clothes, and then at his prison outfit. He thought of Tamal, Ritwick and Arindam. They were still in the cell and here he was out of it. They were perhaps thinking about him. He could feel their thoughts on his person. The clothes he was still wearing were his links to the cell. He had to get out of these and put on his own clothes.

He could not help smiling, when he came out of the antechamber in his pyjamas and kurta, the prison clothes in his hands. "Thank you, sir. Where should I keep these?" he said to the warden.

"You can leave these on the table. My man will remove them. By the way, how far is your home? Do you need a lift?"

"No, I'll walk down. It would be nice to feel the world outside once again, after three days in the cell. It was quite an experience though. I suppose, I'll not regret it. It's opened my eyes to a side of life, I was not aware of."

"I hope you will not come back here again. This is not the place for you. You are from a high family, and therefore, you have to be careful about the people you mix with. Times are bad. Don't allow yourself to be involved in politics. This is my advice to you."

"I'll remember that. But may I request you to look after my friends who are still in the cell. I am feeling bad for them."

"Don't worry. They will be all right. They'll also be released some day: all political prisoners are." The warden smiled and patted Akshyay on the back, "I wish you all the best in life. I hope you will get back to your classes. Which college are you in?"

"I'm not in college anymore. I dropped out midway through the degree course," Akshyay said nonchalantly.

"Why did you do that? You are not a political person, I guess. Then why did you have to drop out of college?"

"Well, to tell you the truth, I just didn't dig going to college. I had nothing to learn there. In fact, I had to do a lot of unlearning after I dropped out. They don't teach anything about real life there. I want to learn about life and for that, I have to live it, don't you agree?"

"I guess you are right. But, if one has to go for a career, a job, one must to have a university degree. Of course, your case is different. You are from a high family. You don't need to work for a living, and hence it is not essential to have a degree. You know, even Rabindranath Tagore did not have a formal education and he too was from a high family."

"Oh! Please don't compare me to Tagore. He was a great poet and philosopher. I am nothing. I am not even in possession of any property as yet. I will have to work for a living. I have a wife; a family to look after."

"Oh really! You are married? I didn't know that. So you are really young to get married? Where's your wife from? She must also be from one of the famous families of Bengal?"

"No, she's not. She's an American Jew. I met her in Rishikesh and we got married there."

"Oh! I see. I can follow you now. You are a hippie . . . An Indian hippie and your wife is also a hippie."

"You're mistaken. Neither I am a hippie nor my wife is one. I don't know what you mean by a 'hippie'. Is it because I think and act differently from the crowd; and my wife's an American girl who's come to India seeking peace?" Akshyay reacted, somewhat charged with emotion.

"No, no, no, don't get agitated. I didn't mean to hurt you or call you names. I don't find anything wrong in hippies. Theirs is a non-violent and unique form of protest against the mechanisation of our society. Why, I also sometimes feel the need to give up this uniform and this place. I want to go Scott free, to where my mind yearns to be, rowing down the mighty Padma River, at breakneck speed, as we all did in our youth. It's a different country now." The warden's eyes suddenly became moist and he wiped away the forming tears with the back of his hand. "You know Akshyay, in our hearts we are all hippies. It's only that we are not courageous enough to follow our innermost desires because of our insecurities and petty foibles. I must admit you are a brave boy and at the same time unselfish, to choose a life that is out in the open, unprotected by the thick walls of custom and tradition."

Akshyay looked at the eyes of the warden, and felt there were people yet in the world, who were understanding and sympathetic. He suddenly began to feel sorry for the trapped-in-the-well situation in which the warden was. "I'm sorry, I have to take leave of you, sir," he said, realising the need to cut-short the conversation and to go home.

"Yes, you must," the warden said, and rang the bell to call in the sentries. They came in and escorted Akshyay out of the room, through a corridor of barracks and finally across a small courtyard to the huge iron gate, with which he was familiar. A small door set in it opened for him and as the gatekeeper checked the release order, which the sentries handed over, Akshyay passed into freedom once again.

Akshyay stood for a while, outside the jail gate and drew in a deep breath. He breathed out slowly, as if expunging the foul air of the jail and all the quaint thoughts and ideas that had assailed his consciousness. He began to feel fresh and light-hearted after a few deep breaths and began to walk down the road on the way to his house.

The trams, buses, taxis, rickshaws, were in their motions. The shoppers and shopkeepers were at their jobs. The men, women and children on the street—they were in their own motions, trapped in their own small worlds. He also felt trapped, even though he was outside the cell. It didn't matter really whether he was inside or outside the cell. He was a prisoner in his own small world.

As he walked along, thoughts of Sarah came back to his mind. She could be on her way to her office. 'Could she be happy to go to office?' He could feel the question prodding his mind. He tried to find an answer that would be in the positive. There weren't any. His own experiences, attitudes and reactions militated against doing a job. He was against fixed timings or living for a vocation, being successful in a competitive corporate scenario. 'What were his objectives?' He asked himself. There were no clear objectives. He didn't know what he wanted from life. He only knew that he had to be different. He could not do the things everyone else did.

He knew that Sarah also wanted to be different. She had come all the way from America, leaving hearth and home. For what did she leave her home? Was it not for a different life? What an irony that she had to succumb to a routine and mundane existence. Surely, she would not be able to accept it. A lurking fear crept into his mind. She would soon realise her predicament and revolt. What would he do then? He recollected that she had taken up the role of a Hindu wife and hence it was a different lifestyle, from the one she had left behind. Still, nothing could guarantee her happiness. He wondered how she had adjusted to his aunt for the last three days. Did they have dinner together? Did they discuss about him? Surely, his aunt must have organised his release. They must have discussed the strategy over dinner several times. Could they have possibly gone over to some influential person's house to arrange his release? He recalled his aunt saying that she had contacts with some powerful people.

Sarah's time must have passed off in quite a hectic manner. There could not have been much time to feel happy or unhappy. He would now have to think of doing something constructive, for her as well as for himself. He wondered what he was doing in Calcutta, in any case, and with what purpose. The property matters needed to be settled as also the question of his mother's treatment. He could not possibly allow her to languish in a mental hospital, while he would be away on his own trip, with his wife. Things have suddenly changed after his father's death. He began to feel that he was not quite free to do as he pleased anymore. The thought of being bogged down spurred him into action. He quickened his pace as he felt an urgency to complete the jobs at hand. He was soon on the familiar stretch of road, near his house and a couple of familiar faces appeared in his field of vision.

When he reached the iron gates of his house, he looked up involuntarily at the veranda to see if Sarah was there. She wasn't and he felt disheartened, even though he knew that she should be in office. He pushed the gate open and walked up the pathway to the house. He went up the staircase and rung the bell. Miss Monica opened the door.

"So you are back, from jail?" She asked with a hint of sarcasm in her voice, which completely threw Akshyay off balance.

"What's the matter? Are you annoyed with me for coming back?" Akshyay retorted and walked in defiantly past her.

"I am not annoyed with you, Akshyay. It's your wife who's really brought us down."

"Why? What has she done?" Akshyay asked surprised, turning to look closely at his aunt.

Miss Monica was silent for a while, making an effort to measure her words. She did not want to precipitate the impending outburst, but nevertheless they came out unbridled. "She has left home."

"When? How?" Akshyay asked, reacting immediately.

"Well, on the very day after you got arrested, she returned from her office late in the night, saying that she had been molested. I wanted to send her to the police station to make a report. She refused at first but when I forced her, she went; but that was the last I saw her. I have checked with the local police station but they have told me that she had not been there at all. I didn't ask them to look for her just to avoid a scandal."

"Why? Was it not your responsibility to find her? I didn't expect this from you."

"What could I do, you tell me? You are in jail. Your wife appears late in the night in a torn sari after allowing herself to be raped . . ."

"I can't believe it. Sarah can't behave the way you have . . . I know her quite well. She is a very responsible person." Akshyay felt something blocking his flow of thoughts.

"That's your clouded vision. I never liked the likes of her from the very beginning. It's the same story again and again. Your father did it before you and now you are doing the same thing. Now we will all suffer for it."

"What are you saying? What did I do to cause your suffering? Don't worry, I will split this place. I'll go away to some far-off joint, where things will be different; where these hang-ups of tradition and custom will not be important."

"Why? Are you thinking of a free society, free sex as well? Is it because of this attitude of yours that you are not reacting to your wife's antics? Has she not done something immoral? Shouldn't it affect you, me and every other person related to us?"

"What do you expect me to do when you tell me my wife has been raped; my wife has left home?"

"Well, I expect you to feel sad and angry at the same time . . . I don't know . . . I mean you should have broken down."

"That's not what a man should do. One should be able to withstand shocks with equanimity. I have learnt that from yogic philosophy." Akshyay felt reassured as he said these words and at the same time a sense of detachment. He felt as if a part of his consciousness was separated from the rest of his mind and personality. The face of Swami Ananda flashed in his mind against the backdrop of the ashram, quiet and serene, beside a turbulent river.

"I cannot understand your philosophy or your attitudes. You are incorrigible." Miss Monica said, in anguish. "You can do what you like, Akshyay. I can only try to guide you. It's my duty to see that you don't go astray. Now won't you go looking for your wife?"

"Yes, I'll have to. That's my duty; I can't remain immune. By the way, did you meet anyone regarding my release?" Akshyay asked, changing the subject.

"Yes, I did talk to an acquaintance. He is a lawyer and he has some contacts with the police and one or two political leaders. Why? Did someone ask you about how you were released?"

"No, I was just thinking."

"It's just possible that the lawyer had organised it."

"Possibly," Akshyay said, indifferently, hinting at terminating the discussion. He felt convinced that his aunt had not helped in his release. He wondered whether the actual culprit's arrest or his own innocence was the real reason. The question seemed to badger his mind. The fear of re-arrest also lurked in his consciousness. The effect of all this was that he began to feel lost, defeated, and powerless.

Speechless and dazed, he turned away from his aunt and went to his room. He looked around and found it very much the same as he had left it. His sling bag was lying as it was on the mattress, which spread across the floor. The sarode and tabla were also there, as if someone had just played on them. His mind went back to the practice sessions with John. Though the place for keeping the tabla and sarode was in another room, on the last occasion they had played in his bedroom. He tried to recollect the last raga they had played. It seemed to be long back in time; it was only with an effort that he recalled that it was raga bairag. He felt he had lost something. He wanted to get the past back into his life once again. He had to get back those days of music, love, and friendship. He had to go away from the arena of violence, hate, and fear.

A yearning for music and love began to overcome him and his thoughts began to float on the ragas and tabla strokes. The tunes of the sarode and tabla began to reverberate in his mind and for a few seconds he closed his eyes to get drunk in its sweetness. Gradually, a hint of a smile formed on his lips as the tension started to dip.

As he opened his eyes, he felt his thought-processes falling in line. Strangely enough, he could now clearly see the course of action that lay before him. The road to the music teacher's house lit up in his mind. He knew that he had to visit that place first. The answers to a number of questions were there. He could find out why the police had released him. He could find out about Sarah, perhaps. He could find out whether the police had arrested the real culprit. He could find a real well-wisher. He could also start his music lessons, and get back the music into his life.

He picked up his sling bag and notebook energetically, and made his way to the music teacher's house. He did not once consider that he was retracing his steps back to the murder site.

CHAPTER - XXIV

As Akshyay walked out of the house, towards the bus stop, his mind dwelt on the probable reasons for Sarah's leaving home. He could not fully believe his aunt; and therefore he felt intrigued as to why Sarah left home. He wondered whether it was her inability to get along with his aunt that compelled her to leave or something else. It also struck his mind that she could have given up being the Hindu wife because he was in jail, charged with murder. She could have decided to just call it a day. She must have forgotten him . . . But how could she forget him? Had he not loved her? Did he not need her? She was the only thing he possessed. Was it her body he was interested in, or her personality and her goodness? Was he secretly enjoying her predisposition of being a Hindu wife?

These and several other questions kept coming in to his mind but he chose not to answer them. He felt he knew the answer. He knew that Sarah would not do anything that would be unacceptable to him. After all, he had accepted her as she was, and on the recommendation of a swami. She was knowledgeable, sober, rational, loveable and above all, a beautiful woman. They were in love with each other. He would rather not rush to any conclusions. He had to meet her first. Probably, the music teacher could tell him where she was, or even John.

The bus soon arrived. Making sure that it was going to Jadavpur, he boarded it. He remembered the last occasion when he had boarded a bus. It was when he was returning from the music teacher's house. Could he have left the torch in the bus? His eyes turned involuntarily to the seats and to the faces of the people occupying them. His attention closed in on a person with a crew cut, thick neck and round shoulders. Could he be a plain-dressed police officer? He preferred not to probe. He turned his mind instead to the passengers getting on and off at every stop as the bus pushed ahead.

It was already midday and the lane that took off the main road, was as usual empty. The shops at the crossing were still open, but the shopkeepers had bored looks on their faces. Some of them were even getting ready to pull down the shutters for the afternoon siesta. As he walked past, he felt their curious eyes on him, as if they were trying to know why they had not seen him for quite some time.

As Akshyay walked along, his mind recapitulated the incidents on the fateful night. Images of the huddled group on the road, the cringing policeman on the ground, the music teacher's anxious face and the series of experiences that had followed, came into his mind one by one. The present seemed also to be part of a chain reaction.

At the doorstep of the music teacher's house, as he rang the bell, memories of the past flooded his mind. This time however, the road he had come through was, in a way, different. The groups of youngsters were not there. He remembered that John had told him about the disappearance of all the teenagers and young men from the locality, after the murder.

The music teacher's wife opened the door. "Oh Akshyay! You are back!" The characteristic smile was missing from her face.

"Yes," Akshyay said, becoming conscious of the change in her behaviour. He wondered how she could know about his imprisonment.

"Why don't you come in?"

Akshyay walked in and followed the music teacher's wife to the drawing room, which was also the music room. He noticed that the sarode, sitar and tablas, in their places, but the music teacher missing.

"Please sit down. He will come down to see you." There was neither any warmth in her voice, or in her manner. Her face was distraught.

"Is anything wrong?" Akshyay asked.

"You'll hear it from him," she said, indicating the door from which he would enter. Akshyay recollected that Hindu women did not utter the names of their husbands, preferring the use of pronouns.

He sat down for a while, wondering what could be wrong except that their son must have gone away from home to avoid arrest. He thought of his attempts to transform him. He was perhaps not a Naxalite any longer. There was, however, no way he could be certain of his compatriots letting him go. Presently the music teacher appeared. He looked tired, but there was a forced smile on his face.

"So, you have been released? We must thank the Lord. It is good that they have let you go. After all, you were not involved at all." The music teacher said these words without looking at Akshyay and as if to himself.

"But tell me, Guruji, how did you come to know about my arrest?" Akshyay said, in an attempt to clear his doubts.

The music teacher looked at Akshyay's face. "They came and arrested my son in a night raid. They also informed me that they had arrested my student, this is you." The music teacher's face wore a sad expression as he said these words, which came out mechanically like inevitable facts.

Akshyay felt uncomfortable in the depressing atmosphere and sought to enliven the scene. "Why did they arrest Shamir? He was already converted, wasn't he?"

"Yes," the music teacher said, looking up at Akshyay's face "Surely he was. I told the policemen repeatedly that my son was innocent but they wouldn't agree."

"What about the other boys in the area? Have they also been picked up?"

"No, I guess not. They have all escaped. Only Shamir stayed back and he got arrested."

"I guess the police would soon release him, when they find out he's not involved."

"No, I don't think so," the music teacher said, his lips suddenly beginning to quiver with emotion. He rubbed his forehead with his palm and said, "He is not as lucky as you."

Akshyay felt uncomfortable again at the comparison between Shamir and himself. He wondered whether the music teacher was jealous of him and then waived the thought on a recollection that a Guru is always a well-wisher and could never be jealous of his pupil.

"I'll try to get him released," Akshyay said, as if to make amends for the evil thought that had come to his mind. "My aunt knows some people who have contacts with the police."

"Do you really think that you were released because of your aunt's efforts?" The music teacher asked rather sarcastically. "No, no, no, it is not so. You were released because of Shamir's arrest. When the police came here to arrest him and informed that you were also under their custody, my son told them that you were innocent. They had snapped at his suggestion then, but I am sure that was the only reason for your release. By the way", the music teacher continued after a pause, "do you know why, in the first place, you got arrested? I did not tell you this earlier. It was the torch. A police dog had traced it to our house. We had to tell the police that the torch was in your hands and that is how the police picked you up. If you had not left the torch on the road, you wouldn't have been arrested. It was only because they arrested you that they found reason enough to arrest my son. They had kept a tab on his contacts with the local young men, who were already marked and so when the opportunity came by, they promptly arrested him. I am sure they tortured him and in his confessional statement he must have repeated that you were innocent. He might have even named the actual murderers."

"I can see clearly now, how I was arrested and how I got released. I think if what you've said about Shamir is true, then they will release him as well. Perhaps they are detaining him for his own security. His comrades, whom he had betrayed, will not stop short of exterminating him. It is in his own interest that he should stay in jail, under the protection of the police."

"Do you really think that my Shamir will be released?" The music teacher asked, with hope lighting up his face. "Will he really be released?" The music teacher's voice had already reached a high pitch. He called out to his wife excitedly, "Are you listening? Are you listening? Akshyay says Shamir will be released."

The music teacher's wife came into the room hurriedly, eager to hear to words again. "Please say it again. Did you say, Shamir will be released?"

Mr.Lahiri's face broke into a smile and his eyes twinkled, "Akshyay says that Shamir will be released." He looked a trifle foolish, as he repeated the words.

His wife's face fell. She could see through the false castle of hope that her husband had built. It came crashing down the mountain slope like a landslide. In anger and frustration she began to shout at her husband. "Will you stop smiling? Pray, why do you allow yourself to be carried away? Are you a child? Akshyay says something and you start dancing. Don't you have any gumption?"

The music teacher stopped smiling and remained silent, thinking why his wife was reacting in that manner. He could not fathom the reason for it and preferred to keep quiet.

His wife continued: "Don't mind my words, Akshyay. I did not mean to hurt you, but tell me: will they release him so easily? He is not from as famous a family as yours. He has also been closely associated with Naxalites. The police know all that. No doubt, he is innocent, as far as the murder of the policeman is concerned, but he was a Naxalite all right. He might have turned out a new leaf, after you had talked it over with him, but the police don't know about that. Therefore, they will not release him so easily. I wonder if you could help him to get released. Akshyay, you are from a well-known family and I am sure you will be able to find out someone who could be of help. You know; Shamir is our only son. We want him back home. I have heard you speaking of your aunt . . ."

"Sure, I did," Akshyay said gaining confidence. He had only some time back withdrawn into a shell, when she had started attacking his guru and implicating him, "My aunt knows some people. I'll tell her to speak for Shamir."

"Will she really do something for us? I've heard she does not approve of your coming here to learn sarode. She wants you to follow the family tradition," the music teacher's wife said, going into her attacking posture once again.

Akshyay could feel that she was keeping something up her Sleeve but he could not guess what it was. "How do you know she'll not help you? She had showed her willingness to speak to some people about me, didn't she?"

"Do you really want to know?" The music teacher's wife continued with another teaser.

"Ah!" The music teacher reacted irritably. "Why do you have to get after Akshyay? What has he done? He is not responsible for Shamir's arrest. It's our own bad luck that he is arrested. Had we checked him earlier, he would not have fallen into this rut, would he?"

"You keep quite. I've had enough of you. What have you done for your son? Do you think that doing `tung tung' is all that is there to do in life. Your responsibility ends there, doesn't it? You men are all alike. You are all seeking your own pleasures, unmindful of wives', or children's needs. Will you now keep quiet?"

The music teacher became silent again, realising that there was no use arguing, with an angry woman. It would lead to more unsavoury comments about his preference for classical music, which would be unbearable. Akshyay also felt caught in an uncomfortable situation, but he knew he had to go through it. He was in a way responsible for Shamir's arrest and that alone justified his mother's anger.

"Do you want to know why your aunt won't help?" The question came again, much to Akshyay's discomfiture. Her eyes were on him.

"Yes I want to know," he said, without meeting her eyes, fearing it could turn her hysterical.

"Well your wife told me about it. She had come here with John and had told me about how she had been turned away from the house by your aunt and how your aunt dislikes your association with us."

"Oh I see! When did she come here?" Akshyay asked eagerly. "Where could she be staying?"

"I don't know where she is staying, but she had come with John," she said matter-of-factly.

"Oh yes, Akshyay," the music teacher intervened, "I forgot to tell you. She came to tell us about your arrest and also about her leaving home. Why, were you not able to meet her so far?"

"I am in fact looking for her. Did she tell you where she has put up?" He remembered that he had come to the music teacher's house for, among other things, information about his wife.

"I am sure John will be able to tell you," the music teacher said.

The mention of John's name sent him on a reverie. He began to daydream of Sarah making an appearance, just then, but gave up the idea as improbable. He focused his attention on the music teacher, his guru. He knew that while he had been thinking about Sarah, they were thinking about their son. The music teacher began to speak about Shamir again.

"By the way, Akshyay, do you still feel your aunt will be able to help? Will she speak for Shamir's release? Do you think she will honour your request?"

"Well, I am not very sure about what she'll say, but I am sure I can do something for my Guru. After all, I must try to give you something in return for all that you have done for me."

"What have I done for you, Akshyay? I have been the cause of your arrest, you know. If I hadn't asked you to come that evening, to speak to Shamir, you would never have had the misadventure of accosting a wounded policeman on the road. You would not have left the torch by his side as a clue. I was a fool to tell them that I had given you the torch. That's how you got arrested, don't you see? I had to give your name to the police when they brought in the torch following the trail of a sniffing dog. I thought you would never be arrested and that the police would be diverted from Shamir's trail. I was right but only for a while, when neither you nor my son were arrested. But then, suddenly everything went topsy-turvy: you were arrested and then my son too. I gave you away and also my son. No! No! No! Akshyay, I have not done anything for you. I have only harmed you . . ." The music teacher covered his face with both his hands and uttered some guttural sounds, as he broke down.

"Will you shut up . . . don't you have any self-respect? Crying like a child? Do you realise what you are saying? Here, Akshyay is talking of doing something to get Shamir released, and you are distracting him with inconsequential words."

The music teacher made an effort to come back to his senses. He rubbed his eyes with both his hands and said, "All right, Akshyay I will expect you to save my son. He is innocent and you know that; I'm sure you can do something."

Akshyay felt flustered at the vacillation in his guru's reactions. He realised that this was all due to his son's arrest. After all, Shamir was his only son and the old couple's lives were in disarray. He felt he must tell his aunt to put in a word. He was sure that his aunt had arranged his release and she could do the same for Shamir too. He would persuade her to help him. "Don't worry", Akshyay said, controlling himself. "I'll persuade her to help him. I know some influential people too, and I am sure I can get Shamir off the hook."

"We will be really grateful to you if you can do that," the music teacher's wife said. "I hope you will really make an effort."

"I said, I will, didn't I?" Akshyay said, assertively.

"Well then, let me get you some tea. Don't go away without it." She got up to leave for the kitchen, as she uttered these words.

Akshyay could make out that her motherly love was desperately trying to blossom into hope.

CHAPTER - XXV

As Akshyay walked out of the music teacher's house, his mind was teeming with thoughts of Sarah. He could not be sure where she could be, but the information that she had come there with John seemed to be like the needle of a compass. It pointed towards him. He would have to meet him. In all probability he would know where she could be staying. He guessed it would be in a friend's place. He recollected that immediately after their arrival in Calcutta they had been going round accepting invitations for dinner parties. Some of his friends and their family members had even offered to help Sarah set up house. They guided her to the right shops for her saris, bangles, sindoor[25] and the other things that a Hindu wife needs.

It was possible that she would be in Satya's place. Satya had been with him in school and he was in the fourth year, Engineering, at Jadavpur University. His two sisters, with whom he had several flings, during his days as a pop star, had volunteered to teach Sarah Indian cuisine. It was possible that Sarah would there. Their house was near his own. Nevertheless, it could be embarrassing to go inquiring there, as it would give them an opportunity to spread rumours about him and his wife. He had first to make sure that she was with them. He felt certain that only John could possibly know.

He took the bus, therefore, to Gariahat and walked straight up to John's place. He was sure that John would be both pleased and surprised to see him. He liked John and knew that he respected him for his knowledge of Indian Philosophy and Music. He recollected John's face staring at him in admiration when he had talked about the relation between the spiritual world and music. He had a feeling that John would help him to trace Sarah. He could confide in him, rather than in any of his Indian friends. At least, he would not spread rumours.

It was afternoon. As he stood wondering whether everyone was asleep at that time of the day, the chowkidar opened the main door.

"Oh! Akshyaysaab[27]! You want to meet Johnsaab? He is not at home . . . but Memsaab is."

"Who is the Memsaab?" Akshyay asked, wondering if it would be one of John's girlfriends.

"I don't know. She came a few days back, late in the night and wanted to see Johnsaab. Then she began to stay here. The landlord had objected to Memsaab's staying here, but somehow Johnsaab has managed him."

"Oh I see! When will John return?" Akshyay asked, half turning as if to go away.

"Why don't you go and find out from Membsaab? Perhaps she can tell you."

"You think she'll know?" Akshyay asked, and then said to himself, 'I think she will.' Akshyay was unable to contain his curiosity. Who is this girl? How is she staying with John? He hadn't heard of John's girlfriend. Could she have arrived recently? He pushed his way past the chowkidar and climbed the stairs to the mezzanine floor, and knocked at the door.

The door was ajar, and so, when he knocked, it gave way. It opened a little. Akshyay stepped back alarmed at the prospect of infringing a young lady's privacy. He could hear no sound save for the occasional clapping from the stairs down below. The chowkidar was preparing tobacco, for chewing.

Akshyay took one look at the chowkidar and gained courage to make another attempt at the door. He knocked again. The door opened wider, but from within there was still no response. Akshyay felt exasperated and knocked a third time. There was still no result; but the door opened a little more. Akshyay could now clearly see a woman sleeping on the floor. She appeared to be wearing a lungi-type cloth round her waist but her torso was completely bare. She was sleeping flat on her back. Akshyay could see her bare body and a bunch of golden hair. He pulled himself away, realising that he was prying. It would be really embarrassing if she were to wake up and find him staring at her nakedness. For a while, he did not know what to do: whether he should go back or stay there and wait for her to be awake. As he pondered over the question, his mind involuntarily took him again to the door. This time he noticed her outstretched hand, and the conch-shell bangles. His curiosity mounting, he looked again more carefully at the hand. It looked familiar.

Wasn't it Sarah's? He looked again to be sure, and true enough the hand was indeed Sarah's and the bunch of light brown hair too. His hesitation simply vanished and he boldly walked into the room. Much to his surprise and pleasure, it was Sarah indeed, sleeping peacefully, on a mattress on the floor. He could not contain himself any longer and was about to wake her up, when he felt something stopping him. He felt that something was terribly wrong: his wife sleeping naked, on someone else's mattress and in someone else's flat.

For a few moments, Akshyay stood still; his eyes fixed on Sarah; his mind witnessing a series of images of John and his wife making love to each other in the most erotic positions. The feelings of anger and jealousy burned in his mind like a full-blown fire. He tried to fight against those thoughts and feeling; to keep them at bay; but they kept coming back again and again. He continued to stand still, looking at Sarah through a mental image of her in John's arms. He was at a loss, unable to resist the flow of erotic images, which seemed to leave a trail of devastation in his memory bank of dreams.

As he tried to control his thoughts, a conflict arose in his mind. On the one hand was an urge to go away from the tormenting site and on the other, a desire to wake her up and give her an opportunity to explain. A flicker of hope lingered in his mind. It threw its wavering light on the scarred memories of his sweet relationship with Sarah. He recollected her clear mind and eyes that revealed a deep blue sea of love. He recollected the sweet smile that lingered on her lips as she talked or listened attentively to words of philosophy, culture, or music. He recalled the image of her light-brown hair. His fingers had so often got entangled, as he had played with the silken strands or let them brush away the anxious thoughts from his brow. The image of the ashram also came to his mind and of Sarah as an ashramite[28], following the footsteps of yogis and yoginis[29] . . . She was a Hindu wife. Could he juxtapose the image with the one that scorched his eyes?

In Akshyay's mind the images were in serious conflict. It was certainly not his Sarah who was sleeping on the floor in a half-naked condition in someone else's flat. Would he wake her? The thought again pestered his mind. He tried to find a good reason to do that, but there seemed to be none. He just stood still, nonplussed, awkward, as conflicting thoughts and images battered his mind.

He lost count of time, as he stood looking as Sarah, stuck between the past and the future, as if separated from time's passage, which flowed past unconcerned. Like in a meditation trip, his mind kept spinning. It revolved around Sarah, his mother and his life in Rishikesh and Calcutta. Images of the jail, the rock band, the trips on LSD, and bhang[30] came in disjointed series from a cavern in his consciousness and seemed to collect in a heap on his mind's surface. He felt somewhat heavy in the head and a simultaneous weakness in his knees and dropped down beside Sarah.

Sarah stirred as his knees touched the side of her stomach and within moments her eyes opened. She saw Akshyay gazing at her face and into her eyes. She had been dreaming of having gone to see Akshyay at the visitor's lobby of the jail, and now she was actually seeing Akshyay's face. She experienced an immense sense of relief, which soon turned into a pleasant surprise. Her emotions did not show on her face because of her state of drowsiness, so much so that Akshyay's first impression of her waking state was her indifference.

"Hi Akshyay! When did you come? How nice to see you," she presently said, as she sat up, still unaware of her bare body.

"Are you really interested to know?" Akshyay said standing up.

"Why do you say so?" Sarah said looking up, baffled at Akshyay's rough voice.

"Do I have to tell you? Don't you realise what you have done?"

"Why, what have I done? Sarah said, getting up and picking up her blouse from the hook on the wall above the mat. "Why are you angry?"

"I'm not just angry. I feel disgusted. I wonder you're still not aware of your abominable conduct, or are you pretending?"

"Why should I? I have done nothing wrong. I moved in here because your aunt refused to allow me into the house. It was the night after you got arrested. What could I do? I had to come here and John was kind enough to allow me in." Sarah said, hoping Akshyay would understand and be calm again.

"That's not quite correct, about my aunt not allowing you in. She sent you to the police station, didn't she?"

"Yes that's right. But it was for no reason at all. My sari was slightly torn, because someone in the party wanted to get warm with me. I foiled his attempts. In the process, my sari got torn. There was nothing in it that would have justified going to the police, was there? In fact, with you in jail, if I had gone to the police station, they would have put me in too."

"That would have been better than this. This is no life for a respectable homemaker," Akshyay said sarcastically. "By the way, what was the need for you to go to any party? Were you celebrating my arrest?"

"On the contrary, I went there on the advice of the proprietor, Mr.Agarwal. He had told me that there'd be some influential persons there, who could get you out of jail. The only reason why I went to the party was to arrange for your release."

"Oh I see! You are ready with answers. There is no way I can verify your statements and neither do I have any desire to do so. You know that of course. You know I am a fool. I'm a fool to have left home; a fool to have left a promising career; a fool to have gone to Rishikesh in search of peace; a fool to have married you and loved you. You have cheated me, Sarah, and right now you are again trying to hoodwink me, trying to justify your actions. Well, I am not going to be a punk any longer, Sarah. You have really been good to me. You have opened my eyes. You know; I always knew that all women are sluts, they only want sex and money. I thought you were different. Well, I made a mistake, and perhaps Swami Ananda too, made a mistake. It was because of him that I agreed to marry you. He told me it would be good for me. Now I know that he was wrong and I was wrong too. I should have known that you were like all the others and not the spiritual type, I figured I would be."

Sarah, who had heard Akshyay without interruption, felt as if an invisible barrier had come up between them. Akshyay was talking in a language she had never heard him speak in. Emotion, scepticism, pessimism and prejudice charged his words. She knew it would be difficult to bring her round to a sympathetic attitude, which could enable him to understand her. Akshyay was not able to accept the idea of his wife staying in John's flat, but she did not understand why he could not trust her. After all, she had told him that she was his wife and true to the concept of a Hindu wife. If Sita could remain in an enemy's house and remain chaste, why couldn't she in a friend's house? It was as simple as that for her. She was not having any affair with John and she was completely and truly loyal to Akshyay. Further, she was true to her trip of being a Hindu wife. There was no question of having sex with John or having an affair with him. She guessed however, that Akshyay would not be able to understand her at the present juncture. He would get to understand her later, in a more stable condition of mind. There was, therefore, no need to argue with him. It would be best to accept whatever he said without protest. These were the thoughts that passed through her mind, as she heard Akshyay, and then she began: "I think you are overreacting to the situation. I can only tell you that it is not what you are thinking. I am, as I was, your wife: true to you with all my body and soul. My objective in marrying you has been to be a Hindu wife and I have done nothing, which has been a deviation from this objective. You may rest assured that I am yours and yours alone."

"I say, I don't give a damn to these damned jargons. I've heard these again and again from many a woman who had come my way. You know, I can see through the deceptive words of a woman. Nothing you'll say can show yourself as anything else than what I've seen: a shameless immoral bitch. That's all I can say. I'd better not say anything more." Akshyay realised that he had said what he should not have. He wanted to change the subject before there could be a backlash. "Now I don't know what I should do with you. Do you have any suggestions?" As he said these words he looked away at the door, as a thought of John's appearance crossed his mind. He clearly saw that he was at the end of the road. There was now a choice before him: to take her away and back to his house or to leave her behind and go away. What should he do? Could he return to his house and tell his aunt about her betrayal? She would not allow a moment to pass without taunting him. How could he tell his aunt that Sarah had been staying with John? He knew he could not mention any other place. His aunt would definitely find out the truth. There would be more chaos then. Again, could he forgive her for what she had done? He felt he could not. He could never forgive people who wronged him or cheated him. He preferred to stay away from the tribe, rather than have a confrontation. What should he do? The conflicting thoughts inside his mind showed on his wrinkled forehead, downcast eyes, and gloomy face. Sarah felt frightened, looking at him. She also felt sad that she had caused him pain, unwillingly though. She decided to make a last ditch attempt to save the situation.

"I think you should take me home. Probably, I can explain the whole thing again to you, when you are in a cooler frame of mind."

"No, no, no!" Akshyay retorted, almost at the top of his voice "You cannot go home with me. You cannot go home with me." The words came spontaneously, like a reflex action, "I have done with you. Leave me alone. I want to be alone, on my own trip."

"You can't leave me here. I'll not stay here any longer than is necessary. I have to go with you," Sarah said anxiously, in a slightly raised voice and looking straight into Akshyay's eyes. She had been, so far, in the defensive, and now she felt she should assert herself.

Akshyay felt uncomfortable at the thought that they were shouting at each other and that it could arouse the landlord or the landlady. The chowkidar could also come up the stairs and try to probe into the goings-on. He knew that he had to take a decision fast. There was no time to fight or argue. Further, John could arrive at any moment and that would lead to further complications. The idea of Sarah having sexual relation with John was convincing. In such circumstances, it was not possible to accept her as his wife any longer. The question of going with him did not arise at all. He felt he should communicate this to her and put an end to the discussion and leave the place. There was no other option open to him. He began: "Sarah let me tell you clearly that I cannot take you home with me for the simple reason: you have ceased to be my wife. You have committed adultery and that too, at a time when I was confined in jail. This was a complete betrayal. Perhaps I cannot explain my condition fully, but you know I was alone in this world and you were my only companion. You can well realise the impact of your action on my sensibilities. But it is not so much my own feelings that I am concerned with; you have broken a family tradition. No one in my family's history has done what you have done. And finally to cut it short, you have become a misfit in our society. I'll be a misfit too, if I continue to be your husband."

"Akshyay, you are jumping to conclusions without as much a clue or even giving me a chance to explain. I am still convinced that I have done nothing wrong. I have only taken shelter in a friend's house. I have not been disloyal to you. Why can't you understand that?"

"I won't be taken in by all that glib talk. I've seen reality with my own eyes and nothing can misguide me now. I'm leaving. I want to get away from this scene."

"You are going to your aunt's place I suppose? Will you be staying there?" Sarah asked, giving up the persuasion for the moment. She felt there was no use trying to convince Akshyay, when he had already formed an opinion of her.

"I'm not sure. For the present, I'll stay with my aunt. I have to find out about my mother. I really don't know what I'll do. It'll depend on the situation. I may even go to Rishikesh and seek Swami Ananda's advice. I don't know. You have put me in a peculiar situation. I'll have to make a fresh start." As Akshyay said these words, he walked towards the doorway, without even taking leave of Sarah.

"Wait a minute!" Sarah blurted out, coming face to face with the inevitable, as it was, "Why don't you give me a last chance to prove myself? You may find, I am not what you think I am, after all."

"There is no last chance, when everything has come to an end. What has happened, has happened—nothing can change the course of action at this stage, and further, I don't have any time. I've a lot to do, and all the more, because I've to start afresh. Therefore, I must bid goodbye and be off." Akshyay cast a last look at Sarah and left the room. He walked down the flight of stairs without looking back; the chowkidar got up to let him pass. He felt he was leaving behind a past: he would divorce it from his consciousness. It was like an island within an island, unable to sink below the waters or join the main land. He felt he was pulling a heavy load behind him and the strings of his consciousness were unwinding to allow him to move ahead. He moved on.

Sarah experienced a bizarre situation coming alive out of the blue and dissolving before her eyes. It caused a chemical change in the imminent course of her life. She remained still, unable to gauge her own reactions for a while. She stood at the doorway, trying to recapitulate the sequences of the play of feelings and emotion, not knowing whether to laugh or cry. She knew Akshyay was wrong. He had reacted incorrectly and that was funny. She also knew that she might lose Akshyay, if she allowed him to get away with wrong ideas. She felt also cheated and misunderstood and sad that she had lost Akshyay. Had she failed in her trip of being an Indian wife or was it another test she needed to pass? She was not able to understand. She only knew that she loved Akshyay and she did not want to lose him at any cost. She felt a sudden choking sensation and tears filling her eyes. As she tried to wipe them away with the back of her hand, she let out a few gasps. Then the tears rolled down her hot cheeks. She broke down. She could not remember when she had last cried. The tears were simply welling up now, and her lips quivered. She covered her mouth with both her hands, sobbing aloud and the tears streamed down and drenched her face and hands.

CHAPTER - XXVI

———❖———

By the time Akshyay reached his aunt's house, he had made up his mind on his future course of action. He would try to find out details about his mother's condition and the time frame by which they would release her. He might then arrange for her stay in the ashram under the care of Swami Ananda. He had tried to picture her sitting peacefully out in the garden, and absorbing the sights and sounds of the ashram and the river. With his mother under Swamiji's care he would be free to follow his cherished desires. He had a feeling that the peaceful atmosphere of the ashram and the simple ways of the ashramites would immensely benefit his mother's delicate mental state. He was certain that the ashram life, free from the pressures and demands of modern society, would be easy to adjust to. In some respects, the ashram could be even better than the mental asylum, where his mother was, at the present, languishing.

Thoughts about his immediate future came to his mind, as if, to alleviate his suffering. He could not let his mind play with his memories of his sweet relationship with Sarah. The only images of her that appeared, were those associated with the trauma he experienced in john's flat. These would send shock waves through his whole being. It was a situation where one has to keep one's eyes open to avoid a bad dream. Thoughts of the future were a logical escape from the painful feelings that sought to engulf his whole consciousness.

"Could you find Sarah?" Miss Monica asked, when she opened the door to let in Akshyay.

"Yes, I found her in John's house," Akshyay said, trying to control his emotions.

"Is something wrong?" Miss Monica asked, noticing the matter of fact tone of Akshyay's voice. "Why didn't you bring Sarah home?"

Akshyay, who had taken a few steps into the hall stopped and turned, stung by the reverse, "Please don't take her name before me . . . I don't want to hear her name again . . . please." He blurted out and then his firmness of manner changed to an imploring one. "Please, don't ever mention her name before me. I have severed all relationships with her. She has betrayed me. She is not my wife anymore."

Miss Monica, unable to comprehend the gamut of Akshyay's feelings, began once again, "Why, what has happened? How is she no more your wife? Have you really deserted her?"

"Yes I have," Akshyay said in exasperation. "What do I do when I find her living in someone else's flat?"

"Whose flat?" Miss Monica asked, getting curious.

"Didn't I tell you? She was in John's house."

"Was John in when you went there?" Miss Monica asked, hiding her curiosity, this time behind an expression of concern.

"No he wasn't. But she told me she'd been living there since the night you prevented her from entering the house."

"I didn't prevent her entry. I just told her to go to the police station to file a FIR. You can't blame me for what Sarah's done."

"No, no, I am not blaming you. I only made a statement of fact. In any case, it's all over now," Akshyay said, attempting to end the conversation. He wanted to be alone for sometime, to be able to make plans for the future.

"All is not over yet, Akshyay. There is some bad news that's just come."

Instinctively getting anxious, he asked again excitedly: "What? What is it?"

"It's about your mother." Miss Monica said, almost triumphantly. It's a letter that's come from the lawyers."

"Where is it?"

"It's right there on the piano. I've read it. It's an open letter, hand-delivered."

Akshyay picked up the envelope and took out the letter carefully, as if it were a delicate thing. He quickly read through the contents and then all on a sudden relapsed into a state of despair. He read the letter once again trying to find something in it, a hidden word or a meaning that could enliven his spirits.

My dear Akshyay,

There is an important letter from the hospital that I should hand over to you, personally. It is regarding your mother. It is very urgent. Come over as soon as you can.

Yours faithfully,

Kamal Roy

(Advocate)

Akshyay could not help feeling somewhat perplexed. He could not figure out why the lawyer had to call him to his place. Was anything wrong? Was she really all right? Have they given up her case as beyond cure? He pictured the face of his mother in the ward and felt sucked into a deep well of despair. He made an effort to get out of the mood through conversing with his aunt.

"What do you feel about this letter? Can you make out anything?" Akshyay began.

"How can I say? I am not supposed to know, am I?" Aunt Monica replied with an expression that seemed to convey, 'what a fool you are to ask me that question'.

"Well, I thought you could help me to find a meaning." Akshyay guessed that he should not have involved her for the simple reason that the lawyer himself had written, that whatever there was it was only for him to know. There was no way out of a discussion now.

"I really don't know what it could be. I guess it's something to do with her treatment."

"You mean she's gone worse, has she?" Akshyay asked.

"No! No! It's not that. They might be wanting, as I told you already, your permission to take up her treatment. You know, for any operation or expensive treatment, they have to seek your assent."

"I do hope it's not something serious. I am looking forward to seeing her fit and . . ."

"Of course, you should", Miss Monica interposed, "don't you remember the will? You'll get your share only if you look after her. And you need the money, don't you?"

Akshyay felt irritated. He knew she was poking fun at him so that he would react, and she could make more fun of him. He decided not to respond to her words and resigned himself to a studied silence. Miss Monica stopped talking, unable to provoke a battle of words.

"I'll go to the lawyer's right away and find out the real reason," Akshyay said, and turned towards the doorway. There was still time to reach the lawyer's office, before it closed for the day and, in any case, he would, if it warrants, go to the lawyer's house as well.

"I hope you'll be back for dinner," Miss Monica said, as he was going out of the door.

"Don't wait for me. I may be late." Akshyay shouted back and went down the staircase.

The lawyer was in the Court's Bar Library, when Akshyay found him. It was already late. Therefore, he asked him to accompany him to his private chamber in his residence. Akshyay agreed and hung out in the courtyard. He ordered a cup of tea from one of the many illegal tea-stalls. The court staff, the petty lawyers, typists, and clients whiled away the time that seemed to hang around like a load on worn out forms. He observed the grim and mournful faces of the people, caught in the web of law and lawyers. His predicament was similar to theirs. He felt the net closing on him: all the chances of escape exhausted. He recounted the events, one after another: the trip of Rishikesh, the marriage, the telegram to return to Calcutta, the music teacher's son, the Naxalite tangle, Sarah's desertion and now the final blow. He could not see beyond the doleful faces in the tea stall; he felt he was like them, chained.

Just as Akshyay's patience was wearing away, the portly lawyer came out of the Bar library, adjusting his glasses.

"I hope, I have not kept you waiting for long."

"Not quite. I didn't mind," Akshyay said, knowing it was a lie. He had been waiting for about an hour.

"Let's go; my car is just round the corner."

At the lawyer's chamber, he felt strangely at home, among the rows of old and dusty books on the ladder-like shelves along the wall: case-histories, books on law and jurisprudence, among others. The knowledge spilled out and seeped into his mind, washing away the heavy feelings of despondency that had been like a weight. The resultant lightness lifted him from the morass of depressing thoughts. The books reminded him of all that he had learned in school and unlearned in college. Even with the mindset of a dropout and his experiences on LSD and hashish, he had seen the shallowness of materialism. He now saw the power of greed and luxuries becoming the guiding factors of progress and development. It was all Maya, a great illusion, which enveloped everything. It held all living beings in its spell. Could he ever be free from it? Well, wasn't he already? The events of the past, which had entangled him, were already unwinding. He had left them far behind. His memory alone was the only link to the past. The future was free. He could almost see before him a new life and a pathway leading to infinity.

He woke up from the reverie, when the lawyer Mr. Roy announced his arrival by clearing his throat and took out a letter from the drawer. After asking Akshyay to take a seat, he pushed the envelope towards him.

"Go on read it," he said, adjusting his glasses, trying to anticipate Akshyay's reaction.

Akshyay read the letter and relapsed into a state of uncertainty and fear. He could hardly believe what he had read and so he began to go through the contents again, lest he might have missed something, which could change the meaning of the sentences. After he had reread the letter for the third time, he slowly lifted his head and looked at the eyes of the lawyer.

"Mr. Roy, is it true? Could she really have escaped from the asylum?" Akshyay asked, his anxiety showing on his face.

"Well that's what the letter says. She had shown signs of recovery and the doctors had planned to release her. Perhaps, they had allowed her some degree of freedom to walk around the place and to meet others. I have heard that one of the trainee nurses is also missing. It is possible that the same trainee nurse might have helped her to escape and provided her with money to go wherever she had wanted to. The police know about it and they are on the lookout for her. They have sent search parties to every corner of the city. They will inform you when they find her. It is also possible that she has recovered. The real need now is to find her out and ensure her safety." Mr. Roy concluded his speech with an adjustment of his glasses.

"What do I do? Do you suggest, I go to Ranchi?"

"What will you do there? Your mother . . . she's not in Ranchi; I'm sure."

"Where could she have gone then? Do you have any idea?"

"I have heard your father saying that she always wanted to go to Darjeeling."

"Yeah! That's because I was in school there," Akshyay said promptly and immediately recoiled as a video-show of his agonising past began in his mind. He started feeling that he had lost his mother once again. It was unusual how his mother was a complete stranger to him. It was his father first. Then the school did its part. He was also responsible. He had removed her from his mind, by his own involvement in the world outside. He had his inner circle of his friends, girl friends, music sessions, his individual ideas and attitudes. He immersed himself into all these and never thought of his mother. He had never, for a moment thought seriously about her: how she was; where she was; or whether he could do something for her. He recollected that by the time he was a grown up boy, in his teens, he had become used to seeing his father alone in the house, and of course, his aunt, who was always there. No one answered questions about his mother and he had stopped asking about her. As time passed, he had become used to not having to think of her existence. The world outside was far too engaging and interesting for him to allow anything else to distract him. He completely caught up in the world of his own actions and ideas.

As he sat before the lawyer, wondering what he should do next, his mind swung back to the time when he had stood before his 'old man'. That was how he used to refer to his father. He himself had been a spent force then. The rock band had broken up; they had blown up the money; he had dropped out of college; the effects of LSD had waned. He had been at the dead-end of his life; he had no idea where to go next. His old man had come to know of his state and had summoned him. He recollected how his father had told him to give up the path he had chosen for himself: to be a hippie. He had told him that if he wanted to experience the spiritual life he should go to Swami Ananda, to the Ananda ashram at Rishikesh. The words of his father, telling him to go to an ashram, surprised him. He could not guess what could have changed his father's attitudes. He had always believed him to be a thoroughly Westernised person with a strong dislike for things Indian. Before he could find out the truth, his father had passed away and the riddle remained unanswered.

The letter to Swami Ananda: his father had left it for him. He was to take it to the Swami. He remembered how his efforts to find the truth about what his father had wanted him to do, went in vain. Perhaps he had wanted him to get a taste of the hard ashram life so that he could come back to the world of flesh and blood on his own. It was one thing to be a hippie and another, to be a sannyasi. He had decided to try out the ashram life and had made inquiries about Swami Ananda. He had learnt that the Swami had left the Ananda ashram and was in charge of a hippie ashram called Swiss Cottage. That was how he had landed there and then things had started to move in yet another direction, until he was once again at a dead-end. Instead of his father it was the lawyer, Mr. Roy, who was now in his father's place: a friend and guardian.

"What do I do now?" He heard himself asking the lawyer once again and he repeated the words to make sure, "What do I do now?"

The lawyer looked at him for a few minutes and said slowly, almost apologetically. "I'm sorry Akshyay, I can't tell you what you can do. I suppose you can only wait. The police will catch up with her sooner or later, and in any case, the nurse, who is missing will surely return and the mystery will get solved. They will be able to find out about her."

"For the present, you will have to watch and wait. The money that was her share is being deposited in the bank. You can only get your share, if you look after her. Since that is not to be, the money cannot be transferred to your name, for the present. Remember there is an amount of five thousand rupees per month for you and a similar amount for your mother. Quite a large sum has accumulated in the bank. We had been using only a small part of it for her treatment at the mental hospital. I can only hope that she is found, declared fit and restored to you."

Akshyay got up from the chair and advanced involuntarily towards the lawyer. The latter stood up almost by reflex action, as Akshyay grasped his hands. "Please Mr. Roy, tell me . . . please . . . do you really think . . . is there any chance of getting her back . . . Please give me an answer, Mr. Roy. I shall remain grateful to you . . . please Mr. Roy."

Mr. Roy, a little flustered, remained silent. He tried to release his hands from his grasp and when he had done it, patted Akshyay on the back, to pacify him.

Akshyay stood with his head bent, feeling ashamed for his behaviour—like a child in the grip of emotions. Could it be his need for money or was it the urge to see his mother, behind his loss of control? He could not be sure. He recovered himself and stood back, looking at the lawyer's eyes. "I'll wait for a while and then I'll go in search of her. I'll have to find her. I cannot leave her out there, alone, Mr. Roy. I will not let her live alone any more."

"That's the spirit, Akshyay. I think you'll be able to find her and then take charge of her. By the way, I hope Sarah will have no objection."

Akshyay looked away, thinking whether he should reveal all to the lawyer. He decided in favour of it. "She is not my wife anymore, Mr. Roy. I have severed all relationships with her."

"Why, whatever happened? She was such a nice person."

"I'm not too sure about that; she has been a deserter. She has left me and that is why I have left her."

"If that's true, I have nothing to say. But I feel she was a nice person: not quite the insincere or disloyal type. I have an aptitude for reading a person's character, from his or her appearance, bearing, and manner. I can vouch for her as being truthful and sincere. I hope you were not mistaken. Did she specifically say that she wanted to desert you; or was it your presumption?"

Akshyay realised that the lawyer had made a valid point and his question was a crucial one. He began to look back at the sequence of events once again. However as he visualised the image of Sarah lying on the mat in John's apartment, the same feelings of jealousy and hate enveloped his consciousness and clouded his thinking. He could not answer the lawyer's question objectively: he could only react. "No! No! Mr.Roy. She is a deceitful person. She's cheated me. I can't have anything to do with her. I hate her! Don't ask me to go back to her and please, don't mention her name before me. It hurts me. It really hurts."

"I'm sorry, Akshyay, I've hurt you. I didn't mean to do that. I was only trying to be sure that you don't make a mistake. It is difficult to judge people by their actions alone and it is always better to give a second chance."

"There's no question of a second chance. I've no time for it. I'm now on a different trip altogether. I have to find my mother. I don't want anything else now."

"Of course, that is an important mission Akshyay," Mr. Roy said with emphasis, adjusting his glasses. "I wish you all success in your venture."

Chapter - XXVII

When misfortune befalls a man it seeks to bear him down. This was what happened to Akshyay. He felt the reverses piled on his head, one on top of the other. It started with the vagaries of his early childhood and a lovelorn teen age. Then came the recent calamities, which culminated at his mother's disappearance from the mental hospital. All these seemed like a long chain of adversities, pot-holing his passage through life. He suddenly felt tired, unable to bear the weight. A desire to off-load the heaviness in his mind began to permeate his thoughts.

Thus, when he entered the house, and lay down on his back on his bed, staring blankly at the ceiling, the idea that flickered in his mind was to escape to freedom. He could not see, at once, how he could be free from the burden of events that had been binding his life. There was no escape route in sight. He could not go away to the Himalayas simply because he had to stay put and wait for news of his mother.

As he lay thinking, it suddenly occurred to him that he could just stay at home and cut himself off the external world. He would shut himself in his music room and meditate till his mind became free and all traces of the dark clouds disappeared. He would not allow the external world to touch him; he will meet no one; he will not allow anyone to enter his small world.

With a fresh determination that seemed to also recharge his body, he got up from bed and picked up his sarode. He walked briskly over to the music room that overlooked the backyard. An inner door opened to an attached bath and toilet. There was no furniture save for a carpet, which covered the entire floor. A cane mattress lay unfolded along the wall on one side. He could sleep on it and also use it as an asan for his meditation and music sessions. Akshyay placed the sarode astride the mattress and went back to get the tablas. He also got a few books on yogic philosophy and a book entitled 'Tibetan Book of the Dead', which he considered to be a great book on meditation. He had come to know about it, from one of the members of the rock band, and he had got hold of it, after a long search among the bookstalls in College Street.

As he sat on the mattress, closing the door behind him, he quickly re-evaluated his decision. He had decided to get into this room with the explicit idea of freeing his mind. He would have had to wait, in any case for news of his mother and utilise the waiting time effectively, meditating and playing music. He would be able to pick up on his music lessons for one; and for the other, he could put to practical use his knowledge of the theories of yoga and meditation. Above all, he would be able to cut the chain of action and reaction; cause and effect; the law of karma: all of which seemed to have bound his life in misfortune. He would attempt to break the chain and be free.

He had heard that the yogi is always in bliss because he is free from this chain and the consequent cycles of happiness and unhappiness. Could he also achieve the same level? Would he be at all happy, in such a state of bliss? Did he really want to be in such a state? Wasn't the world of flesh and blood, joys and sorrows, pleasure and pain, action and reaction, cause and effect, more attractive because of its sheer variety? Was it not a reaction to the effect of calamities that had made him seek happiness? Was it not a sense of imprisonment in feelings of sorrow that had prompted him to seek freedom? There were no clear answers to these questions that prodded his mind. He had to find out for himself. Somehow he felt that his plans to close himself in the room would give him enough time to think on these issues and come out with a proper understanding of his own life.

He set about, therefore, to shut himself in the room. He called Abdul and gave him instructions to bring in breakfast and meals at fixed timings. He should knock at the door and wait for it to open, before ushering in the food plates. He should come back about an hour later and pick up the plates, which he would keep outside.

Akshyay also gave him instructions about turning back any visitor with the standard reply that Sahib is on a meditation trip. Lakshman should tell Aunt Monica that Akshyay would not be available at the dining table for the next seven days or so.

He then closed the door and sat on the mattress, the sarode in front and the books on yoga on his right. He felt an urge to play his favourite tune on the sarode. At the same time it struck him that he should begin by reading one of the books on yoga to tune his mind to the task before him. He concluded that there was no use debating which he should take up first: music or reading. He was there for complete detachment and inaction. Almost involuntarily his eyelids closed as his mind positioned itself between the eyebrows. He began to meditate.

The days passed one by one, and Akshyay got totally immersed in his self-imposed confinement. True, it was a subconscious fear of the outside world that kept him in, surfacing whenever the urge to go out pushed him. He drove away the temptation to go back to the world outside. He did this by diverting his mind forcibly to playing a tune on his sarode or reading a chapter from the books on yoga or getting back to meditating. He had some faint idea of death meditation as expounded in the Tibetan Book of the Dead. Whenever the desire to go out of the four walls became unbearable, he would just lie down and think he was dead.

He knew that he would have to reduce the intake of food, since he was conserving all the energies within his body, and mind. His mind seemed to have begun to acquire enough elevation to witness his thoughts and feelings with some degree of detachment. After the third day, therefore, he left a note outside his room to replace breakfast and dinner by a cup of tea and a glass of milk, respectively.

In the meantime, Miss Monica began to wonder about what was wrong with Akshyay. Why had he chosen to shut himself up in his room; why he had stopped meeting anyone; why he was not coming to the dining table? She felt it was a strange reaction, for a young man, whose wife had deserted him. She had never considered Sarah seriously as Akshyay's wife and as a family member. This was not because she was an American girl and a hippie, but because she did not act in the way she expected her to. She felt that Sarah had been putting on an image: trying to be something she was not. It did not surprise her that

Akshyay had finally found out her true character and broken all ties with her. She felt their marriage was false, as was their way of life.

It was good that Akshyay had seen the truth for himself, but she could not understand what he would gain from meditation, shutting himself in his room. He had been leading a wayward life, without direction and involving in activities that would not lead him anywhere. That he had chosen to shut himself in and meditate showed up the same streak of madness, inherited from his mother. She had called up the lawyer that morning to find out what had transpired between Akshyay and him. He learnt that Akshyay had left that place saying that he would be out in search of his mother, after waiting for a few days in the city for some news of her. From her discussion with the lawyer she concluded that Akshyay was in a state of double shock and he needed time to recover. It was therefore good for him to remain confined.

On the seventh day of his self-imposed confinement, Akshyay felt some changes taking place in his self-perception. The compassionate, gentle, music-loving, sex-|crazy, childlike, emotional, revolutionary, deeply religious, modern, sophisticated, physically strong, well liked, personality, seemed to have transformed itself. It was now a mind full of ideas and images, surrounding an invisible source light. The light seemed to spread over everything whenever he closed his eyes.

That morning, after his cup of tea and bath, as he sat down in clean pyjamas and kurta and closed his eyes, a strange iridescence seemed to fill his consciousness. He could see through his mind's eye a spreading, red, light, like the morning sunlight, illuminating the plains of his mind. The familiar images, which his mind carried, images loaded with grief, fear, love and guilt, appeared to vanish, as the darkness of a room as the lights switch on.

With his eyes still closed, he sat in the padmasan posture and concentrated on the point between the eyebrows. A red ball of fire was all he could see and as he continued to stare at it, his whole being seemed to merge in it. He could feel he was rising with it up and away from his body. He went up, floating in the space between the floor and ceiling. He perceived himself as two different entities. One, a formless and free being; and the other: his own personality lodged in his body and sitting below. He could be either entity by turns. When he entered his body below, he could feel all the pleasures and pains of living. Similarly when he moved up to merge in the formless state above, an awareness of limitless freedom and buoyancy overtook him.

Akshyay's mind traversed between the form and formless states for quite some time until his conscious mind asserted itself. Then he opened his eyes. He could discern the feelings of sadness and despair, which had weighed him down, belittled, in the face of a new detachment of mind. He was in this state neither sad nor happy. He was neither full of desire nor longing: all of which had always been lurking in his mind. He was now without the sense of being deprived or cheated. The past seemed to be at best a distant dream, which hardly affected him. He felt that he had become self-sufficient, in as much as, he could spend the rest of his life in a similar detached environment, pursuing his studies and music. He had a talent for music and therefore it was easy for him to comprehend a life of music. Philosophy and the meaning of life interested him. He would study of the ancient Vedas and Upanishads, Bhagabat Gita and other religious texts, such as the Bible and Koran. This would occupy his life in a peaceful locale, with no one to disturb him. For the present, he could not think of another marriage, but if he did meet the right person, he could marry again. The thought of marriage was not in his mind. The thoughts that emerged in his mind were his plans for the immediate future. The meditation trips had given him a realisation of the insignificance of the events in one's life, when compared to the limitless consciousness, which is a part of his own mind. One has only to enter the vault of the brain and see the events in the fiery light of the intellect. The feelings of joy, sorrow, fear, pity, and anger will be scattered and dissipated.

He could not forget his delicate feelings for his mother and the unnerving experiences in jail and with Sarah. He could only perceive them differently. He could not allow these to affect him any longer. He had had the taste of freedom.

The thought of freedom brought into his mind his present condition of confinement. It was ironic that he had tasted freedom in a confined state. However, he had to go out now and carry on with his plans.

What were his plans? When he asked himself this question, he did not have a ready answer. Yes, he had told the lawyer that he would go in search of his mother. Could he possibly to do that? He felt it was an absurd idea, in the first place. Where would he look for her? Would it be Ranchi? It was unlikely that she should be staying in that city after escaping from the mental asylum there. What should he do then? Should he wait any longer: shutting himself up in his room? There was no use in it. He had already achieved what he had wanted. He had achieved a frame of mind, which was really high.

Where would such a mind be useful, but in the pursuit of philosophy and religion? He had to go to Rishikesh for that, to some of the Vedic centres that were there. Indeed, it was Rishikesh, where he had to go to in any case. Didn't Swami Ananda tell him to come back to him if there was any problem in their marriage? He recalled Swami Ananda's words. He would have to go to Rishikesh to tell the Swami, about the break-up with Sarah.

He got up from the mattress, opened the door and stepping out, walking straight into the drawing room, where his aunt sat, reading the newspaper.

"Good morning!"

"Oh Akshyay! You're back!" Miss Monica exclaimed smiling, raising her eyebrows. "So how was your meditation? Did you get over your problems?"

"Well, I have," Akshyay said, confidently. "I am feeling happy again."

"So what do you want to do now? Have you had breakfast?"

"Yes, I have already had my cup of tea . . . but I can do with some toast and omelette. I have work to do today."

"Are you going out?"

"Yes I'll have to go to the lawyer's to find out if there's any news of my mother."

"There isn't any. I checked three days back."

"Well that was three days back. There could be some now. I also have to take a loan from him."

"Why? Why do you want a loan from him?"

"I have to make a trip to Rishikesh and start afresh there."

"What do you mean?" Miss Monica said outraged. "Do you want to be a hippie again?"

"No, not quite. I'll meet Swami Ananda and tell him about our broken marriage. I'll also explore the possibility of studying the religious philosophies of the world."

"Why can't you do that here; there are so many teachers here, in this city, aren't there?"

"True there are; but the atmosphere is not conducive. One gets engrossed in other things. I am not looking for a degree, in any case."

"Oh I see! I really can't understand you, Akshyay."

"It's simple, you know. I just want to be different. I don't dig the life you want me to lead."

The next day, Akshyay took the train from Howrah Station, for Dehra Doon. He had managed a loan of five thousand rupees, which would see him through for at least three months at the ashram. He was not sure whether he would stay there. He could think of moving up into the Himalayas, to Kedarnath or Joshimath or some of the other places on the banks of the Ganges, Alakananda, Sone or Mandakini. In any case he would consult Swami Ananda. He might be able to guide him to the right path.

When he landed on the platform at Rishikesh, he remembered having a bath in the river, which he had enjoyed so deeply on the previous occasion. He wanted to have a dip again now, to refresh himself. He began to walk briskly, therefore, towards the ghats. The shops on either side of the road were selling framed pictures of Gods and Goddesses. There were those selling warm clothing and blankets for the pilgrims too. The tangawallas sat smoking and chatting in small groups. These scenes evoked memories of his last visit to this town. He felt light-headed and delighted. A feeling of expectancy lurked in his mind, bordering on the romantic. He walked towards the river with the same feelings that someone experiences on the way to the house of a paramour. He could not understand the feelings, but he broke into a run at the sight of the river, which leapt over the stones to greet him, the silvery waves shining in the morning sunlight.

Akshyay took off his clothes and waded knee-deep into the water. The water was not as clear now, since the rains had begun, and the round stones below were no more visible. The water, however, was still cold and Akshyay felt refreshed, as a new sensation replaced the fatigue in his bones, washed away by the swirling stream.

He dried himself with his gamcha and put on a fresh kurta and pyjama and with his sling bag on his shoulder, headed for the ashram. As he walked through the cobbled lanes, the same feelings of expectancy again overtook him. He wondered whether it was for the parathas that Panchu prepared last time or any other thing. He was hungry no doubt, but the nervousness that gripped him was due to something else. Was he afraid of meeting Swami Ananda and telling him about how he had deserted Sarah? Would he fault him for deserting her? Was it the fear of facing Swamiji that made him feel shaky? It could be; but he failed to understand why he was walking at a brisk pace towards the ashram.

It was not long before he saw the white building of the ashram, the gate between the walls and the marigolds still lining the path. The sound of the rumbling river was punctuated by birdcalls and the soft breeze rustled through the leaves. He walked in and as he turned back after closing the gate, he saw two women in red-bordered saris, sitting in Padmasan under the Banyan tree, their eyes closed. He advanced a little further to have a closer look, when he suddenly recognised them. A feeling of surprise and joy filled his heart. The two women were his mother and Sarah.

END NOTES:

—◆—

1 Tonga: A horse-drawn carriage; and the drivers are called tangawallas
2 Ghats: Steps on the riverside to facilitate public bathing.
3 Gamcha: A piece of cloth, the size of a towel, used for drying the body after bathing.
4 Jhankar: The fast strumming of sitar
5 Rahara: The solo performance of a tabla player.
6 Dharamsala: A free rest house for pilgrims.
7 Padmasan: A yogic posture
8 Dakshina: The offerings made to a priest after the puja is over.
9 Purohit: A priest of a temple.
10 Ulu: A shrill sound made by Indian women during marriages and pujas, by wagging the tongue.
11 Fhul Sajja: The night after the wedding on the nuptial bed.
12 Charanamrit: Holy temple water.
13 An earthen cup.
14 A lakh: One-tenth of a million.
15 A popular hot fast-food item: potato curry contained in a conical shaped flour paste and fried.
16 Rewas: The practice of a raga on a musical instrument; also includes practice of vocal classical.

17   Sabasan: A yogic posture and exercise, in which one lies down as if dead. It is a great form of relaxation and rejuvenation.

18   Sita: Rama's wife in the epic Ramayana.

19   Draupadi: The common wife of the five Pandavas in the epic Mahabharata.

20   Adda: Casual group discussions among friends usually by the roadside or in a teashop.

21   Guru-Sishya: Teacher-disciple.

22   Panwalla: One who sells pan; a mild intoxicant of betel leaf, betel nuts and lime.

23   Khambaj: A raga.

24   Chowkidar: House keeper or caretaker.

25   Sindur:A red powder used as a bindi and between hairline parting by married women.

26   darwan: A housekeeper cum guard.

27   Saab : Saab stands for sahib, a term used to address a white person or an officer.

28   Ashramite: One who lives in an ashram.

29   Jogini: A woman practising yoga.

30   Ganja: An intoxicant.